On Streets of Gold

TO: Eric
God Bless
- Reid M.

heaven & earth series
book one

On Streets of Gold

a novel

Reid Ivan MacLean

TATE PUBLISHING
AND ENTERPRISES, LLC

On Streets of Gold
Copyright © 2011 by Reid Ivan MacLean. All rights reserved.

No part of this publication may be reproduced, stored in a retrieval system or transmitted in any way by any means, electronic, mechanical, photocopy, recording or otherwise without the prior permission of the author except as provided by USA copyright law.

Scripture quotations are from *The New English Bible*, The Delegates Of The Oxford University Press and The Syndics Of The Cambridge University Press, 1961, 1970. Used by permission. All rights reserved.

The opinions expressed by the author are not necessarily those of Tate Publishing, LLC.

Published by Tate Publishing & Enterprises, LLC
127 E. Trade Center Terrace | Mustang, Oklahoma 73064 USA
1.888.361.9473 | www.tatepublishing.com

Tate Publishing is committed to excellence in the publishing industry. The company reflects the philosophy established by the founders, based on Psalm 68:11,
"The Lord gave the word and great was the company of those who published it."

Book design copyright © 2011 by Tate Publishing, LLC. All rights reserved.
Cover design by Shawn Collins
Interior design by April Marciszewski
Author Photo by Eric Wynne

Published in the United States of America
ISBN: 978-1-61346-915-6
Fiction / Religious
11.11.02

To Jan, my best friend, confidante, and loving wife of forty years.

Acknowledgments

I want to acknowledge the work of several authors whose writings have given me insight into the world of heaven, hell, angels, demons, and all things supernatural. I make mention of Mary K. Baxter and her revelations recorded in her work: *A Divine Revelation of Hell*; Dr. Tim Sheets and his work, *Heaven Made Real*; Dr. Billy Graham and his work, *Angels: God's Secret Agents*; Frank E. Peretti and his work, *This Present Darkness*; and Dr. Henry C. Thiessen and his work, *Lectures in Systematic Theology*. Lastly, and most importantly, I acknowledge the Holy Spirit and God's Word, my ultimate sources of inspiration in the writing of this novel.

"The twelve gates were twelve pearls, each gate being made from a single pearl. The streets of the city were of pure gold, like translucent glass."

                        Revelation 21:21, New English Bible

Chapter One

Nothing seemed out of the ordinary as he surveyed the park from his favorite bench. All the things he loved about this delightful place were intact, though he didn't seem to be enjoying them as much. Perhaps the overcast sky, with its hint of rain, had dulled his senses.

Suddenly, out of the corner of his eye, he noticed a slight movement on the ground. He turned to see the strangest thing. There before him was a large squirrel, acting, to say the least, rather peculiar.

It wasn't so much how he looked, as his actions that appeared odd. The furry creature was hopping back and forth from foot to foot, performing what looked like some sort of dance ritual. Its head jerked slightly backwards, first to the left, then to the right, beckoning like a dog wanting someone to chase him.

The old man's first thoughts were that the thing was rabid. He immediately grabbed his cane, tapped it violently on the ground, and flung some of the pathway gravel in the direction of the squirrel.

Then it happened.

In an audible, distinct, high-pitched voice, the squirrel began to speak.

"Put the cane down, pops! What are you trying to do, hurt someone?"

Stunned, the old man recoiled. His cane went flying off into the greenery. What in the world was going on?

"Take it easy," said the squirrel in a huffy voice. "My name is Malak and I'm here on assignment. You happen to be that assignment."

"What assignment?" the old man blurted out as he tried to calm his shaking.

Malak chattered back, "Many times throughout your life you've secretly asked for understanding, for deeper meaning into what life is really all about. You've done so from behind a mask of science and scorn that has fought against your ability to get closer to the truth."

"What on earth are you talking about?" asked the old man, his voice wrought with indignation.

Even before the answer came back, he realized a sudden calmness had descended over him. It seemed almost tangible, like a blanket placed gently over his shoulders, its warmth bringing a feeling of peace and contentment.

Even Malak, whoever or whatever he was, seemed different than he had just moments before. The furry, attitude-packing rodent suddenly seemed more friend than foe.

"How do you know anything about me?" the old man asked in a much calmer voice.

"I know a great many things about you," said the rodent chatterbox. "I know your name is Ben T. Jacobs. I know you live alone in an apartment on the south side of the park. I know you were a physics professor at Saint Mary's University for forty years. I know your wife, Melanie, died five years ago. I know you have a daughter named Sarah, and two grandchildren, Esther, age ten, and Joshua, eight.

"Now, stop right there!" said the old man, his sense of calm turning back to agitation. For a moment, awareness of his talking friend faded. He looked up to see a young mother pushing a baby stroller coming toward them. What would she think? What would she say?

Oddly, she never gave them a second look.

For a split second, the befuddled professor thought of calling Halifax Herald reporter Aaron Cummings and telling him what was going on.

That's what I'll do. I'll call him, he thought. Reality, however, quickly presented a brick wall. The professor didn't own a cell phone, and there were no phones in the park. Besides, he figured any reporter worth their salt would surely think he had gone off the deep end.

He thought a second time about calling Aaron, forgetting again that he didn't have a phone.

Aaron had once been a student of the professor's. In recent years their paths had crossed several times. The professor had always found Aaron to be a polite, eager-to-learn kind of student, but there was always a cloud of mystique that seemed to follow him. It was as if Aaron was hiding a deep, dark secret that he was never quite ready to share.

The professor's thoughts turned once gain to the young mother pushing the baby stroller.

Could it be that nothing out of the ordinary, at least in her eyes, was going on? This, indeed, seemed to be the case. As for him, he had a gut feeling that this strange twist of events was somehow just the tip of an iceberg.

"Relax, relax!" said Malak. For a few seconds, the old man had almost forgotten his buck-toothed friend.

"Okay, squirrel, or whatever you are, I insist you tell me how you know so much about me and just exactly what's going on."

"All right, all right," Malak blurted back. "But before we get down to nitty-gritty things, I want you to know that I'm expecting you to get over talking to a talking squirrel. I want you to understand that I sometimes find talking to humans even more bizarre. In my world, you people are often so very difficult to understand," he said, squiggling his nose up and down, faster and faster as his voice rose higher and higher.

"And I wonder what world you come from?" the old man muttered sarcastically under his breath.

"I can tell you a few things about my world, but others are best left untold for now." The old man's face registered the shock at Malak having heard what he said.

"I have been given more information on you than you could imagine," said Malak, who no longer conversed from the ground but from the opposite arm of the bench.

The old man's curiosity was definitely stirred. He began to bombard the squirrel with question after question. Hour slipped into hour.

Malak's tone suddenly became curt as dusk hurried the fading colors of a beautiful sunset.

"Darkness is descending over the park. I want you to go back to your apartment until tomorrow. Come back at the same time and sit on this exact bench."

In a flash, Malak leaped from the arm of the bench to the ground and scurried out of sight.

The old man stood, found his cane in the nearby bushes, and began to make his way down the path in the direction of home.

Glancing at his watch, he couldn't believe that six hours had gone by. A thousand jumbled thoughts raced through his mind. All contained fragments of the same question he kept mulling over as he walked along: Did what he thought just happened, really happen?

Deep in thought, he failed to realize the rapid change in his surroundings.

Not only was it almost dark, but the wind had picked up as well. He began to wish he had not taken the outer, less-traveled path from the park. He tried to console his jitters by telling himself the distance to the street and his apartment was only the equivalent of about three city blocks, two of which he must have journeyed by now.

Each step he took seemed more ominous than the last.

The wind had actually begun to howl as if a tunnel had been created between the wooded area to the left, and the tall, black wrought-iron fence to the right.

Suddenly the loud harsh call of at least two or three blackbirds, high in the trees above his head, broke the eerie silence.

Startled, the old man missed his footing and fell headlong into the path.

He got up as quickly as he could, desperate to reach the gate at the end of the lane that led onto the street. In the panic that ensued, he hadn't noticed the gash on his right hand, not until he saw the blood oozing from the cut and flowing down his arm.

His heart began to pound as he half ran, half hobbled, what he knew, or hoped, was only a short distance to the gate, a distance that suddenly seemed an eternity away.

Swoosh! What was that?

There it was again, this time from behind but coming straight at him. He realized the squawking birds hadn't flown off into the night. Instead, they began to swarm and swoop down at him, first in twos and threes, and then in groups too numerous to count.

He could see the light outside the gate ahead, no more than two hundred feet away, but he couldn't seem to get to it.

Then came the voices.

"You won't make it to the gate."

The voices were anything but friendly, as had been his conversations with Malak. Instead, they were sinister, cold, threatening.

"Help me," he remembered crying out in a weakened voice of desperation.

"No one can hear you," came a voice that seemed to emanate from the center of the flapping, menacing birds.

Light!

He was aware that bright, soft light was suddenly filling the pathway in front of him and behind him as far as he could see down the lane.

The light not only dispelled the darkness and drove away the birds, but it also stilled the wind and brought a calming to everything along the path. It also exposed an abrupt wall of darkness on either side.

No longer did the old man feel the need to run. To the contrary, he found it quite enjoyable walking the remaining short distance to the street ahead.

When he reached his hand up to open the big, iron gate, he jumped back quickly, astonished at what he saw, or rather, what he didn't see. There was no cut on his hand, no blood. It was as if he'd never fallen and never been injured.

Startled, he flipped his hand back and forth, over and over, looking for the cut. It wasn't there.

Pushing the gate open, he walked out onto the sidewalk. As he did, he realized he had emerged from one world into another. As he glanced back, the light that had befriended him retracted in tumbleweed fashion down the path and out of sight. Blackness filled its void.

As quickly as he could, he made his way to the set of traffic lights at the corner, crossed the street, and briskly walked the fifty yards leading up the lane to his apartment complex.

Once inside, he made his way to the elevator, glancing continually over his shoulder. He was glad when he entered and was able to press the tenth floor button without anyone, as far as he knew, seeing him.

The old man's hand trembled as he tried to fit the key into his apartment door. He thought for a second, rattled as he was, that he might have been trying to enter someone else's apartment. He glanced quickly up at the number on the door. It indeed read "1007."

Finally, he got the key to fit. He turned the handle and the door swung open. Stepping into the entryway, he flicked the light on and quickly went from room to room turning on all the remaining lights.

He took a good look around. Everything seemed in its proper place. He noted the clock on the kitchen wall said ten after ten.

Exhausted beyond measure, both mentally and physically, he headed for the bedroom, collapsed fully clothed on the bed, and fell immediately into a deep sleep.

Chapter Two

The morning sun filled the old man's room. He remembered feeling its warmth on his face as he tried to ease into consciousness.

The ring of the phone at his bedside quickened the process. Half awake, he leaned over and removed it from the cradle. Before it even reached his ear, he could hear the panic in his daughter's voice. "Dad, are you okay?"

"Yes, darling. What's up?" he replied.

"What's up!" she shot back quickly. "I called you eight times since yesterday afternoon and left messages on your answering machine, but you didn't call back. Where were you?"

He was now fully awake and quite speechless.

"Dad?"

"Yes, I'm here."

He quickly sat straight up in bed, his mind racing, trying to process what had happened to him since yesterday afternoon. He tried to calm his voice, not wanting to further alarm his worried daughter.

"I'm fine, Sarah. Thanks for your concern. I was in the park from about mid-afternoon until sunset. When I got home, I was so tired I went straight to bed and didn't bother to check my messages."

"Okay, dad. I'm glad you're all right. It's just that you gave us a fright."

"I'm sorry, Sarah."

"It's okay. I'm glad nothing is wrong. Gotta run with the kids. Will talk to you later."

"Okay, take care." *Click.*

"*Well, at least I didn't wake up in a straitjacket,*" he mused to himself, half chuckling that he could find any humor in the events of yesterday.

What on earth had happened? And his hand. *What was that all about?* he thought as he turned it over and over looking for something but finding nothing that would prove he had fallen and cut himself badly.

Where to begin with the thousand questions he wanted answered? He caught a glimpse of himself in the dresser mirror and decided a shower, shave, and fresh clothes were definitely a good place to start.

The perked coffee did the trick. He could smell its sweet, enticing aroma wiggling its way under the bathroom door as he stepped out of the shower.

Feeling refreshed and hungry, he made a stop in the kitchen en route to the living room and his favorite chair, coffee in one hand and a bagel in the other. Plunking his food on the coffee table, he opened wide the curtains to let in the brand new day and soak up the panoramic view of the park below.

Such were the things of his daily routine. For the moment, he felt safe but scared that routine and normalcy were slipping away.

After a quick glance across the expanse of the park, beautifully arrayed in its finest greens of summer, his eyes were drawn to the outer pathway that ran south to north. It sure looked a lot different in the morning sunlight than it had just hours before in the dark of night.

As he stood there staring, he began to think about his life and the darkness of the past five years without his wife. Perhaps the powerful light that dispelled last night's darkness was a sign of things to come.

Melanie had been the love of his life, and he missed her dearly. The two were university sweethearts who married in their mid-twenties and spent the next forty-two years finding ways to outshine each other in the realm of love and mutual respect.

His mind flashed back to a small wall hanging that had been on their bedroom door for almost their entire married life. It read: "Happiness is being married to your best friend."

Perhaps the poster's fate was symbolic. It seemed when Melanie died and it came down, so did his happiness. The tattered reminder of what used to be was somewhere in a closet in his apartment. It seemed he couldn't throw it out, but neither could he overcome the pain of seeing it hung in a new place that he couldn't share with her.

So was theirs a perfect life? Did they ever fight?

Sure they did. Well, I guess you couldn't call their disagreements fighting. They were more like spats that ended in laughter over the silliness that caused them.

There was, I guess, one thing, however, in the last ten years of their marriage that caused some division. Melanie had found what he called "religion" and she called "a relationship with God," or, as she liked to refer to Him, her "Lord and Savior, Jesus Christ."

Sarah and the children had followed in her footsteps, but not him. No, not him. He had firmly stood his ground against what he often referred to as "that nonsense." After all, he had dedicated his entire professional life to physics and teaching others to be rational and to never get caught up in what he often told his students was nothing more than "euphoric pie in the sky."

To him religion was a joke. Now, he was beginning to wonder, after yesterday, if the joke was on him.

A tear rolled down the old man's cheek as he reminisced how he now believed he had failed his beloved in not being more understanding of her beliefs and in the love she found in the one she so freely called her Savior.

How he wished she was alive so he could put his arm around her and apologize for often feeling jealous of her new-found love. He had to admit she never gave him any reason to think that way. After all, he knew only too well that because of the love she found in her God, their marriage and her love for him had magnified.

He began to catch a glimpse of how wrong it was for him, and those who, either openly, or behind her back, let her know they thought she'd gotten a little crazy with all this "religious" stuff.

Now as he stood staring out the window, his emotions raw and exposed, he wondered if it wasn't he who was crazy for not following her in the deeper walk she found. And speaking of crazy, he laughed out loud at what his colleagues would think if they knew he had an afternoon appointment with a talking squirrel.

Before he knew it, his soul-searching morning had vanished.

It was close to noon.

He threw a frozen dinner in the microwave and began sifting through several days of mail piled up on the kitchen table. As usual, the exercise produced little more than a few bills and a lot of flyers.

The all-too-familiar sound of the microwave bell broke the silence. His face displayed a sheepish grin as he thought of how disappointed Melanie would be in his messy apartment and horrid eating habits.

Melanie! Melanie! He couldn't get her out of his mind. If she were alive, he knew she would be the only person on the planet with whom he could share the events of last night.

Wanting to scream, he actually visualized himself standing at the edge of a large canyon yelling his lungs out and then waiting for the echo to bounce back over and over again. It was at least some form of communication.

Was he losing his mind? He thought for a moment about what his colleagues would think of his situation. Imagine, their co-defender of the science world, the professor who always had rational answers to everything, all of a sudden having answers to nothing.

After wolfing down his now-cold dinner, he grabbed his hat and cane and headed for the door. Although it was only one thirty, he thought the park would be a little more calming than the closed space of his stuffy apartment.

When the elevator door opened on the ground floor, Matt MacKeen, the building's superintendent and handyman, offered his usual, "Good morning, Professor. How are you today?"

Matt had been a student of his for many years. He liked the boy. He remembered him as a good student who had done well in all his classes. Now, as fate would have it, their paths crossed again. Matt had taken the super's job because it was close to the university and gave him a roof over his head while he worked to complete his doctorate in child psychology. For the professor, the young man's face was always a welcome sight, a reminder of a past he so often wished he could go back to.

Matt opened the door and the old man stepped into the sunshine and down the lane toward the park.

Chapter Three

He checked his watch. It was exactly two o'clock in the afternoon as he swung open the wrought iron gate and entered the park grounds.

Three paths led into its beauty. Anxious and nervous at the same time, he chose the outer trail he had traveled the night before.

Everything seemed the same, yet different. He laughed as he tried to process such a thought. How could everything be the same, but yet be so different?

There before him towered the same row of tall pines reaching majestically skyward. He and Melanie had nicknamed them "tree soldiers" because they seemed to be guarding the flowers, ponds, statues, and all things green that composed his beloved park.

As he strolled along the pathway, he couldn't get over how at peace he felt.

The air seemed charged with expectancy. It reminded him of the feelings he had as a young boy on the first day of school after summer holidays. Such was a time when most lads pretended they were sad that summer was over, yet down deep they were anxious and excited about going back. Who would be their new teacher? What would he or she be like? There would be new things to learn. What would that be like?

Before he knew it, he had reached his familiar bench. Sitting down, he crossed his legs and rested his cane against the seat.

Not in a long time had the old bench seemed so warm, friendly, and inviting. He wondered how many hours of their marriage he and Melanie had spent sitting there, especially in the years just before she died.

Somehow he felt closer to her at that very moment than at any other time since her passing. Extending his arm as far as he could reach across the back of the bench, he closed his eyes and pretended to be once again gently rubbing her shoulder and nudging her closer to him.

Suddenly a voice uttered the words: "Would you like to see her again?"

He opened his eyes expecting to see Malak leaping onto the bench, but there was no Malak. There was only a man sitting with his back to him some thirty yards away, near the fountain to the unnamed soldier. Two children played nearby, giggling as they stared and pointed at the shiny coins in the water.

Where had the voice come from? He thought about what was more startling: the fact that no one was within earshot, or, that the clear voice that sounded like Malak's, had offered such a strange request?

Puzzled, he stood up to take a good look behind the bench. He even glanced underneath it to make sure Malak wasn't playing tricks on him. As he looked back in the direction of the fountain, he noticed the man on the bench was walking toward him.

The closer he got, the more the old man was aware of something odd about the stranger. It wasn't so much the way he looked or walked, as it was his big, wide grin that seemed to exude familiarity, a familiarity that was beginning to make the old man nervous. Whoever he was, he hoped a giant bear hug wasn't about to overtake him.

Now they were standing face to face, no more than two feet apart.

The stranger spoke first. "It's me, Malak! Do you want to make that visit or not?"

Shocked, and feeling a definite buckling in his knees, the old man struggled to land himself on the bench.

Malak's quick, strong arms, and what felt like a cushion beneath him, softened the landing.

"Take a deep breath and relax," said the new version of Malak.

The old man picked up on the brash, quick tones of speech he had come to know from his previous encounter with four-legged Malak. This was definitely Malak but minus two legs, more height and no fur.

Malak sat down beside him, seemingly oblivious to the shock he had inflicted on an old man still trying to catch his breath.

"I suppose you're wondering about the squirrel thing?"

The old man didn't answer the question immediately. He was too puzzled about what was going on.

Finally his tongue caught up with his thoughts. "Well, as a matter of fact, I'd feel a whole lot better knowing exactly who you are, or what you are, and just where it is you come from."

A smile came over Malak's face, one that gave the old man hope he was about to get some answers.

Malak cleared his throat.

"What you see before you is a young man who looks to be in his twenties, vibrant, strong, and good looking, though not human. Because I'm not human, I can boast as if I were. Though I speak in jest, understand that this is not a riddle, for I am merely being playful. You see, I have watched humans for centuries do such things as boast, and I must say I cannot grasp their reasons for doing so, or their silliness.

"Now let us address the matter of Malak the squirrel. Obviously, squirrels are only animals and cannot speak. Speech is characteristic of the spirit. I appeared to you first, and spoke to you through the squirrel to throw off your reasoning and make you think outside your comfort zone. It seems to have worked as it definitely got your attention, leaving you vulnerable and in a state of helplessness.

"My assignments quite often only begin when such a state has been reached by the one I have been sent to help. Had I appeared to you first as a man, especially with your keen intellect"—Malak smirked politely to himself—"you would have wasted too much time trying to intellectualize me away. To use one of your earthly sayings: 'You would not have been able to see the forest for the trees.'"

Malak definitely had the old man's attention.

"Now to the question of exactly who I am. I am an angel sent from God as His messenger to you."

Somehow the old man had guessed what was coming. The answer rang in his ears as more of a relief than anything else. He was definitely glad that his mind had not reached the outer limits of insanity, and that he was at least beginning to see Malak as once again a friend rather than a foe.

"Angels exist in another realm seldom understood by humankind. People, for the most part, have romanticized them into little, chubby-winged creatures with golden curls who strum harps all day as they float by on fluffy clouds. Nothing could be farther from the truth."

Curious as the old man was to soak up all that Malak was saying, he could wait no longer. Apologizing for the interruption, he brought his new angel friend back to the question of seeing Melanie.

Before his lips formed the words, Malak began to answer.

"Yes, I can take you to the other side where you will see your beloved, but you must understand something. It is important to know that heaven is not a place for earthly man. Human beings cannot enter heaven in fleshly form, for it is a spiritual place inhabited by spiritual beings."

Malak chuckled.

Something had obviously changed the serious look on his youthful face to a smile.

"It's sort of like you humans in your space suits flying around in metal ships. Without the ships, and without the suits, you could not survive in such an environment."

The old man, who had been listening intensely, turned slightly as the laughter of nearby children caught his attention.

When he turned back, Malak was gone.

Chapter Four

Being a man of science leaves little tolerance for loose ends.

At least that's what the old man used to think. Now he wasn't so sure.

He would be the first to admit that Malak's most recent, abrupt departure frustrated him, but at the same time, it made him laugh, something he hadn't done a lot of in the past five years.

As a matter of fact, he was becoming aware once again of this strange peace that was enveloping his life despite the bizarre circumstances going on around him.

As he thought about where Malak had gone, he realized he was somehow sure he'd be back. A silent voice, an understanding deep inside, seemed to be giving him assurance that everything would be all right.

I guess—he thought—*I must be learning to trust again.*

Trust had certainly dropped out of his world when Melanie died.

Since her death, he had come to believe that the God she trusted certainly wasn't trustworthy. Now, he was no longer so sure.

If God was the giver of the peace he felt, and if He thought enough of him to send an angel, maybe, just maybe, he could trust Him a little. And besides, he couldn't shake Malak's words about seeing Melanie.

How could he possibly get to see her again? Surely an angel would not be so cruel as to merely tease him about something so important?

The old man made a conscious decision to slow down his racing mind in favor of enjoying the park and what was left of the day.

A soaring hawk caught his attention.

Hawks, effortlessly strutting their stuff in the blue sky above, were not uncommon in the park. His eyes had locked on this particular one because of its now-rapid descent toward the small grassy knoll near the fountain.

The dive target became all too evident with the loud squeal of a fat field mouse caught in its talons and carried off through the trees.

Nature, he thought, had so many lessons to share with those who slowed down long enough to take notice. At least this was how Melanie always saw the big picture. He realized he was beginning to see it that way too.

All around him, nature, as Melanie would say, had stamped its marks of beauty and order on a planet so well designed that there had to be a master designer.

As he drank in the beauty of his surroundings, he was suddenly aware of something strange happening in his body. He began to feel nauseated and cold. How could this be in the heat of such a beautiful day?

His chest tightened and sharp pains shot down both his arms. His eyelids drooped to slits allowing in less and less light. The pain in his chest felt like a truck had parked itself across his rib cage.

He became aware of people stopping and gathering around him and could faintly hear a man, obviously on a cell phone, frantically calling for help. Then everything went black.

The next thing he recalled was a feeling of weightlessness. He found himself actually floating about ten feet above his own body and could clearly view everything that was going on.

There his body lay, sprawled out on the ground for all to see. He remembered thinking what a spectacle it all was.

The wail of sirens pierced the hot, humid air, heightening the tension of what had, just minutes before, been a snapshot of serenity.

Paramedics pushed through the crowd and began to work frantically on his pale, still body.

He remembered being able to float with ease in any direction he chose. With just a thought, he could move up, down, or sideways in order to get a better look at the macabre scene as it played out below him.

His next recollection was one of extreme acceleration. The peaceful floating had transformed into rapid speed. Where was he going? What was happening?

The scene he had been watching disappeared in a second.

He was aware of being inside something resembling a tunnel, one without defined walls; at least he wasn't aware of any that he could make out in so dark an environment.

He remembered wondering what was propelling him forward. The strange, rapid travel mode caused the old man no sense of alarm. To the contrary, he was rather enjoying the trip.

The only other thing he could remember vividly in the blackness was the sense that someone, or something, had extended what seemed to be an arm across his shoulders.

Whatever it was, it was definitely guiding him rapidly along an upward path whose destination he assumed would be heaven and his beloved Melanie.

His guide, who had thus far not spoken a word, was strangely familiar.

The best guess he could come up with was that Malak, the only spirit being he knew, was somehow at the helm.

Later that day, at an aging four-story office building across town, a broad frown swept over the face of a young man talking on the phone. Prior to the call, he had allowed his mind to drift off to a faraway place. His sagging posture now straightened like a pin as his brain registered what he was hearing.

According to the caller, the man's old friend, Professor Ben T. Jacobs, had suffered a heart attack and lay comatose in the hospital.

Herald reporter Aaron Cummings grabbed his coat and headed for the door.

Chapter Five

A low, rumbling sound was the first hint that something was wrong.

The smooth ride gave way to shaking and dipping worse than a plane fighting extreme turbulence.

Malak still seemed to be in control, but the gentle arm across the old man's shoulders now became more of a clutching grip as they jostled back and forth, up and down.

Then, for the first time since taking flight, he began to make visual contact with his surroundings.

What he saw, he wished he hadn't.

At first he could make out only fragmented glimpses, snippets of grotesque faces and creatures riding horses almost as ugly as their riders.

The rapid acceleration began to slow down. The more it slowed, the more visible their surroundings became.

The old man began to figure out that some sort of a battle was going on.

The ugly creatures and their hideous mounts began to pop up suddenly in front of his face as if he had been watching a 3-D movie.

Movement through the tunnel completely stopped.

He could hear the sounds of thundering hoofbeats getting closer and closer, louder and louder. The clanging and clashing of swords, combined with blood-curdling yells, grew more intense.

"Quickly, hurry, this way."

It was Malak, as the old man had never seen him before. This time the old man's eyes locked not on Malak the squirrel, or Malak the young man, but, rather, Malak the winged creature dressed in a white gown and sash and with a large sword strapped to his waist.

Cocky Malak he wasn't.

His head jerked rapidly to and fro. His eyes shot back and forth in quick succession. The old man quickly became the object of a shoving match as a grotesque creature appeared out of nowhere and began clutching at him with its octopus-like arms.

The thing's breath was enough to kill a person before its tentacles could do any damage. Getting free seemed impossible no matter how hard he struggled.

Suddenly, a blinding flash of bright light appeared, followed by the swish of steel as it cut through the grasp of the creature. In an instant it vanished, yelping like a scalded dog. A faint wisp of reddish vapor trail was all that remained.

There before the old man stood a warrior from the opposite side, an opponent of the devilish thing that had tried to drag him off to who knows where.

Who was this being?

Before the old man could even form the question, the soldier in white was gone.

Malak quickly grabbed the old man and flew him high above the battle scene. From their perch they could see the chaos unfold below.

"What's going on Malak. Am I dead? Who am I? Where am I? Where am I going?"

Malak wasn't too keen on answering questions.

"Quiet... lower your voice. The battle down there is mostly over you and those like you. Zadar is angry and has vowed to stamp out the travel plans of those from heaven's armies sent to get you and the others who have not been redeemed but have been given the unusual chance to go to the other side and live to tell about it."

"Hold it!" the old man cried out as quietly as he could and still be heard.

Before he could finish his sentence, Malak pushed him down and pulled him behind a thick, opaque, boulder-like mass about the size of a small shed.

There were no trees, water, or land around them, at least none that he could see. Instead, there seemed to be layers upon layers of vapor, each varying in degree of density and transparency.

The old man couldn't blame Malak for not sitting down at that particular moment to a cup of tea and a geography lesson. Obviously, dealing with the chaos came first.

They seemed safe, at least for the time being

Malak continued to scout their surroundings with a seeming ability to see in all directions at the same time.

No aspect of the battle, or its deafening sounds, escaped his constant glare. Unfortunately, from the look on Malak's face, it was obvious to the old man that the forces of good weren't doing as well as he had hoped. Part of the reason was that the dark forces far outnumbered those valiantly trying to fend them off.

Because he had no awareness of time, he couldn't gauge how long the battle was lasting. He guessed it had been at least a half hour since they had first been tossed from the tunnel's path.

Malak continued trying his best to keep as little as possible of the ugly scene from the old man he had been sent to protect and guide.

The first hint that the battle had ended came with an emerging sulfuric smell, much like that of rotten eggs. Blackness was choking out any remaining pockets of light.

A presence slowly but surely began to emerge.

It appeared first as a shapeless blob, large and looming. Then it began to slowly take shape.

Fear gripped the old man.

He become aware that whatever this thing was, it knew their hiding place and was coming right for them.

The old man, not wanting to look, tucked in behind Malak's extended wings and closed his eyes.

It wasn't the fear of being found, nor the possibility of having to soon look at yet another grotesque beast, that scared him most. It was the hideous, mocking laughter that filled the air as Zadar, and a dozen or so of his cronies, burst into their space.

"Seize them!" he barked as his underlings charged toward them.

Malak drew his sword and quickly sent two of them yelping off to lick their wounds. It wasn't long, however, before he was unable to overcome the sheer numbers arrayed against him.

The unblocked blade of one of them pierced Malak's shoulder.

The frothing fiends nipped and chewed at one another in a frenzied rush to get at Malak in his weakened state.

In a flash, Malak shot straight up and out of sight as the pack of demons fell headlong into one another landing in a heap.

"Forget about him, you imbeciles. Bring the prize to me," yelled Zadar.

"*The prize?*"

As he sat there dejected, bewildered, numb to his surroundings and feelings, he tried to grasp what could be the ungodly reason anyone would consider him a prize.

One of Zadar's thugs threw a collar and chain around his neck and dragged him to the feet of his master.

Now, there was a sight.

Once again the smell was as bad, if not worse, than his adversary's appearance. He remembered thinking that a thousand pair of dirty socks couldn't do justice to the rancid odor emanating from Zadar.

There he sat, a pompous, fat, beanbag of a creature, almost as round as he was tall.

Junior demons scampered across each other's path in an effort to fuss over and preen the disgusting thing. Three or four fanned him while the others fiddled with what appeared to be a mess of oily, grotesque hair, best described as what steel wool might look like on steroids.

A demon handed him the chain around the old man's neck.

Zadar proceeded to yank the tether, jerking the old man off his feet and within inches of the demonic commander's face.

A hot blast of breath that smelled like sewer forced the old man to turn his head away.

"Look at me," Zadar roared. "No one turns their head in my presence. I am Zadar, commander of Satan's Alpha armies in the fifth zone. I demand the utmost respect and you will give it to me."

By this time, the old man didn't much care what the fat, moron commander wanted, or got.

Feeling totally demoralized and more tired and sick than afraid, he merely nodded acknowledgement in the direction of Zadar.

"You have no right to be on any journey to the places where our adversaries dwell. No right!" The eyes of his captor bulged larger each time his voice rose. "I personally will take you where you belong, you silly little fool of a man."

With a wave of Zadar's flabby arm, the rag-tag band of demons cleared a path. Their commander arose, the old man in tow, and disappeared into the darkness.

Total blackness had returned and with it the rapid acceleration he had experienced in his tunnel journey with Malak, only this time, his escort was anything but a friend.

As for their direction, if he got it right, they weren't headed up, but instead, were on their way straight down.

Chapter Six

Down, down they spiraled into blackness so dark he couldn't see his hand in front of his face.

The old man, if not for the intensifying heat, would have sworn they were on an Olympic luge run, complete with banking turns and the sensation of almost blasting off the track at any second.

As for the pilot, bad-breath Zadar was anything but a gracious host. Gone was Malak's caring arm of assurance and protection, replaced with a tight rein on the old man's chain that left him gasping at every turn.

Dry, choking heat intensified the deeper they went. Smoke, at first only a slight occasional whiff, grew worse. The air began to resemble the stench and dryness of being down wind of a roof-tarring job on the hottest day of summer.

Within minutes, things got a whole lot worse.

Voices, mocking voices, joined the horrible mix of the old man's disastrous ride. Each seemed to be trying to outdo the others in terms of hideous groans and laughter. The deeper they descended, the louder they got.

The full weight of what was happening suddenly struck the old man's entire being with the force of a wrecking ball.

He became acutely aware that in minutes, perhaps seconds, he was about to descend into the depths of hell.

Every fiber in whatever kind of body he was presently in kicked into high gear. The horror of what he now knew was about to take place gripped his very soul.

Never had he felt so helpless.

He wanted out, but had no way to escape and knew it. Deep inside he knew it, like a trapped animal facing death knows his fate and fights violently to escape.

In desperation, having never felt so forsaken, he cried out for help. No one answered back.

Instead, the demon voices mocked him all the more, taunting him, claiming ownership over him, and promising him a life of chains and torment for eternity.

The gloom and the relentless horror of his situation pointed to an end to everything he had ever known that was good and decent.

He thought of the possibility of never seeing Melanie again.

Where was God?

Where was the truth of the promise given to him by Malak that he would go to her? Was God a liar? Was Malak a liar? Was his promise nothing more than a sick joke?

Were these his final thoughts? Was hell's fiery, bony hand about to reach out and claim him?

The old man didn't recall anything too dramatic about the landing. The motion simply ceased and there they stood. There was no crash, no abrupt bump in the darkness.

A welcoming committee of sorts jostled and pushed their way forward for a gawk. Their overwhelming ugliness and sickening, taunting rants frightened him, but for the moment he was more caught up with the fact they were standing on solid ground; that is, if it could be called ground.

Where they stood resembled a field of smoldering lava that hadn't quite cooled. Fiery specks of reddish-orange embers could be seen amidst the pockets of gray smoke that rose up all around them.

Not every spot where they stood was alike. Pathways void of the molten-like mess interspersed the landscape.

Simultaneously, with Zadar's first step, a deafening roar of cheers arose from the hellish peanut gallery.

Shouts of "Welcome to hell!" drooled from the mouths of about three hundred of the ugliest creatures one could possibly imagine.

Their intent became immediately obvious. They were there to welcome home an important commander and to hear the victory tales surrounding the capture of the old man who was still puzzled about all the fuss.

Were there not bigger fish for hell to fry?

As a crowd-pleasing gesture, Zadar yanked on the old man's chain, hauled him to the ground, and proceeded to grind his foot into his face.

Torture, torment, and degradation were obviously a hit in the little bit of hell the old man had seen thus far.

Zadar flew into a rant about stopping the rise in the number of earthlings being allowed into heaven and then sent back to earth to spread their "poison."

"This is not written in the book," he shouted to the gang of goons who hung on his every word. "We will push the High and Mighty back on this one and score a victory in the battle to throw Him off His throne."

The words had no sooner left Zadar's vile mouth when the ground began to rumble and shake violently.

Plumes of black smoke arose instantly all around them. Showers of hot coals flew in all directions as the demons ran for whatever cover they could find.

The old man remembered seeing hotshot Zadar leading the exit parade. There he was pushing, shoving and stomping on anyone who got in his way.

If there was any consolation for the old man in all that was going on, it was in the delight of no longer having Zadar's fat foot squashing his face into the ground.

The shaking seemed to last several long minutes. When it stopped, the old man found himself alone for the first time in a long time.

Surveying his surroundings, he noticed cracks of one inch to approximately eight inches had gouged the terrain all around him.

Sitting in the midst of the chaos, he bowed his head, already slightly lowered by the weight of his chain, and cried.

Never had he felt so alone, so forsaken.

As he looked through his tears out over the blackened mess, he was suddenly aware of a glowing light behind him. Too beaten and weak to fully turn his head, he sat motionless in the stillness and watched the light expand around him like a butterfly slowing unfurling its wings.

With the glow came a sense of well being, a sense of peace and warmth, unlike the stifling, sickening heat of the hell that had become his home.

Gently, soothingly, a pair of hands touched the chain around his neck. Instantly it fell to the ground. With its fall came a total relief from the pain plaguing his body. His mind was doing cartwheels trying to figure out what was going on.

The light grew stronger in the seconds it took him to turn around.

There before him was the most beautiful being he had ever seen. The brilliance of His presence forced the old man to quickly shield his eyes with his forearms.

As best he could make out through the slit of the opening, this amazing creature was of average height, dressed in a full-length white gown with a golden sash. His hair was white and his eyes were like flames of fire.

The old man couldn't detect any outstanding physical features, but outward traits were not the essence of this being's beauty; that is, except for His eyes.

He was instantly aware that all the poets of the earth, from all generations, could not pen the words to do them justice. They emanated love in its purest, indescribable form. Captured within their glow was the embodiment of compassion. Pure goodness, mercy, and empathy shone out from them in all directions.

Within seconds, the old man fell prostrate on the ground. There seemed no other choice in the presence of such majesty. Everything within the old man's being was electrified with the need to respect, to worship whoever, or whatever, this was.

Feebly, almost in a whisper, and with his eyes still shut, he found the courage to ask, "Who are you?"

"I am the Alpha and the Omega, the beginning and the end. I am the great I Am," he said, not as a boast, but rather as a matter of fact.

The old man got the message loud and clear. He knew enough of the Bible and Melanie's love for it to know he was in the presence of God's only begotten Son.

No wonder he felt like bowing down.

No wonder his body trembled.

No wonder he was too terrified to open his eyes.

Chapter Seven

"Fear not, hell is not your home. You will not be forced to stay here," were the first words Ben heard after being told to stand. To say they were music to his ears would be an understatement.

"Come with me and I will show you what human eyes—except you and a small number of others—only see when it is too late and they cannot turn back," said the Lord, in a voice charged with sadness.

The old man felt totally at peace as he stood there frozen in awe and wonder at where he was and who he was witnessing. His mind flashed back to the sporadic moments of peace he felt in his topsy-turvy life since his first encounter with Malak.

He now knew, beyond the shadow of a doubt, that true peace was not an emotion, or a feeling, it was a person. That person was the God-person whose presence now engulfed him, held him under its dome, frozen in a state of tranquility.

Suddenly the glow, the light surrounding the Lord, began to move slowly but surely forward.

As it moved, the old man moved with it. A thousand questions raced through his mind. He was actually in the presence of the Almighty and could have them all answered, but he could say nothing. His thinking process seemed suspended in time, his tongue frozen.

As he soaked up his surroundings and the present situation, he thought back to a Bible study he remembered Melanie teaching in their living room years ago. It was on the glory of the Lord.

During such times as Bible studies, the old man was always pleasant to Melanie's invited guests, but declined taking part. Instead, he sequestered himself in his study until they were gone. What Melanie didn't know was that he always kept the door open a crack so he could hear what they were saying.

And now, here he was in the very presence of the one she taught about and held in such great esteem. He now knew what "glory" was because he was standing in it, surrounded by it. He had come face to face with the "King of Glory" and was now moving in His cloud, an area, as far as he could tell, about the size of a city block.

As the cloud moved, its light revealed a host of demonic riders just ahead. Screams and a litany of curses could be heard all around them as some launched attacks while others raced to both get away from the light, and at the same time, herald the arrival of their most feared enemy.

Very little was said as they journeyed on, the Lord arrayed in brilliance almost too bright to behold, followed just behind by the old man, who was on such a euphoric high that he couldn't speak, even if he had wanted to.

It wasn't long before it became apparent that traveling alongside the Creator of the universe had its definite advantages. One big one was the shield of protection it offered. The sphere of glory, as they moved forward, definitely kept the increasing hordes of attackers at bay.

It certainly wasn't because of their lack of effort, as some of the bolder ones tried to push through the waves of glory but fell short every time. They reminded the old man of giant hornets trying to smash their way through large sheets of impenetrable glass.

As they moved closer to their destination, it seemed it was the big-gun, big-ego officers of the hordes who seemed the most intent on stopping them. The more junior in rank were intent on just trying to escape as the chaos intensified. All of hell appeared abuzz with the news of who was moving through their blackened wasteland.

The Lord turned to speak. As he did, the old man again shielded himself from the brilliant light that shone out from those piercing eyes.

"So that you will better understand our journey, I will tell you what hell is like. Contrary to the lies of the adversary, this place is very real. It is laid out in definite divisions of horror and degradation. One of them is the area of the pits, which we will visit now.

"You will soon understand that there is no escape for its inhabitants," He said, His voice quivering as He spoke.

"My love and the redemption I purchased on the cross are sufficient for all who repent and turn to me while alive on the earth. Once death has occurred, it is too late.

"Also take note that the senses of hell's captives are more acute than on earth, thus making their pain here much worse. Stay close to me at all times while we are here."

The old man instantly moved closer; there would definitely be no need to be told twice.

He was also informed that in most situations from here on in, the forces of evil would no longer be able to detect their presence, though those held captive would be able to recognize them—something obviously necessary for any meaningful observation and interaction to occur.

The stench was the first thing the old man noticed.

For a moment, he thought back to his college days, and the summer he worked at the city incinerator.

His job was to weigh the trucks as they drove onto the large scale at the entrance to the building. He would weigh them full, and then empty on their way out, thus providing a way to determine the weight of the trash. He never quite forgot the rancid smells that seemed to stay fixed in his nostrils for the longest while.

He now realized those smells were like perfume in comparison to the horrible, rotting odors he had begun to encounter. The offense, he would soon realize, came from burning, rotting flesh, rising up out of the pits that ran for miles in all directions.

Each pit seemed to be approximately eight to ten feet wide. He would have to get closer to see how deep they were. The screaming coming from each was the most pitiful sound he had ever heard.

The blackness, the heat, the horrid smells, and the haunting screams all contributed to his wanting to vomit and to be anywhere but where he was.

The LORD, in a soft, gentle voice, suggested they stop and the old man rest before going on.

"I know this is difficult for you, but please understand why it is necessary. I want you, and all of the others who have been allowed to break into this world, to understand my appreciation for the work you have done, or will do, when you have returned to earth. Your task is to tell others of the hell awaiting the rejection of my love and forgiveness, and the heaven that awaits those who accept it.

"I am sure you have realized from the opposition you have witnessed that the deceiver does not like what you are being allowed to do.

"One thing about the adversary, that you will find out only too well as we approach the pits, is that he is the father of all lies. There is nothing and never will be anything good in his blackened heart. Because he will not repent, he has been judged and will take his place in the lake of fire at the appropriate time.

"Understand before we view the pits that hell was never intended for man. It was made for Satan and his angels of rebellion. The adversary is a deceiver and a liar. Unfortunately, he is good at what he does, and has convinced far too many souls to reject me and choose eternal damnation with him and his cohorts.

"When you return, tell the world of my love. Tell them that I have won the victory over death and hold the keys to hell. Tell them it is not my desire that any should perish and come here but that all should come to the knowledge of the gift of eternal life I have for them. Tell them I have provided the cross as the way out but the choosing has been left to them according to their own free will."

The old man realized that the LORD's words to him were delivered void of what his senses had beheld just moments before. The smells, the screams, the ugliness all around him, seemed somehow suspended.

Tired, he fell off to sleep, not knowing how long the reprieve would last.

Chapter Eight

As he slept, Ben dreamed a most unusual dream.

It seemed he was floating, as had been the case after his collapse in the park, only this time he appeared to be looking down over a large building. As he drew closer, he realized it was a hospital, and he was headed straight down toward a particular room.

As he hovered near the ceiling, he could vaguely make out the image of an older man hooked up to a plethora of machines and tubes. A young woman leaned forward over his bed in what appeared to be an intense one-way conversation. The fact that the man wasn't responding to her didn't seem to bother her in the least.

As he pushed through the ceiling barrier and entered the actual room, its occupants became shockingly familiar. The man in the bed was himself, and the young woman, his daughter, Sarah.

I guess, by now, nothing in this strange journey surprised him.

For a few seconds, all he could think of was how glad he was to be away from the horrors of hell.

Dream or no dream, he now found himself unable to think about passing up a chance to relate to the world he was familiar with.

He wanted so desperately to reach out and touch his daughter, put his arms around her, talk to her, hug her, and hold her, but no matter how hard he tried, the spirit body he was in did not allow the contact.

He remembered thinking how strange it was to be staring at his own body just lying there in the bed hooked up to so many tubes and machines. He thought about how he looked more like a mechanical porcupine than a human being.

Sarah held his cold, ashen hand. She spoke in a bubbly, enthusiastic voice, which, at first, seemed odd to the old man, given the circumstances.

"Dad, dad, I'm so excited," she announced. "Last night I had a dream from the Lord, and He showed me many things. He told me that he had taken you on a journey and that He had a task for you to fulfill. When it is finished, you will be allowed to return to earth, where the medical world will be shocked that you are out of the coma and alive and well.

"Oh, Dad! I had been so worried about you this past week but now all my fears have been removed. I know it was the Lord who spoke to me in the dream and that because He never lies, He will do exactly what He said He would."

Joy engulfed the old man's spirit as he hovered unnoticed in a corner of the ceiling, unable to speak to his precious daughter. He was so appreciative that she had been given hope in what seemed a hopeless situation.

On that thought, his dream was over.

As he awoke, so did his dormant senses. Back were the horrible smells, the heat, the screams, and the stark reality of where he was, including the hellish fire pits that he so wished he didn't have to face.

But though the magnet of hell had once again drawn him to its side, so too had the wonders and the peace of the Lord. The warmth of His countenance compensated for his cold, stark surroundings. The hand of the Lord beckoned to him as they began to move across the forlorn landscape to the first of the pits.

As they approached the one closest to them, he could hear the screams of a woman's voice. He would find out later that most often the gender of anyone in the pits was only known by the voice projected from each hellhole.

Looking down into the pit, which appeared to be about eight feet deep, he observed a most pitiful sight. A gaunt, skeletal creature clawed incessantly at the walls of her pit moaning, yelling, begging for someone to come and get her out.

The sides of the prison and its bottom were lined with hot coals that burned without end. Shreds of burning flesh continued to fall from her tiny frame, unrecognizable as once having been a human being. Worms, mysteriously unaffected by the flames, crawled continually in and through the remains of this tormented soul.

In its center was a small, pulsating, bluish-gray form about the size of a man's fist. He was told this was the actual soul of that particular person. Each person in the pits had such an entity.

As the old man watched, her cries grew louder. "I want my reward; I want my reward," she kept yelling.

Jesus, who had been standing afar off, drew closer. As the edge of the light of His presence touched the circumference of her pit, she lowered the tone of her rant. Immediately she switched tactics and began to plead her case.

"Lord of the universe," she cried out. "I know who you are. Let me out of here and I promise I will serve you."

Jesus, sitting calmly by the edge of her personal hell, began to speak.

"While you were alive on the earth, you led thousands astray through your witchcraft and your encouragement of the occult, even to the point of sacrificing and desecrating human beings."

"But I had such power," she yelled. "I had colleges, towns in my grip. Satan's power flowed through me. I was a kingpin in his earthly battles. He promised I would rule and reign with him in his kingdom. Now all he does is laugh at me as I burn in this hellish hole. Let me out and I will serve you, I will never go back to him."

"My child," Jesus answered, "it is too late for you. Many times I called you to repentance. I visited you often in the nighttime, pleading with you to abandon your ways and accept my forgiveness, but you would not listen and have thus chosen your course."

As the LORD turned to move away from her, the old man noticed a tear fall from His cheek to the ground.

They had not moved two feet from her pit when the most ungodly string of curses he had ever heard were directed at the very one whom she had but moments before pledged her allegiance to and promised to serve.

As would be repeated time and time again, those in the pits would promise anything and lie about everything to scheme a way out of their ghastly, fiery hell.

The next pit they visited was about one quarter of a mile away. Several hundred were visible all around them as were the unforgettable screams coming from each. The old man wasn't told and wasn't sure why only certain ones were marked for closer observation.

As they approached this particular pit, he could hear a man repeating himself in a loud voice. "There must be some mistake; check again, I'm not supposed to be here. Please, this is a huge mistake. I'm not supposed to be feeling pain. I am not supposed to be here, I tell you!"

The man immediately recognized the LORD as He moved toward the edge of the pit.

"Ah, LORD, there you are. I'm so glad you've come to get me. How could such a mistake have been made?"

"There's been no mistake," said the LORD, as he peered into the hole. The old man, who had been several steps behind Him, caught up and was now also looking into the pit. What he saw surprised him.

The man was a mess but didn't seem to be in as much a state as the poor soul who had been into witchcraft.

Knowing the old man's thoughts prompted a reply from the LORD.

"My son, looks are often quite deceiving. This man's hell is different from hers by design. Satan's torture in each pit is usually quite different. Having spent all of their lifetime getting them here, he knows only too well what upsets them and triggers their pain. It is those things he then tortures them with without end."

The man in the hole continued his rant.

"Lord, you know I lived a good life and hurt no one. You know only too well of my good deeds, now get me out of here."

As the old man stood in the Lord's shadow listening to the dialogue, he couldn't help but think how convincing the man sounded. He even looked both proper and sincere. Though his clothes were blackened and tattered, most of his flesh was intact, though shriveled and deformed.

What struck the old man the most odd was that though the flames licked all around him and worms had begun to crawl through his mid section, one could still see about two thirds of a bow tie hanging from what shreds were left of his shirt collar.

"All of your righteousness is as the filthy rags I see before me," said the Lord to the man. "You know only too well, as I do, that your memory and that of all the others here is not only intact, but more acute. Therefore, you cannot pretend you have forgotten how you lived your life on earth.

"You were ashamed of me and the cross your entire life. Choosing not to accept my righteousness, you chose instead your good deeds, sweeping your sin and what you were really like under the carpet.

"Your good deeds were always so that others could see them and you could gain some benefit for yourself. It was always I and no one else who saw how you treated your wife and children behind closed doors.

"Only by renouncing your sin and taking on my righteousness could you have changed. Your outcome could have been so different had you listened to me all the times throughout your life that I came to you and offered you my love and forgiveness, but you refused."

The words of the Lord seemed to penetrate the pitiful man in the bow tie to the core. The last they saw of him, he was coiled in the fetal position, cowering in the corner of his pit. Though dejected, his voice still worked well, as evidenced by the curses he let out as they walked away.

As they drew close to the third pit the Lord had chosen for observation, the old man could hear what seemed to be the oddest thing in such a place—the words of the Gospel being preached.

With fervor and gusto, someone in the pit kept shouting out: "Repent, for the kingdom of God is at hand."

A demon, who obviously couldn't see either the Lord or the old man, peered over the edge of the pit and mocked its owner.

"Yes, preach that one again, that was a good one. And how do you find the accommodations in your new kingdom?" laughed the demon as he began to walk away from the edge of the preacher's pit.

"Don't laugh, you foul creature; the Gospel of the Lord brings repentance and salvation."

As the demon moved off to another pit, the Lord slowly approached the edge of the hole, the old man following close behind.

What he saw ranked right up there with the other top disgusting things he had witnessed being dished out on hell's sickening platters.

The babbling words of the preacher in the pit emanated from what appeared to be the remains of a grossly ulcerated tongue. The grotesque-looking organ—at least three times normal size—protruded disproportionately from the charred skeletal form that shouted in pain between bouts of preaching.

The Lord, aware of the old man's total shock and puzzlement about the large tongue, offered an explanation.

"The tongue is symbolic of those I have called to teach and preach my Word. Not many are called to the task because of the pressures and attacks associated with the challenge. Few can handle the holiness and truth necessary to be my spokesman. The failure always comes when they begin to shy away from preaching the cross and its message of love and repentance. The watering down of my words becomes their downfall."

As soon as the LORD finished His explanation, the shouts of the preacher picked up.

"LORD, see how I'm suffering for your Gospel. I shouldn't even be here. The demons mock my preaching and do not listen."

"My son, it is not here and not now that I called you to be my vessel. Yes, you did preach for over twenty years, but not the full truth of my cross. Truth cannot be mixed with what is false. You began your course well but did not finish it. I wanted you to always tell my people of the rewards of following me after repenting of their sins, but you would not tell them. Instead, you spent the greatest portion of your ministry watering down my Word and making light of sin, often referring to it as just a matter of interpretation and a state of mind.

"Good works replaced the preaching of repentance and became the banner of your demise. Because people under you never repented of their sins to receive forgiveness and eternal life, their blood now rests on your soul.

"Error begets error. As you moved slowly away from truth, false doctrine nipped at your heels until it brought you down to the level of justifying horrible sins you fell into, all the while convincing others and yourself that you were following Me.

"I came often to you to explain these things, as did others I sent to you, but you would not listen. Instead, you chose to follow the father of lies, whom you serve here now."

These were the LORD's final words to him. They were followed immediately by a violent outburst of screams and curses from the preacher's pit. The mask of this poor soul had been removed.

The old man felt sick to his stomach as he pondered how horribly sad things were in this horrid place.

Chapter Nine

The peace of the LORD's presence was the only thing sustaining the old man. He knew deep down in his soul that only God Himself could keep him from going insane in such a place as this.

He tried, as a diversion, to focus for a moment on the peace and serenity of his park bench and life as it used to be, but the screams and choking smells of burning flesh would not allow the luxury.

The LORD beckoned for the old man to follow Him. Together they began to make their way down a lane he hadn't noticed before.

After walking for several miles, the old man realized the farther along they went, the fewer pits he saw. The smells began to dissipate, and the screams became fewer and fewer until they finally could not be heard at all.

The terrain around them began to change from flat plains to a series of steep hills dotted with ragged rock outcroppings.

As they descended to the bottom of the highest of the hills, a most bizarre sight caught the old man completely by surprise. There before him was a brightly colored bench sitting in the middle of a large, open park area covered in the most luscious green grass he had ever seen. Its texture was like velvet, and it swayed back and forth, stroked by a cool breeze and accompanied by the soft, low sounds of music that quickly enraptured his whole being.

The glorious glow of the Lord's presence—switched off as they traveled through the pits—had returned, enriching the beauty of this heavenly spot.

"What's going on?" he asked of the Lord as he quickly plopped onto the bench, hoping that it indeed was real and not one of hell's sadistic tricks.

"What you see before you is real in the sense that I created it for you. When we leave, it will leave with us."

So there he sat in his little oasis, smack in the midst of a blackened hell.

The old man couldn't thank the Lord enough for the reprieve.

"My nature has always been to create peace in the midst of chaos. It has always been my desire to have fellowship with man, to have creation worship its creator. The beauty and peace before you is but a sample of what has been prepared for those who have chosen to spend eternity with me."

Ben listened but couldn't quite take in all the Lord was saying. His whole being seemed suspended, frozen in the joy of his new surroundings.

Not only did his field of view include a bench and luscious grass, but also a crystal-clear spring bubbling up in the midst of several beds of flowers of every color of the rainbow, and a few more he had never seen. There was even a smattering of fruit trees adding to the beauty of this place.

The old man couldn't get over how the vibrancy of the colors in his tiny utopia was far superior than anything he had ever seen on earth.

His new little world seemed surreal, especially in light of the blackness and smoldering landscape just beyond the park.

Yet, as he sat there, he could definitely feel the thick lush grass beneath his feet. And the smells were beyond anything he had ever known. Each seemed bathed in sweetness similar to what he had experienced whenever he got close to the Lord. It was almost like everything in the place drew its life from Him.

He began to feel like a kid in a candy store as he surveyed his good fortune and wondered how long it would last.

The Lord, meanwhile, was nowhere to be seen, though His presence was certainly both evident and felt in every square inch of this incredible spot.

The old man didn't want to focus on where the Lord had gone. For now he simply chose to bathe in the tranquility of his surroundings. And besides, he had been around the Lord long enough to realize He was trustworthy and would be back.

Giddy with his good fortune, Ben for a moment thought of himself as being in the center of an enormous cage, with the wild animals on the outside and him safe on the inside.

After a long spell of just sitting there, mentally bathing in the splendor of his surroundings, the old man decided to walk the perimeter of his new abode.

His first steps off the bench were heavenly. The velvet-like grass was not only a delight to walk on, but was also therapeutic. A sense of rejuvenation and refreshment poured over him each step he took. As a matter of fact, he felt so good that walking quickly turned to running. Age obviously had no bearing in this environment. His seventy-two years quickly turned to thirty-two—at least that's how he felt as he ran across the landscape.

His jubilation proved, unfortunately, to be short-lived. Having initially focused mainly on the bench in the center of the park, he hadn't checked out what was beyond the blackness along its edges.

Climbing to the top of the hill, he discovered a large, flat area about the width of a football field that made its way almost completely around the compound and served as an ideal look-off for observing the plains below.

As he scanned the terrain from his hilltop view, he became aware of distant images coming into focus. Crouching low to the ground, he scurried quickly behind a large boulder. Peering out, he caught a glimpse of two demons moving quickly on foot through the rocks and approaching the park compound.

As best the old man could make out in hell's depleted light, each demon was in competition to see who was the ugliest.

One, about five feet tall, looked a lot like a giant rat in a hooded robe. The second, about three and a half feet tall, resembled an overweight cobra that half slithered, half walked around and through the legs of the other. Both were spewing verbal abuse, arguing intensely over something that each said was the other's fault.

The sound of approaching hoof beats silenced their mouths as they quickly scratched and slithered their way to cover. It was soon obvious that the twenty or so riders kicking up the black dust in the distance were some sort of demonic posse in pursuit of the rat and snake pair.

Finally, after about ten minutes of silence, they once again emerged from the shadows and resumed their argument.

"It's your fault that we're on the run," the rat-like one said.

"It most certainly isn't; it's your fault," said the other. "You were the one in charge of the section of pits they visited.

"How was I to know who they were?" screamed the one with the snake face.

"Shut up for a minute, and let's think this through," the rat demon shot back. "The way I see it, we have only two choices. We either continue to run and hide or turn ourselves in to Satan's henchmen."

"Wow, what great choices," the snake demon hissed sarcastically as he slithered past the legs of his rat sidekick, who couldn't resist nipping at him as he passed by.

"Cut it out!"

"Now, listen. I say we continue to try and make it to the walls of one of the tunnels and hide out there as long as we can. Surely the lowly vermin there would be honored to have someone of our stature dwelling among them."

Both were in agreement that if they gave up they would surely be tortured for eternity as one of Satan's caged pets.

The rat demon quickly scurried to the highest point he could find and returned to report no sightings of the band of hunters who sought them out.

Within seconds of the *all clear* being given, the oddball pair of demonic rebels was off in search of a tunnel to hide in.

The old man shivered as he silently bid them good riddance and watched them fade into the bleak landscape, neither aware of how close they had come to his paradise hideout.

Feeling safe, he headed back down the hill to his little oasis and its park bench where he could sit and once again enjoy the splendor of the Lord's provision.

Chapter Ten

The old man leaned over and plucked a pear-like fruit from a tree that had extended its branches over his bench just far enough to offer shade and a temptation of food.

As he bit into the fruit, he realized it was both bitter and sweet; *symbolic*, he thought, of his present circumstances.

Crossing his legs and arms, he wiggled his body into a comfort zone and decided it was a good time to relax and take stock of his situation.

How strange, he thought, *to find myself in such a place as this, and sitting on, of all things, a park bench.* It was hard to forget the last park bench he sat on, or to be more technical, fell from, landing in a heap on the ground.

So here he was in a world so bizarre as to defy reason—something he had quickly come to learn bore no credentials in the places he now found himself.

Though he felt peaceful and content in his little haven, he could not shake a gnawing feeling of loneliness, of being incomplete, of something missing. It didn't take him long to realize the source could be summed up in one word—Melanie.

He knew now more than ever how badly he missed her and how determined he was to find her, especially since he had a promise from his heavenly friends that his mission was in their hands to grant. Feeling rejuvenated, he decided to set his eyes anew on the prize of finding her.

As he consumed the last bite of his heavenly fruit, loud words of invitation broke both his train of thought and the silence of the park.

"Come and dine."

Turning around quickly to determine the source, he nearly fell off his bench in shock. There before him was a table about thirty feet long, set more extravagantly than anything he had ever seen or could possibly imagine.

The LORD Himself, in a white full-length gown trimmed in gold, sat at the head. The glory and splendor of His presence immediately lit up not only the table, but instantly filled the entire park as well. A lone, empty chair, about ten feet to the Master's right, sat unoccupied.

The table itself was covered in a thick, white cloth embroidered throughout in gold-stitched patterns. Gold candelabras stood equidistant across the expanse. Brightly colored flowers—many of the species he had never seen before—adorned the table, their exotic fragrances filling the air with heavenly smells.

Gold was everywhere. All of the various shaped dishes, food containers, goblets, and cutlery sparkled, and danced in the light of the LORD's glory.

Then there was the food.

The smells wafted through the air, arresting his nostrils. The steam from the meats, seafood, and vegetables arose from the table, capturing his palate and watering the inside of his mouth.

His eyes could scarcely take in the variety as he scanned the feast. Desserts—his favorite things—were there in equal abundance, a collage of all things imaginable, each arrayed in a multitude of swirls and curls and dressed in every shade of chocolate and caramel known to man.

Before his eyes could complete the survey, the LORD motioned for him to come forward and be seated.

As he took a step toward his chair, he saw for the first time an entire host of heavenly beings, two of whom gently placed an arm under each of his and began to escort him to his place.

At the same time the most incredible soft music he had ever heard—each piece a praiseful anthem to the Lord—filled the air. The source became obvious as a host of angels became a choir and hovered about ten feet above and behind the Lord.

Divine scenes such as this began to unfold, one by one, as if someone was flicking switches to light up a baseball stadium for a nighttime game.

Next up was the top of the hill that enclosed the park. There stood a host of twenty-four warring angels, swords drawn, standing an equal distance apart around the entire perimeter.

Each appeared to be approximately ten to twelve feet tall and clothed in long, white gowns that flapped like flags in the warm gentle breeze. They wore sandals on their feet and breastplates of gold with matching helmets. A golden trumpet hung at the side of each sentinel.

As the pair of heavenly dinner escorts reached the table, one pulled back the chair to seat him and then both disappeared.

The old man pondered how being in the direct presence of the Lord was such a hard thing to fathom. He thought, as an example, how impossible it was to reach out and touch Him. He instantly knew that to do so would not only be disrespectful, but impossible, not to mention dangerous, as the power of His glory would surely disintegrate the one who tried.

No one, he thought, *except someone who experienced it, could understand what it was like to be in His presence.* It definitely held his emotions on the brink of tears. He realized this certainly had nothing to do with sadness. To the contrary, as he would later come to know, it had to do with His holiness, the very essence of who He was.

So there the old man sat in awe, perfectly still, head slightly bowed, and terribly afraid to speak.

It wasn't long before the silence was broken by a voice behind him uttering the words, "Well, Mr. Jacobs, where would you like to begin?"

That voice.

It couldn't be. How could it be? Could it be? Sure enough, it was.

The shock of hearing his name was minor in comparison to realizing it was Malak behind the voice asking the question.

As the old man glanced over his right shoulder, he caught sight of a gold-edged serving cloth hung over Malak's extended arm. His glance continued upwards until he made contact with the twinkle in Malak's eyes and the boyish grin on his lips.

The old man glanced quickly at Malak's left shoulder for signs of a wound. None appeared.

Malak spoke first as the old man couldn't seem to get his tongue in gear.

"You're wondering about the wound? It has healed quite nicely. It would take more than a pack of dimwit demons to put me out of commission."

Malak glanced quickly over at the LORD to see if there was a hint in His expression regarding his choice of words. Having discerned no serious rebuke, he continued to speak.

"I will be your main server for the banquet that has been prepared for you. If you're not sure where to start, may I suggest we begin with some of your favorite seafood appetizers?"

Leave it to Malak to know what I like to eat, the old man mused to himself. "Sounds like a plan," he answered sheepishly, half afraid to even blink in such an atmosphere.

With a nod from Malak, six servant angels appeared, three on either side of the table. Neither spoke to the other, but each knew exactly what to do without Malak uttering a word.

Thus the feast began.

Hour after hour the angels waited on the LORD and His lone guest.

It became evident early on just how contrasted the banquet was, in emphasis and purpose, in relation to any similar earthly function he had ever attended.

Neither the food, nor the presentation, nor the ambience, became the focal point of the heavenly feast.

Here in the middle of hell, fellowship—God meeting with man, man meeting with God, in raw-gut conversation, no holds barred—was the centerpiece.

As the serving of the food wound down, the conversation picked up.

It didn't take the old man long to realize he was somewhat of a novelty to the inquisitive angels who had come to serve him. It turned out, ironically, that they were as nervous of him as he was of them.

Throughout the formal portion of the evening, each had sized up the other like schoolgirls giggling over the boys at their first dance.

As it turned out, the LORD, who leaves no stone unturned in everything He does, had handpicked each servant angel allowed at the feast.

The fellowship with the angels would become the old man's introduction to the fact that not all angels are created equal. Malak would teach him that just like human beings, they do not all look alike and certainly do not all perform the same tasks. Classification, rank, government, and purpose are all part of their structure, all part of who and what they are.

As for his six new angelic acquaintances, he found one in particular stole the show.

Ben conceded that far too often it was the human tendency to stereotype everything. Such a thought formed the genesis of why this particular angel brought him so much amusement.

Mosoo was the angel's name.

Awkward, but with an inquisitive nature to the point of asking rapid-fire questions every minute of a conversation, Mosoo brought the old man almost to tears with laughter as he tried his best to come up with answers.

A wing-tip calamity with a water vase that spilled its contents all over the table was but one example of Mosoo's entertainment. The incident invoked a half-stern look from Malak, but nothing more than a few giggles from the others.

The old man couldn't help but realize throughout the evening that one particular question kept coming up in one form or another. Each of his six new friends kept refocusing on why the old man was considered so special and worthy of such a feast.

Repeatedly they wanted to know why the Lord was so passionate about human beings, who far too often, as they saw it, were so unkind and so rejecting of Him.

Their honest words of inquiry pricked the old man's heart. A tear began to form and fall slowly down his cheek as he thought of the Lord's goodness to Him.

For the first time, he truly realized how much he was loved and what a sacrifice it was for the Lord to die on such a cruel cross for the sins of mankind and, more personally, for his own sins.

The Lord gave the angels a task that took them away from the table. He then beckoned for the old man to come and sit at the chair directly alongside Him.

Head bowed, he obeyed the command.

He had never been this close to the Lord. Only a foot separated the old man and this Majestic Being. Tears now flowed uncontrollably down his cheeks. Too embarrassed to look up, he just sat there, hands folded, staring at the tablecloth.

Slowly and gently, the Lord reached over and touched the old man's clasped hands. As He did, it was impossible to miss the ugly nail scars on the master's hands as He consoled His teary-eyed subject.

For the first time, the full impact of the Lord's sacrifice at Calvary hit the old man with the force of a barreling freight train.

"My son, I have seen the changes in your heart, changes that have been ever so gradual since Melanie accepted my sacrifice. I've watched over the years as love has chipped away at your hardened heart. I've seen it soften and then grow cold when I took your beloved home to heaven.

"It brings me great pleasure to see love finally win out over your life. Your decision to accept my love will be monumental for you. You are my son and I have much work for you to do."

As the master finished speaking, the angels returned and began to sing loudly, all the while dancing around the table, the LORD, and the old man.

It all seemed so strange. He had officially become a Christian in this tiny piece of heaven plunked in the middle of a fiery hell.

Chapter Eleven

Citadel Hill was one of her all-time favorite places to unwind from life's hectic pace.

Since it was Saturday, Sarah brought Esther and Joshua with her. During the week she was always by herself, mostly on lunch breaks since she only worked a few blocks away at one of the downtown bank towers.

Her promise to the children was that they could fly their kites on the hill's slopes while she watched, read, and guarded their picnic lunch. She knew, of course, that there probably wouldn't be a lot of time for reading if past kite excursions were any indication. Rescuing plummeting kites and untangling string would likely occupy most of her time.

So far, so good.

The wind on the hill seemed just right for kiting. A flood of warm, persistent breezes swept over the green slopes and rushed down toward the harbor.

Short sprints down the hill brought surefire success as the brightly colored birds soon soared higher and higher, bobbed, and pushed to new heights. Obviously ecstatic, Esther and Joshua held on tightly to their masterpieces.

Sarah laughed to see the loves of her life having so much fun.

As she looked out over the harbor, she thought how glad she was to be living in Halifax, Nova Scotia, the city of her birth. She had traveled extensively across Canada, the United States, and Europe after completing her commerce degree at Saint Mary's and before getting married, but nothing thrilled her more than to come back to Halifax. It was home.

In recent years, she also traveled for the bank, something that occupied more of her time than she liked to admit. But without a husband and no second salary to help out, she had too few choices and little room to complain or maneuver.

She and George, just like her mom and dad, had met at Saint Mary's. Unlike her mom and dad, their marriage lasted only three years. When it was over, she was left with a two-year-old and a newborn to care for.

"Irreconcilable differences" was how the divorce papers put it. According to his lawyer, lily-white George felt he couldn't take being married to a "zealous fanatic," his favorite buzzwords for her conversion and attempt to live according to what she believed. The truth be known—and she had found out—George was having an affair, his second in the first two years of their marriage.

The only good thing about the whole mess was that she got full custody of the children—and he got what he wanted—bimbo number two.

It all seemed so sad. He didn't even fight for visitation rights, something he simply threw away in his blind pursuit of another trophy.

For the moment, she chose to push such thoughts away and focus on the slow, steady pace of a pilot boat guiding its assignment up the harbor.

Slowly it led the huge container ship past Georges Island, past the Angus L. Macdonald bridge, and then the A. Murray MacKay span at the Narrows. Its final destination would be a swing to starboard into the Bedford Basin and a berth at the Fairview Cove container pier.

The goings-on in the harbor always fascinated her. They were so often an escape when too many things made too many demands on her time.

Why worry? she would always tell herself. She knew, having been a Christian for ten years, that doing so changed nothing. She knew only too well that the LORD would help her solve what so often seemed unsolvable.

This was indeed what her heart told her, but she had to admit that some days she listened to her gut feelings and focused on circumstances rather than solutions.

Today seemed to be one of those down days.

She didn't have them all that often, but when they did come, they took a serious bite out of her emotions. She kept thinking how totally abandoned she felt when George left her with no means of support and two kids to care for.

At that point, her life seemed to be over. Its cruel waves seemed to have landed her on a beach of despair like a stranded whale, unable to breathe.

But God, as He always did, came through. This time He used her mom and dad as His extended arms.

Dad had the basement of their Fairview home turned into a small living quarters, and in they moved with what little furniture they could scrounge.

All seemed well.

A friend of her dad's heard of her plight and lined up a job interview at the bank. Landing the job after six months of searching not only boosted her morale but, more importantly, put money in her pocket to support herself and the children.

Her mom, right up until she got sick, was a fulltime nanny to the children, a real blessing for a single parent trying to get on her feet. So much, she mused, for what used to be.

Her deep thoughts were interrupted by the sounds of laughter as the children frolicked, eyes heavenward at their kites, now mere specks against the blue sky.

Sarah, unaware she was being watched, adjusted the picnic umbrella, trying to get the correct angle to shade the sun as it quickly approached high noon.

She glanced to the bottom of the hill at the arms of the old town clock for the exact time, and in anticipation of the firing of the noonday cannon from atop the garrison behind them.

Hidden in the belfry of the historic landmark lurked two unsavory characters, each of them intent on not only disrupting her thoughts, but on causing whatever harm they could to her and the children.

Such, she would soon realize, was the reality of warfare that so few earthlings are aware is going on simultaneously, and on so many levels.

In hell, her father's heavenly entourage was about to be attacked by everything the beastly place could conjure up, while here on earth, a sinister stalking was underway bent on the destruction of an unsuspecting mother and her kids.

Boom!'

It was the deafening sound from the cannon blast, a noise loud enough to raise the dead.

Sarah thought she would be used to it by now, but somehow the shrill sound could still catch her unaware, especially if she was deep in thought just seconds before its intrusion.

Though she jumped, the children, caught up in the enjoyment of their kites, hardly flinched.

Meanwhile, in the belfry of the town clock, the plot had hatched.

Two dog-like creatures emerged from behind the clock's base and headed straight toward the children at rapid speed.

They were dogs in the sense that they had four legs and a tail, and they growled, but beyond that they were too grotesque to be considered anything resembling earthly canines.

From what Sarah could make out from a distance, they seemed to be more head and teeth than anything else.

Like any mother, she was aware of the drama the second it began to unfold.

In a flash, she jumped to her feet and began to run toward the children at the same time as the creatures. In her heart she hoped beyond hope that she could reach them before they did.

As she ran, she noticed yet another blur of movement closer to the children than either she or the menacing beasts. A man in an orange jacket moved in front of them just seconds before the animals pounced.

As the pair lunged skyward to get past the man, he too shot straight upwards at least twenty feet into the air. When he landed, he had each of the growling beasts by the tail and began to swing them around and around at amazing speed.

After several rotations and a powerful thrust, each was flung high into the air and out of site above the crest of the hill.

Tears streamed down the faces of the children as they screamed and raced toward their mother as fast as their little legs could carry them.

Frightened and shaking, they grabbed and embraced her waist, each trying to out-squeeze the other.

"It's okay; it's okay, calm down. Everything's going to be all right. They're gone. You're safe. I've got you. It's all right. You're okay."

Joshua, between sobs, was the first to realize he didn't have his kite.

"Mom, mom, my kite! I let go of my kite."

"Yes, I know; it's okay."

"So did I," Esther sobbed.

"I'll get you each another one. None of us are hurt, and that's all that matters."

"Mom, where is the man in the orange jacket?" Esther asked.

All three suddenly became aware that their rescuer in the orange jacket was nowhere to be seen.

For now, all Sarah wanted to do was get the children off the slopes to somewhere where there were people.

The entrance to the fort was only a few hundred yards away. The place would be crawling with tourists and a much-needed feeling of safety in numbers.

Quickly gathering their belongings, they headed for the entrance.

Explanations of what had happened would have to wait.

Chapter Twelve

Sarah fumbled in her purse for money to pay the booth attendant. Try as he may, the young man in the Parks Canada uniform couldn't disguise his look of concern as he greeted the disheveled trio.

"Is everything okay?" he asked.

Judging by their demeanor and the look of fear on their faces, it was easy to see why he asked the question.

"We're fine, thank you," Sarah replied.

She knew it wasn't exactly the whole truth, but she also knew the truth would create more questions than she had answers.

Sarah wasn't ignorant about spiritual warfare. After all, she had studied the Bible and several books on the subject. But now she had come face to face with the stark contrast between book knowledge and real life.

Then there was her dad.

Surely here was a case in point of the colliding of two worlds: the physical that we can see and touch, and the spiritual or supernatural that's seldom seen and doesn't exist for those who simply choose to blot out or ignore what they don't understand.

The physical dad she was close to, the one she loved and respected all her life, lay in a comatose state in a Halifax hospital with next to no chance of recovery, at least according to the doctors.

But she knew, deep in her heart of hearts, that her real dad was alive in a world she had never seen. Though scared out of her wits, knew she had the Bible and a dream from the LORD as anchors to hold onto.

Lately, it seemed, those two worlds had been fighting fiercely for control of her mind and life. Now, with the attack on her kids, things were getting a lot more personal, and a lot more serious.

With tickets, brochures, and lunch in hand, the trio walked the few yards from the booth to the young sentinel at the entrance to the drawbridge. The weathered gateway led across the moat and into the fort.

The sentinel was quite a sight, dressed from head to toe in his red uniform, an exact replica of a 78th Highlander, the British regiment of soldiers garrisoned at the Citadel from the founding of Halifax in 1749 until 1906.

The children were always fascinated by how long he could stand on guard in such a motionless, statue-like stance.

It wasn't the bright-red uniform, nor the long, impressive rifle that most often caught their eye. Rather, it was his tall, black, ostrich-feathered headgear with its strap under the chin. They would always stare directly at it for however long it took for a breeze to whip up and get its feathers swaying. Both agreed it reminded them of tall grass blowing in the wind.

Walking the short distance across the bridge and through the arched granite tunnel leading into the square, a person could—if they listened carefully—almost imagine the sights and sounds of an active garrison of days gone by.

But in today's world (unless a reenactment was underway), the loud firing of rifles was replaced by the silence of digital cameras as crowds of tourists tried to capture the past with present technology.

The pebbled square of the fort bustled with activity as the crowds jostled, seemingly in all directions, crisscrossing the open area heading for the specific spot they wanted to visit first.

For Sarah and the children, that spot was the nearest piece of grass they could find to spread out their picnic blanket and satisfy their hunger.

No one spoke a word as they climbed the stone steps that hugged the inner walls of the fort and led to the grassy slopes overlooking the moat below and the city beyond.

Sarah convinced her clutching children to move far enough away from her side to spread out the blanket for their picnic.

She resolved to overcome her frightened demeanor in an attempt to give the children a sense of assurance that they were out of harm's way and that she would protect them.

As they plunked themselves down on the blanket, their nervous silence was interrupted by a growling noise coming from Joshua's famished stomach.

A simultaneous giggle erupted from the three of them as the closeness of sharing lunch became a small but much needed pinch of normality.

Minutes dragged into what seemed hours before anyone spoke. Esther broke the silence.

"Mom, why did those things come after us?"

"Yes, Mom, why?" echoed Joshua.

Sarah took a deep breath and paused for a moment before answering.

"Children, do you remember the story in the Bible about how Jesus allowed demons to enter a herd of swine and how two thousand of them went wild and threw themselves off a cliff?"

"Yes," they both replied.

"Well, we see from that story that somehow evil angels, or demons, as the Bible refers to them, can enter into animals and drive them mad. Although, in this case, the creatures that came after you seemed to be a different breed of evil, one that we don't fully understand. Your mother is so sorry that we have to discuss these things, but above all else, we must realize that God is greater than any force of evil."

"Yes, mom," piped Joshua. "Do you think He sent the man in the orange jacket? Do you think he was an angel?" He was speaking so fast she could barely make him out.

Sarah smiled and marveled at her children, who surprised her with their eagerness to discuss their horrible ordeal.

"Well," Sarah replied, as she tried to gingerly answer the children's questions, "the man in the orange jacket must have been an angel. No one but an angel of the Lord could have done what he did."

"That's right, mom," said Esther.

Her wide-eyed son kept blurting out, "Wow, an angel!"

Esther came back with yet another question. "Mom, is Grandpa going to die like Grandma Melanie did?"

The question caught Sarah off guard.

She had guessed by now that the children were venting anything and everything they had on their minds, obviously prompted by the ghoulish attack they had just been through.

"No, Esther, Grandpa isn't going to die in that hospital. He's going to return to us just like your mother said he would. Don't you remember the assurance the Lord gave me in the dream?"

"Oh, that's right. But how long will Grandpa be there? When will he wake up? How long can a person stay sleeping like that?"

"I don't know, Esther. I think people have been known to remain in a coma for many months, sometimes years. All I know is that your grandpa will come back to us just like the Lord promised."

Sarah embraced a welcomed lull in the rapid-fire questioning. The silence was indeed golden, but short-lived.

Neither Sarah nor the children heard the stranger approach.

All three had become absorbed in their own little world for the past hour, oblivious to their surroundings as they tried to sift through what happened to them.

"Hi, how is everyone?"

Sarah, startled by a voice behind her, sprayed her mouthful of lemonade all over the blanket.

Each of the children simultaneously let out a yell.

"Oh! I'm so sorry, I didn't mean to startle anyone," said the stranger. "I just came from visiting your grandpa and I wanted to assure you he's being well taken care of."

All three huddled closer to each other.

"Who are you?" Sarah blurted out.

"Just a friend," the stranger answered. "I guess you might say a lifelong friend."

"What did you say your name was?" Sarah asked as she tried to wipe the lemonade and food particles off the blanket.

The stranger didn't answer.

Though there seemed to be nothing to fear, exactly who he was and how he knew her dad, was a mystery she instantly wanted solved. But the more she asked, the more he skirted the question.

After offering a few additional assurances about her father, the stranger began to walk away.

"Well, I must be going now," he said, as he backed away slowly. "Stay close to the Lord." Those were the last words he spoke as he reached the top of the stone steps leading down to the courtyard.

As he turned to wave good-bye, there was something about his clothing that left Sarah and the children stunned—the stranger was suddenly wearing an orange jacket.

"Wait! Wait! Don't go!" Sarah cried out as all three of them jumped from the blanket and ran after him.

It was too late.

It took only seconds to reach the top of the stairs, but by the time they got there, the man in the orange jacket was nowhere to be seen.

Chapter Thirteen

The sights, sounds, and smells of battle thickened.

"Up here Ben, come up here!"

It was the first time someone had actually called him by his first name since his journey began.

Their little oasis—a place the old man hoped wouldn't become their Alamo—was under siege. But for now, there was calm in this dark place, calm despite the rumblings, yelling, and the sounds of approaching hoof beats.

Ben thought about how he would like to be as steeled as those around him. All of the spiritual beings seemed to draw their peace and strength from the presence of the Lord in their midst.

"Ben! Ben!" came the call a second time.

As he looked up to the top of the wall to identify the voice, he caught sight of the largest and most striking angel he had seen thus far.

As he thought about going toward him, he realized that without having taken a step, he was positioned alongside this gigantic creature who he guessed was nearly three times his own height.

A reflection of light from the angel's sword bounced into his eyes. When the flash eased, it became a mirror pointing at Ben and reflecting what should have been the old man's image. Instead, a young man about the age of thirty in a flowing gown was staring back at him.

When the shock ceased, he realized he was the man in the sword's mirror, minus forty pounds, white hair, and a pearl-handled cane.

Wow! he thought. *Is that really me?*

The angel spoke, but Ben didn't answer.

The winged warrior took his cue from the dazed look and dropped chin of the professor at his side.

The angel put down his weaponry and assumed a seated position. Doing so allowed the old man to better converse with this majestic being.

"I want you to see and understand what is going on," said the angel in a booming voice. The loudness of his words had nothing to do with his size, but rather the necessity of being heard above the din of battle preparations.

As he spoke, the wind parted a mass of blond curls, revealing the ruddy complexion of this handsome creature with the solid square chin, high cheek bones and the biggest set of soft, pale blues eyes Ben had ever seen.

Several questions darted through Ben's mind, pushed aside by the intensity of what was unfolding in the distance below.

The twenty-four angels positioned atop the bluff were obviously commanders who took their orders from the big angel seated at his side. One by one, and sometimes by twos and threes, they would appear in front of him chattering incessantly about points of strategy and position. As orders were handed out, each dispersed down the slopes and across the rugged terrain to the battlefields below.

The angel stared intensely back and forth across the dimly lit horizon like an eagle preparing to swoop down on its prey. Opponents slowly advanced toward each other as if figures on a giant chessboard spread out across the landscape.

Horses and riders were now visible in the distance.

"Are you wondering why we fight with ancient armor and ride on horses?" the angel asked as the vigil continued.

Still in awe and half afraid to speak, Ben mumbled something affirmatively while trying to hide his surprise that the angel knew his thoughts.

"Assault rifles, laser-guided bombs, and nuclear weapons are not of this world and were never meant to be in yours," said the angel, not in a condemning voice but more in one of melancholy tones. What unfolded next was a lesson from the winged logician on a few of the differences between the natural and supernatural world.

"God the Creator made the heavens and the earth. He created man out of dust, breathed life into him and put him in charge. We angels know this to be the truth because we were there."

The young professor's ears perked up at the thought of the angels having been witnesses to an event that took place so long ago.

The angel continued. "Man, who proved to be no match for his adversary, not only failed and rebelled against God, but he also brought about the blackest day ever in the heavens and on earth—the day His Son, our master, shed His blood and died on a cross to pay the penalty for man's sin."

The professor wasn't sure if angels cried. All he knew was that there was a definite quiver in the big guy's voice as he briefly turned his massive frame around, blocking a view of his face.

Composing himself, he continued to brief the professor and finish the query on the difference between arsenals in the seen and unseen world.

"Weapons in earth's world equal power. In the many dimensions in which we exist, they are of no effect and are both useless and powerless. Earth is but a reflection of heaven gone mad because the Holy One has allowed humankind freedom of choice. Man by excluding God, has run it amok."

Ben knew a lecture when he heard one. He hadn't spent over four decades in the classroom not to recognize an intense talking to, diced with a wee bit of scolding.

Fascination gripped him as he hung on every word the angel spoke. He began to realize that before him was a window into the makeup of these servants of God and man.

As time went on, he realized in greater depth just exactly how compassionate and totally dedicated they were to their master. He was also gaining greater understanding of their inquisitive nature and puzzlement when it comes to the strange ways of man—the creature they are sworn to serve and protect under God's direction.

"God the Almighty is all powerful," the angel continued. "He contains all power and is all power. We move and carry out His plans with the power He gives us. We can operate in many dimensions that you cannot in order to conduct His bidding, be it here in hell, in heaven, or on earth.

"You must always remember, my friend, that God is counting on the Christians of earth to use His power for good. A day of reckoning will surely come for all who choose not to do so.

"The battle about to begin before you is an example of what power in the hands of the evil one has come down to. His insane hatred of God has led to the trickery and destruction of untold millions of lives who have abandoned God and pursued a promise of power the devil cannot deliver. This day you will see the power of your God unleashed through His mighty warriors who will have victory over the enemy and secure your freedom from this place."

The professor turned and walked to the opposite edge of the look-off to check out the status of the compound below.

The first thing he noticed was the definite dimness where once had been the glorious light of the Lord's presence.

Movement had come to a standstill. He quickly rubbed his eyes and looked again. There was no heavenly anything to be seen anywhere. Gone was the beautiful greenery, the fruit trees, the table of feasting, the servant angels, and worst of all—the Lord.

The general hadn't missed the shock registered on Ben's face as he looked back toward him.

"They're gone, professor."

"But where? How? Why?" asked the frantic and disgruntled student of this strange place.

Thoughts of the horrors of hell began to paralyze his mind. It was an understatement to say he was scared. He could feel himself grow cold and begin to shake.

The giant angel changed again from stern general to compassionate being.

Warmth increased steadily as a definite arm embraced his shoulder. He felt himself being gently turned around and motioned in the opposite direction.

"Focusing on what was will not bring you what will be," said the angel, as he softly patted Ben's back and beckoned for him to sit at his side.

"If you can use a few words of advice, I challenge you to trust the LORD with all your heart. As angels, we have trusted our master for thousands of years. You humans, if you don't mind me saying so, often can't seem to trust Him for a day."

A booming, boisterous laugh followed his words. The comment, and the laughter, brought a smile to Ben's face.

"I guess he has a point," Ben said softly to himself.

The angel's outburst triggered a peace that settled over Ben, quieting his nerves and delivering a needed dose of assurance that everything was going to be all right.

"Get some rest," said the angel. "This battle won't last long. When it is finished, we will go down together to lead the charge out of this place."

Exhausted, the old man, who chuckled to himself because he was now a young man, decided to take the angel's advice.

In the midst of his laughter, he had to admit he liked how he looked and felt in this younger version of himself.

Before he nodded off, he thought he should at least find out his guardian's name.

"What do they call you?" Ben asked.

"I am God's war angel. They call me Michael, the archangel."

Chapter Fourteen

Matt MacKeen had a problem. His strong feelings for Sarah weren't going away and he was too scared to tell anyone, especially her.

Living and working in the same apartment building as her father had both good points and bad. The good points were the opportunities to catch a glimpse of her, and the odd chat when she and the children came to visit.

The bad points, as he saw them, could all be attributed to him, including his shyness and inability to keep his foot out of his mouth, or his face from flushing every time he was anywhere near her.

His infatuation with Sarah was not an overnight thing. It was more of a marathon that started thirteen years earlier when they were both attending Saint Mary's.

He was an awkward, gangly, socially inept eighteen year old from the town of Lunenburg, on Nova Scotia's south shore, the son of parents who made a humble but honest living from the fishing industry, or what was left of it.

She was a bright, preppy, opinionated eighteen year old with a bouncy head of red hair and an attitude of confidence that he instantly admired.

Sarah grew up in Halifax, the daughter of well-educated parents, one of whom was his all-time favorite professor, Ben T. Jacobs. He often wondered if he liked Professor Jacobs so much because he was such a good teacher or because he was Sarah's father. Perhaps it was a little of both.

Matt let his mind wander back to the first time he met Sarah. It was, of all things, in a lineup registering for a sociology course.

She had spoken first. "I hate lineups. Don't you?"

Before he could answer, she had spoken again.

"I can't understand why, in this age of computers, they make us queue for courses."

"I can't either," he finally had blurted out.

"My name is Sarah. What's yours?"

"Matt MacKeen," he had answered back.

In the half hour it had taken to get to the front of the line, Sarah had told a total stranger her life story. Matt had only managed to get in a thumbnail sketch of his life between pauses about hers.

Perhaps it had been her smile, her spunk, her kindness in making conversation, or maybe all of the above. All he knew for sure was that from that first day he met her, she had caught his eye and captured his heart.

Matt glanced at his watch, surprised at how much time he must have been daydreaming and how he was almost late for class.

Finishing the last of his routine checks of the apartment complex, he bolted for the elevator, slipping a second arm through his backpack as the door opened and quickly closed behind him.

Matt thought some more about his shy nature as he half walked, half ran the few blocks down Robie Street to the university. Surely he had become more outgoing over the years since he first met Sarah.

He wondered though, what good coming a little more out of his shell had done for him, since Sarah surely wasn't interested in him after all these years.

He did feel sorry her marriage had failed and she was a single mom with two children to raise without a dad.

When Matt left Saint Mary's after completing his master's degree, he thought all was well with Sarah and George.

"Ah, George Crosby." Matt could feel the hair rising on the back of his neck as he thought about him.

I guess sometimes love really is blind, he thought. He could have told her from the start that George was no good for her and that he was more in love with himself than he was with her.

For the past six years, Matt had put his own life on hold. His aging parents weren't able to keep up with the pressing demands of running the fish plant in a changing world where there were too many big players, and too few fish to play with.

Matt was unable to perform miracles for his parents, but did manage to keep them from losing the plant and keep them afloat until the right buyer came along and bought them out.

Now they lived—with smiles on their faces—in sunny Florida for six months, and in a quaint little mobile home outside Lunenburg, the rest of the year.

After the deal went through, Matt had decided to resume his education. His first thought was to write to Professor Jacobs to ask his opinion on whether he had what it took to complete a doctorate in child psychology.

The professor's kind words and encouragement, not to mention his glowing letter of recommendation, had tipped the scales toward yes, so here he was back in Halifax living a life where he was always short on cash, but happy doing what he wanted.

Matt certainly owed a great deal to professor Jacobs. Not only did he encourage him, but he also let him know the super's job was available at the apartment complex. Getting it meant he had a place to live and money to go to school.

Professor Jacobs's present medical state brought Matt a lot of worry and concern. Even more so, he was worried about Sarah.

They hadn't really spoken much since her father's heart attack and subsequent coma, but he did bump into her every now and then when she came by to pick up her dad's mail and check on the apartment.

Matt had gone to see his beloved professor a few times at the hospital, usually when he felt no one was around. He hadn't been there in over a week and didn't want to go back. Standing there looking at him hooked up to all those tubes and machines and unable to talk, was too depressing, too sad to deal with.

Matt's foot had just landed on the first of several granite steps leading to the large wooden doors of Saint Mary's main building, a quaint, three-storey stone edifice built in the early 1800s.

Before he could take a second step, a loud, clear voice broke the crisp, fall air. "Matt, go to the hospital at eleven o'clock and visit Professor Jacobs."

Quickly retracting his foot to ground level, Matt immediately turned around to see who was speaking. There was no one there.

Removing his backpack, he sat down on the steps to regain his composure and try to figure out what was going on.

He had to admit he was totally confused.

The voice was clear, distinct. Was it audible or just inside his head? He suddenly wasn't so sure. All he knew was that the words not only continued to ring in his ears, but they began to penetrate his thinking. They were, at the same time, both friendly, but insistent.

Rattled as he was, he decided to skip his class and begin the walk back up Robie Street to the Queen Elizabeth II Health Sciences Centre, Halifax's largest hospital complex, commonly referred to as the QEII.

As he began the fifteen-minute walk north to the QEII, an argument unfolded in his mind. One of the voices seemed bent on talking him out of going to see the professor.

Why bother going? He can't hear you, he's a vegetable, go back to the apartment building. Forget about what you heard, or thought you heard.

The words—not his own—were sinister and cold with a twist of meanness.

Matt kept walking as the word war raged on.

On Streets of Gold

When he reached the corner of Spring Garden Road and Robie Street, a tugging sensation, half a nudge, half a pull, tried to redirect his path.

Such mind games were new to Matt. He couldn't quite get a handle on what was going on, but he was aware the tit for tat battle was way off the charts of normal reasoning.

Matt made his decision.

He decided to go with the friendlier, audible voice telling him to go to the hospital and discard the cold, unfriendly attempt to get him to go east on Spring Garden Road and back to his apartment building.

He checked his watch. It was ten fifty-five as he turned in the lane leading to the Robie Street entrance of the QEII.

As he entered the lobby, he couldn't believe who was no more than ten feet in front of him fumbling in her purse.

"Matt, oh I'm so glad you're here," said Sarah. "Are you here to visit dad? How did you know I was here? How are you doing?"

Some things never change, Matt thought to himself, as he smiled at Sarah while asking her which question she wanted him to answer first.

Sarah smiled back.

"I guess I'll never get the knack of how to slow down my racing tongue."

Matt wondered why she seemed so nervous around him, something he had never noticed in her before.

The elevator door opened and in they went.

Sarah pressed the button to her father's floor and turned back toward Matt. Both of them just stood there, staring at each other. Both their faces were slightly flushed. As the door opened, Matt motioned for her to go first. Through the elevator foyer, a right turn to the big glass doors, and the first left down the hall brought them to the third door on the right, her father's room.

Standing outside the door in full war garb were two huge angels, one slightly taller than the other, one dark skinned, the other Asian, both rugged in appearance.

Neither were visible to the old man's visitors, and probably just as well.

The pair of angelic guards, unbeknownst to Sarah and Matt, were joined in the vigil by twenty-five warring angels on the roof of the building and another three inside the room hovering near the ceiling above the professor's bed.

The pair of visitors tiptoed into the room, slowly easing their way up to the edge of the bed.

Sarah spoke first. "Is it my imagination, or is there an unusual amount of light on the wall and ceiling above Dad's head?"

"Yes there is," Matt whispered softly.

Both shrugged their shoulders at each other, neither quite sure what was going on.

"Dad, it's me," Sarah said softly, clearing her throat after several minutes of silence. "I'm sure you'll be glad to know Matt MacKeen is also here to visit."

Sarah failed to fight back the tears that began to flow down her cheeks.

Matt, unsure of what to do, went with the feelings in his racing heart. He slowly reached over and gently squeezed her trembling hand—a bold move for a shy guy.

Chapter Fifteen

Michael was right about the length of the battle.

His accurate prediction would soon become apparent to the young professor who tossed and turned into consciousness after a hard night on the rough ground.

The first attempt to open his eyes was met with such bright light that he had to work his way slowly from squint to wide open.

As he stood to his feet, the source of the light became evident. The majority of the twenty-four commanders under Michael's command, along with several junior officers, had gathered at the top of the bluff overlooking the battlefields below.

Their dazzling radiance chased away what was left of the dark and brought a sense of relief to Ben.

Shouts of victory broke out all over the angel-filled ridge.

Some were hugging; some were jumping; some galloped back and forth across the ridge; still others gathered in small groups and lifted their voices in praise to God. One thing was for sure—all were jubilant.

At the far end of the look-off, Michael had gathered his weaponry, mounted his enormous white steed, and headed in Ben's direction. Those in his path quickly stepped aside, cheering as he made his way toward the young professor.

Reaching Ben, he bent down, grabbed his hand, and with one swoop of his powerful arm, landed the professor on the back of his horse.

Off they rode, down through the rugged terrain and across the rolling hills to the plains below.

The short journey on this magnificent beast was like nothing he had ever experienced. Motion took on more of a glide than a ride. At times the horse's hooves touched the ground, at others times they did not. Angel and man became one on this incredible animal that seemed to know exactly what Michael was thinking, what direction he wanted to go in, and how fast.

Michael, indeed a formidable sight, was without a doubt the revered leader of the host of angels, well liked and well respected. Cheers erupted in whichever direction he turned as he galloped across the plains.

But not everywhere was there cheering and jubilation.

As they approached the front lines, moans and groans grew louder. All around were the wounded and those who comforted them, helping them up and voicing encouragement.

What struck the professor odd about the scene was the absence of blood. Hundreds of the thousands who fought had obvious wounds, but no blood oozing from them. The ground lacked any sign of the red lifeline that spilled out everywhere when men slaughtered men on earth's battlefields.

The professor's scientific mind teemed with curiosity over what he was seeing. These angel warriors were obviously injured and felt pain, but there was no blood.

"Your questions will all be answered soon enough," Michael informed the professor, who was becoming accustomed to the fact that these spiritual beings knew what he was thinking before he spoke.

By now, the commanders who had been on the ridge, found their way down to the battlefields to begin preparations for an exit from this hellish place.

"Gather up the wounded and be gentle with them," shouted Michael to the commanders who in turn echoed the orders to the junior officers in the field.

Within minutes the task was complete, and the exit began.

The acceleration was beyond anything imaginable. Thousands of the heavenly warriors, all in one accord, shot straight up—a direction most pleasing to the young professor who had locked his arms tightly around as much of Michael's waist as he could reach.

Everywhere blackness dogged the light.

Thick, black, menacing clouds rolled by, spewing hot, sooty vapor across their path as they journeyed through the sickening soup of hell.

Satan's demons were nowhere in sight.

Commanders of the defeated legions were somewhere in the bowels of hell licking their wounds and making excuses to the prince of darkness for their humiliation at the hands of the heavenly host.

It was difficult to tell how long it took to break through hell's final barriers.

All Ben could remember was that it was fast and powerful, as if a missile had been fired from a submarine on the ocean floor. The action shot the heavenly entourage into the glorious light through some sort of a portal-like gateway.

The rocket-like propulsion landed them into a sphere he quickly recognized as the surface of earth.

Never did it look so marvelous.

Everywhere the eye could see, blue replaced black as light gobbled up darkness.

As best he could tell, their exit point was somewhere near the island of Bermuda, at least that's what he knew, though he had no idea how he knew.

In what seemed to be only the blink of an eye, the blue ball of earth diminished to the size of a marble and then disappeared.

The world of physics never seemed quite so exciting to Ben T. Jacobs as it did at that moment as he grappled with how he and the band of angel warriors were able to achieve the flight they were achieving and at the speed they were traveling.

The professor's knowledge of particle physics tantalized his mind with so many questions and so few answers.

Academia bowed to reality as he tried to process his rapid travel mode, where he had been, how he got there, and where he was going.

One thing was for sure, there was no sense thinking the science of what was happening to him was impossible. Such reasoning doesn't wash when you are flying through the air at unimaginable speeds.

The professor's knowledge of light and the speed at which it travels consumed his thinking.

He knew that it was a scientific fact that light travels at a speed of 186,282 miles per second. By way of example, he had often used the illustration of a bullet traveling at the speed of light. Before you can take your finger off the trigger, he would tell his students, you will have traveled around the earth seven times.

The example was always popular as a picture of light's incredible speed. The professor was also quick to point out to the students the fact that light travels 670 million miles in one hour's time.

These facts were indeed mind-boggling especially in view of the fact that he knew they were clipping along at quite the speed.

I wonder if we are travelling at the speed of light, he thought to himself.

Michael interrupted his thoughts with the fact that they had slowed down long enough for him to catch a glimpse of the earth, but they usually traveled much faster.

How amazing, the professor mused, but he couldn't stop thinking about their bodies.

Peter Pan he knew he wasn't, but who was he? And what kind of a body could defy known science in such dramatic fashion?

As far as he could tell, he and Michael were somewhere in the middle of a huge contingent of spirit beings headed back to their base, or wherever it was they were headed. His judgment came not by sight but by deduction.

A total feeling of contentment and safety enraptured the young professor.

He could literally feel waves of warmth emanating out in all directions from where he and Michael seemed to be positioned in the pack.

At this point in the journey, there was once again very little light, an occurrence he attributed to long having passed away from earth's atmosphere.

"A trip to heaven takes approximately an hour," said Michael matter-of-factly.

"We will slow down because of the wounded and arrive tomorrow in the early afternoon. When we get there, we will separate. You will be dropped off in a region near one of the gates and we will journey to our base at Angelica."

That was it.

Michael had dished out the phenomenal information in as nonchalant a manner as you would order a burger at a fast food restaurant.

Finally, and *Melanie*, were the only two words that came to his mind.

Ben T. Jacobs could think of nothing else.

For him, nothing else really mattered.

Chapter Sixteen

Melanie loved homecomings.

For her, they were some of the most enjoyable events on the planet. She often referred to them as heaven's piñatas waiting to burst and spill their contents over her life.

As her mind filled with thoughts of the necessary preparations, she pondered in her heart the question of who the guest might be.

There was never really much fanfare associated with a homecoming announcement. Usually it was just a matter of an angel showing up at the door with the information on where to go. He or she would give the details, smile, and leave.

Within seconds of the door being shut, occupants of the house would jump for joy. That joy, in turn, would soon spill out into the neighborhood as those near your home caught wind of the blessing coming your way.

Those nearby were often other relatives and friends you had come to know and love, some you had met for the first time at other homecomings.

Melanie Jacobs could hardly contain herself wondering if today's guest of honor might just be her beloved husband. She thought of him often, though not as one would pine over a lost lover on earth.

Everything in heaven was different, though the planet itself bore many physical similarities to earth.

What a paradox, she thought, as she allowed herself to think on things of earth.

Her beloved Ben was her soul mate, her husband, her lover, father of her only child, her best friend. In him she felt complete, fulfilled. On earth, the two had become one flesh.

But things were different here.

In one sense, the focus of fulfillment was no longer a spouse, but rather God Himself.

What was this love?

How would you describe it to an earthly audience? You couldn't, was her conclusion. Yet there were some things that could be said.

On earth, she remembered how life was an ongoing mix of striving, struggling, pain, and constant unknowns, combined with too few pleasures thrown in when all was well and sense prevailed.

Then the cycle would begin again. A letdown would come and you would start all over again to climb back up to some semblance of reason and hopefully happiness.

Here it wasn't so.

There was no striving, no struggles, no pain, no unknowns, no letdowns, and everything made sense.

So where did Ben fit into the picture? How was it she longed for him if she was so complete in such a paradise?

The answer, she thought, was found in an understanding of God's goodness and an understanding of how He majors on completeness, fulfillment, and finishing what He starts.

Melanie liked to think of heaven as one big graduation, a learning center where God offers each individual a chance to complete and bring to fruition the gifts He placed in them at birth.

In other words, each good gift, each honorable desire, each fruit seed given an individual and nurtured on earth, would be given the chance to produce and go on producing healthy fruit in heaven.

She and her two best friends, Mary and Martha Johnson, would often get together for hours on end to ponder such things.

Oh, how they enjoyed their times of study and praising the Lord for his marvelous wonders that lay like nuggets below the surface of understanding, waiting to be dug up and embraced.

In terms of her relationship with Ben, she hadn't discussed it with the Lord, but knew that she knew, deep in her heart, that He was going to endorse the continuation of their bond in heaven.

On earth, it was a good marriage that produced much fruit.

Its perpetuation in heaven seemed logical to her. She knew from God's declared Word that if she delighted herself in Him, He promised to give her the desires of her heart.

She also knew that according to His Word, there would be no marrying in heaven. Now that she was there, she understood how the two ideas seemed incompatible. But were they?

Obviously, reuniting with a spouse in heaven was not a plan for everyone. Marriages rife with contention and strife on earth certainly weren't going to cut it in heaven.

As for new relationships focused on marriage, she knew there was really no need for them here as there were so many other things to occupy any need to be fulfilled. In other words, it wouldn't be necessary to complete something that never started.

Melanie giggled as she thought of showing off her mansion, her heavenly home, to Ben.

Contained within its walls was absolutely everything that was her. The thought of an awestruck Ben taking in its magnificence and God the Father's loving attention to every detail, brought her a flood of happy thoughts.

She had observed, firsthand, that every mansion in heaven is handmade by the finest craftsmen of all ages and with the best and most lavish materials, many never seen before on earth. The one and only common thread is that God Himself is the architect of each and every home.

She thought about how, because He took the task upon Himself, each mansion is unique in design and character and reflects the fact that every human being He ever created is unlike anyone else.

In other words, each mansion in heaven is like no other; each is stamped throughout with the individual tastes of its owner.

Melanie pondered for a moment about the skeptics she had met on earth who had scoffed at talk of mansions in heaven. She wondered how many who laughed would gladly trade places with her now.

How silly, she thought, *to think that God could not do such a simple thing as individualize a mansion for each of us.*

Melanie also thought about the billions and billions of people who had ever walked the earth and how no two of them were exactly the same; no two (with the exception of identical twins) had the same DNA, the same thumbprints, or the same retina patterns.

She laughed out loud as thoughts about genetics and other science-related things came to mind. These were things more typical of Ben's thinking.

Ben, Ben, Ben! She couldn't get him off her mind.

She knew now that Ben must be the homecoming guest of honor. Why else would she be this excited? Why else would she all of sudden be thinking so much about him?

Two hours had already passed since the angel brought the news of a homecoming.

Melanie projected herself to the home of the Johnson sisters, three miles east along the same river that snuggled its shores up to their property line, properties all three considered among the finest real estate in heaven. Then again, everybody in heaven thought the same thing about their own mansion specifically designed for them.

Martha answered the door. Her sister Mary was worshipping God in the study, totally oblivious that anyone had even knocked on the door.

The three of them often got a chuckle out of the similarities between the sisters and the Mary and Martha of the Bible, who, by the way, they intended to visit one of these days.

The relationship reminded them of how God indeed had a sense of humor and was not at all the stern task master painted by the enemy to keep as many as he could away from the Master's love.

Hostess Martha grabbed Melanie by the wrist and pulled her in so fast she almost yanked her arm off.

"Mary, please come down here; Melanie needs our help."

Three hours and five plates of refreshments later, the task was complete.

A grateful Melanie bid her friends good-bye and headed out on foot along the river pathway leading home. She wanted to take in the beauty of the riverbank walk until she got tired and would then do a transport the remainder of the way.

Transport by thought was one of heaven's greatest features, as far as she was concerned. It sure beat earth's dependence on cars and their hassle, noise, pollution, and overall nuisance.

Tucked neatly in her pocket was a folded list of guests, foods and all the other preparations required for the homecoming mansion party.

Melanie left the list on the usual spot just inside the main foyer. Mosoo, her peculiar but much-loved house angel, would find it there and carry out the orders to the letter.

She laughed over her last thought. Knowing Mosoo as she did for the past five years, there would probably be a few minor goofs but it really wouldn't matter.

Tired from the long day, Melanie decided to turn in.

Entering her large master bedroom with its stunning canopy bed, she noticed something different on the pillow.

A closer examination revealed a single red rose and two of her favorite chocolates in the center of a handcrafted solid gold dish. Close by was a note. Picking it up, she read, "You were correct about your guest. Ben will arrive tomorrow. Get a good night's rest."

It was signed, *"Your heavenly Father."*

Chapter Seventeen

The poets and painters of all the ages could not do justice to the beauty of approaching the planet heaven.

Darkness slowly but surely gave way to discernable light, like the first crack of a magnificent dawn.

Michael and the large contingent of warriors had slowed their speed allowing Ben a bird's eye view of the approaching planet.

Angel warriors around them, including the wounded, were visible once again.

As they broke into the first stages of the planet's light, a strange thing began to happen. One by one, those who were being supported, some carried by their fellow angels, began to show signs of recovery.

There was obviously healing in the very faint waves of light emanating from the planet. The healings continued in number and degree the closer they drew to heaven's brightness.

Thousands of other angels, from the direction of heaven, began to appear. Shouts and unbelievable singing filled the air as those approaching applauded the returning warriors.

The planet was now quite visible, as were the brilliant colors radiating from it. Its own color was an amazing green as opposed to the blue of earth as seen from outer space.

Ben would find out later that there were no major seas on the planet. Waterways consisted of a plethora of rivers and lakes, complemented by lush green landmasses teeming with vegetation.

Perhaps the most stunning feature of their approach was the increasing brilliant, rays of golden colors coming from the northernmost tip of the planet, now quite visible and about the size of a large basketball and quickly getting larger.

The dazzling northern display, he was told by Michael, with obvious pride in his voice, was a reflection of God's city of gold.

Ben's jaw began to drop as the planet's surface grew closer and closer.

Angels, by his estimation to be in the tens of thousands, were now everywhere.

Light, light, and more light took the form of colorful beams shooting outward in all directions, crisscrossing and bouncing everywhere, in, through, and off the shapes of the mass of heavenly creatures.

There stood Michael, God's fearless war angel, in the midst of heaven's light show.

The last time Ben saw him, he was waving good-bye, a broad smile on his face, accompanied by a so-long-for-now salute.

Ben felt bad. The parting had taken place so fast that he never had the chance to bid him farewell and to properly thank him. But, for the moment, his gratitude was superseded by the delight of having his feet back again on solid ground.

It seemed as quick as it began, the light extravaganza was over, the angels were gone, and Ben found himself alone in Paradise.

Though he had obviously never been to heaven, where he stood looked familiar. He definitely felt he had seen this particular array of lush grass, fruit trees, flowers, and water springs before.

As he turned to look in the opposite direction, his suspicions were confirmed with the sight of what appeared to be his beloved, solitary park bench about sixty feet in the distance.

The whole scene was exactly what the LORD had created for him in the midst of the dreadful hell they had fought their way out of.

Everything was the same with one exception—someone was seated on the bench where he once sat.

A feeling of well being followed him as he glided across the carpet-like greenery toward the bench.

Not until the stranger turned around to greet him, did he realize the occupant was not at all unfamiliar.

There sat Malak sporting his boyish grin and that mischievous twinkle in his eyes.

"Hello, professor. Welcome to heaven."

"Heaven!" He was in heaven!

All of a sudden the reality struck him with full force, as did the shock of once again connecting with Malak.

"I've been sent here as your guide. I will stay in the background, take you places you may want to go, and answer questions you may have."

Malak had barely finished his sentence when Ben blurted out his first and most important question, "Where can I find Melanie?"

At that moment, he really didn't care how lush the grass was, or how sweet-smelling the flowers were. He figured since he had literally been to hell and back, he now wanted to see the one person he was told he could see—Melanie.

Yes, he knew he had been converted and loved the LORD, but there was still a big something in him that cried out to see his beloved Melanie.

Malak smiled, arose from the bench, and started to walk away.

"Come with me. We'll talk as we stroll along."

"Where are we going?"

"There's a little riverside region called Harmony just inside the limits of the city about an hour's walk from our gate of entrance. We first have an appointment at the wall and should arrive there just on time."

"Will Melanie be there?" asked the professor.

A simple yes was Malak's reply.

Finally! thought Ben to himself.

Maybe it was the deep realization that he would soon see Melanie that made Ben relax a little, that made him more trustworthy regarding Malak, the Lord, and all of heaven's efforts to bring him here.

So this was heaven.

What were his thoughts? What did he think of it? So much raced through his mind that he hadn't really had time to formulate any kind of an opinion.

As they began their walk, Ben laid aside his thoughts of Melanie and started to drink in his surroundings.

No words could ever really describe heaven. If he were allowed only one, Ben thought his choice would be the word "beautiful."

It seemed lame, but how else could one sum up such a place as this?

Ben knew his knowledge of scripture was limited, but for some reason his recall of anything he'd ever learned on earth, had instantly become acutely accelerated the moment he entered heaven's atmosphere. He was suddenly aware that he could remember every verse he had heard or read, especially those he used to eavesdrop on when Melanie had her Bible studies.

One verse in particular now seemed to pop out at him: "Eye hath not seen, nor ear heard, neither have entered into the heart of man, the things which God hath prepared for them that love him."

He thought also of the Apostle Paul who had once been to heaven and returned to make the statement that he heard "unspeakable words, which it is not lawful for a man to utter."

Maybe, he thought, it was timing that kept the lid on the secrets of this place. Then again, as he looked around, he realized the difficulty of describing such beauty, also had a role to play.

In many ways, the slice of heaven he'd seen thus far was much like earth, except it was thousands of times more beautiful, more crystal clear and inviting to the senses.

Ben had not been that much of a nature lover on earth, but here it seemed easy to fall in love with every tree, flower, plant, and blade of grass.

Some of the plants he recognized, some he didn't. It was the same with the trees and flowers. Whatever the difference in heaven, one thing was sure; all the greenery was somehow teeming with energy and vitality.

Then there was the air he was breathing.

Every breath seemed to invigorate and energize the body. It was as if beams of freshness were being sent down to your toes and back again with each step you took.

Ben couldn't help wondering if earth had similar qualities before the fall of man and the consequences of sin, not only on the soul, but the body as well.

"We'll soon be there," said Malak.

In the past few hours they had made it almost to the top of a very large hill. The farther up they climbed, the more brilliant the light became as it shot amazing colors over the tops of the trees and down upon them.

Ben's heart began to race with the thought of seeing what was on the other side. Malak's wings, he noticed, beat a little faster as their approach narrowed.

"Come on, Ben, we're almost there," said Malak.

"I'm coming, I'm coming," mumbled a short-winded Ben.

Chapter Eighteen

A lot had happened since Matt reached over and took Sarah's hand at the bedside of her dad.

Sarah was caught up with the timing.

"*Why now,* Lord*? Why didn't I have these feelings for Matt before I met George?*"

Sarah knew the answer before she asked the question.

George made her laugh. Ever the Romeo, he was full of fun, or at least seemed to be. He was popular, good looking, the kind of guy who was always the life of the party. *But,* she thought, *nobody was laughing now, and the party turned out to be a disaster.*

It was hard not to think of the warning signs that were there, all of which she ignored. Her mother gently tried to tell her, like every mother does, but she was never in the mood to listen.

She thought back to how Matt always seemed to be around her on campus. Sadly, she never clued in as to why he showed up in a lot of the same places she did and why they seemed to take a lot of the same courses.

She felt embarrassed that she never detected his feelings for her as she went along her merry way, en route to disaster.

But that was then, and this was now. Besides, she had decided it was time to end the browbeating.

Sarah thought about how bizarre it was that one's feelings could cover such a range in so short a period of time.

It had only been a few weeks since she stood with Matt at her father's beside, but, in those two long weeks her emotions had gone up and down like a roller coaster that never seemed to stop.

Since they both liked coffee, Matt had invited her that day to join him in the hospital cafeteria.

Sarah had reached across the table for the sugar. At the exact time, so did Matt. Their hands collided awkwardly with his ending up on top of hers. He left it there for a second, and then quickly pulled it away. Sarah smiled, but said nothing about the redness of Matt's face.

It was fall in Nova Scotia.

Sarah peered out the window of her Fairview home, her eyes taking in a yard full of leaves so red, so golden, so yellow. She was convinced that God surely could not have made a prettier place than her province, especially in the fall.

Sarah, the mother hen, was smiling at the sight of her children raking the lawn under the supervision of Matt.

She marveled at how great the three of them got along, and how well Matt interacted with Joshua and Esther.

The thought no sooner left her mind when the trio got into some sort of a tussle over who had the highest and neatest pile. Within seconds, three neat piles destined for a home inside large orange bags, somehow ended up once again scattered all over the lawn.

Three kids (one supposedly an adult) lay on the ground in fits of laughter.

The sight brought much joy to the heart of one Sarah Jacobs, who in recent years had almost forgotten how to laugh.

An hour later, the three outside joined Sarah inside for some hot chocolate topped with marshmallows.

Homework followed for the kids, a warm fire, and a long conversation in the living room for Sarah and Matt.

For a long time they spoke only about the children, their likes and dislikes. Sarah had gone to the closet and retracted several photo albums over which they perused, joked, and laughed.

Matt laughed at Sarah's enthusiastic commentary on every photo, her pride bubbling over with each explanation of where the picture was taken, and how old the children were when the masterpiece was snapped.

As soon as the cover closed on the last album, Matt asked Sarah if anything was wrong.

"Why do you ask?" Sarah replied.

"You forget, I've known you from a distance for a very long time," said Matt. "I can usually guess when something's bothering you."

Sarah was quite surprised at Matt's intuition. She had become quite adept at hiding her feelings, yet he seemed to know she was upset over something.

"You're getting a bit creepy," she joked.

"Creepy in a nice way, and yes, you're correct."

Sarah was not as caught up with how he seemed to read her emotions as she was with the fact that he really seemed to care about her feelings.

The whole thing was a bit daunting, unnerving in the sense that she had gotten along without a man for this long and along the way had developed a sort of sixth sense in the area of caution. She realized she had also become like a mother bear protecting her cubs when it came to her children.

Sarah wondered if perhaps everything was moving a bit too quickly, not so much that she minded, but she had to admit she was afraid.

"You're afraid because of past hurts and how much you love and want to protect your children. Am I correct?" asked Matt, kindness exuding from his smile and those soft eyes.

"Yes," said Sarah in her best serious face, followed immediately by a burst of laughter in her most not-so-serious face.

"I guess I've prayed for so long for God to send something good my way that I've forgotten how to recognize His goodness when it gets here."

"The LORD always knows what He's doing," said Matt.

A puzzled look swept over Sarah at Matt's last remark. His words were definitely a lead into the second part of what was bothering her.

Having made such a blunder in picking George as her mate, she definitely wasn't about to make the same mistake again.

Her mom, bless her heart, had cautioned her about marrying George because he was not a Christian, stating her case emphatically that the two would never be compatible.

Young and impetuous, she went ahead, convinced she would be the first person ever to prove wrong the saying: "You can't make a silk purse out of a sow's ear."

Never one to be shy, she blurted out a question for Matt.

"And when did you, Mr. MacKeen, start talking like a Christian?"

"When I became one," Matt shot back without missing a beat.

His answer was both a shock and a curiosity.

Questions by the dozen raced through her mind. *Matt a Christian? When did all this come about? Why was I not told before?*

Sarah just sat there and said nothing.

Matt smiled.

Could he read my mind? Sarah wondered.

Matt cleared his throat and began to tell Sarah a story that left her spellbound, almost speechless for one of those rare times in her life.

It seemed Sarah's mom was the one who led the shy young man to the LORD.

Matt had attended Melanie's Bible study off and on for two years prior to her death. It all started with a conversation Matt had with Melanie at Saint Mary's. Matt had asked how Sarah and the children were doing in light of the family breakup.

It seems Melanie asked him to keep her and the children in his prayers. When he replied that he didn't know how to pray, Mrs.

Jacobs replied it was time he learned and invited him to start attending her Bible study.

Matt accepted, but had to admit he saw the attendance as more of a chance to get closer to the Jacobs than it was to get closer to the Lord.

Nonetheless, it wasn't that long into the studies that Matt realized his need to accept the Savior's sacrifice on the cross. Melanie led him in the sinner's prayer and the rest was history.

Matt and Melanie hadn't intentionally agreed to keep his conversion a secret; it just sort of went that way. With Melanie's sickness, and later her passing, the secret just never found its way to Sarah.

Sarah's eyes were as big as saucers.

"There's something else," said Matt. Reaching into his pocket, he pulled out an envelope, well worn and dog-eared. As he passed it to her, she noticed it was addressed to her. She immediately recognized the hand writing as her mother's.

"What is this?" she asked, her hands trembling at the thought of something with her mother's handwriting on it and addressed to her.

"It's from you mother. She asked me to keep it, not to open it, and to give it to you, but only under certain circumstances."

"What circumstances?" Melanie asked in a somber voice.

Matt's face turned red. He blurted out that he was only to give her the letter if at any time the two of them felt a spark for each other that was honest and genuine.

Each looked at the other as if they had seen a ghost.

"Open it, if you feel you want to."

Sarah had been standing with her arms folded. She decided to sit down, hoping to ease her shaking.

Carefully and slowly, she began to open the letter.

She never made it past, "My Darling Sarah," before the tears began to flow and the words began to blur.

Matt, who had been sitting in a chair opposite her, stood up, walked across the room and joined her on the sofa. He put his arm around her, held her to his chest, and let her cry.

"It's okay, Sarah; it's okay. I'm so sorry you're upset by this." Matt offered her a tissue. She took two.

Drying her eyes, she again picked up the letter and read its contents.

> My Darling Sarah,
> The fact that you are reading this brings me great joy. It means you have discovered the real Matt MacKeen, a good and gentle man who loves you and loves his LORD. I recommend him highly to you with my blessing should you decide to pursue your relationship. Say hi to dad and the children for me. I can't wait to see you all some day on the other side.
> Love, Mom.

By now both Sarah and Matt were crying up a storm. A box of tissue, almost empty, sat on the sofa between them.

Neither said a word. They just kept holding each other, pulling out tissues, and wiping away tears.

Chapter Nineteen

Reaching the crest of a magnificent hill and viewing, on the other side, a solid wall of jasper the height of a twenty-four-storey building was indeed breathtaking.

The wall before them, as explained by Malak, sat on a foundation of blocks of precious jewels, each forty-eight feet high and five hundred miles long.

There were twelve such blocks in total, laid end to end all the way around the circumference of the city. Each block bore the name of one of the twelve apostles of the Lamb.

Add to the sight an enormous gate carved from one solid pearl, and it had the makings of enough shock power to keep a person in awe for a very long time. At least that was how Ben felt at his first glimpse of the heavenly Jerusalem spread out before him.

His right hand instinctively rose to his forehead as he tried to shield his eyes from the glare of the bright colors bouncing off the wall.

For a minute, Ben thought Malak had gone off on one of his disappearing acts. He was so caught up with what he was seeing that he didn't know his angel friend was standing right alongside him smiling, even chuckling at the bedazzled look on the professor's face.

"Let's make our way down, Professor. We've still a ways to go to the gate."

On Streets of Gold

Startled to hear a voice, Ben turned, gave Malak a nod, and began to follow him.

Malak filled him in a little on the way down about the wall and the city beyond.

He explained to Ben that the walled city actually had twelve gates similar in nature, each named after one of the twelve tribes of Israel. Each is five hundred miles apart and there are three on each side. The city itself is one thousand five hundred miles square. It is fifteen hundred miles long, fifteen hundred miles wide, and fifteen hundred miles high.

The professor could understand the length and width of this massive city, but he couldn't quite grasp how it could reach fifteen hundred miles high.

Malak answered the question Ben hadn't actually asked.

"God's city begins here at the wall and climbs gradually upward taking in a series of foothills, mountains, and valleys in between. It eventually reaches to a peak of 1500 miles at its highest point, which is Mount Zion, the dwelling place of the King of Kings and Lord of Lords."

Makes sense, thought Ben, quite stunned at what lay before him.

As they walked toward the gate, Ben tried to imagine a city of that size on earth. As he thought about it, he realized it would have to take in an area greater than one third of the United States. In his mind, he visualized a rectangle drawn through the country's midsection from the Canadian border to the Gulf of Mexico.

As they got closer, Ben counted twelve huge angels—obviously guardians of the entrance to the pearl gate. Each flitted in and out, back and forth through the glistening entrance to the city of gold.

Boisterous singing began to fill the air. It grew louder and louder as their approach narrowed.

They were now a mere sixty yards from the massive gate.

As they drew closer, he could see that it was meticulously carved and inlaid with inscriptions. The foundation stone under this particular gate was a solid emerald. Its color blended together with the beams of light coming from the jasper wall and the pearl gate to produce a sparkling show of glitter, the likes of which boggled the imagination.

People by the hundreds began to pour out of the gate and quickly fill the surrounding area. Some stayed near the walls; others began to move toward Ben and Malak.

The non-stop singing continued to fill the air.

At first Ben couldn't quite make out the words, but as the singers began to surround him, he could hear their voices blending together singing in unison: *"Praises to our God who has brought you here, we thank Him for His mercy, His love, His care."*

They kept repeating the same words over and over.

Suddenly a sound like the sound of many waters burst through the gate, its glory flattening the people. Ben fell to the ground as well.

In an instant, he knew what it was. The glory of the LORD was flooding through the pearl gate, and no one could stand upright in its presence.

When he and the others were finally able to look up, the LORD Himself was standing in their midst.

"Welcome, my son!" were the words He spoke softly and with such genuine warmth, love and sincerity, as to penetrate to the core of his soul.

Ben knew it was the LORD even before he looked. That same presence, that same voice, had approached him in hell and yielded him senseless in the midst of its overpowering majesty.

"Ben, I have someone I want you to meet."

As the LORD took two steps to the side, a figure resembling that of a woman with long hair and outstretched arms slowly began to emerge from the cloud of glory that surrounded the Master.

Locking of eyes, locking of arms, and the shedding of tears best summed up the goings on at a tiny spot in heaven where Melanie and Ben Jacobs stood, oblivious to the claps of the welcoming crowd.

For the longest time only eight words were spoken, four by her, and four by him.

"I missed you, Ben!"

"I missed you, Melanie!"

These were all the words that seemed to matter for the moment. Meanwhile, the LORD was nowhere in sight.

Melanie took Ben by the hand and began to stroll through the gate. Tears ran freely down their faces.

There were so many things the two of them wanted to know all at once. Melanie was especially inquisitive about Sarah and the children, but the noise and excitement was too intense for meaningful conversation.

The crowd followed close behind them, jostling, laughing, talking.

"Who are all these people?" Ben shouted, trying to raise his voice above the din as they passed through the glistening pearl gateway.

"They are all mostly relatives and friends that have died in Christ and have come here. Some of them you will recognize at the homecoming party. They all know you and soon you will know them."

So there they were by the hundreds, passing through the gate, Melanie and Ben in the lead.

Melanie leaned over and whispered in Ben's ear not to squeeze her hand so tight. He laughed while adding that he had no intentions of losing her a second time.

"Melanie, you're so young, so beautiful, so radiant, so full of life."

"You're not so shabby yourself, Mr. Ben Jacobs."

Stepping foot for the first time on a street in the New Jerusalem had no comparison to anything on earth.

Ben remembered the trip they took to Disney World the year before Melanie died. When they entered the gates of one of the four kingdoms, an awesome atmosphere struck them squarely in the face.

Passing through a gate here was similar but a thousand times more special, more exciting, more breathtaking.

Everything here was affected by God's presence. It was like a heavenly charge had electrified every particle, every square inch of this place.

The thing most eye-catching and impossible to miss was the massive boulevard of pure gold spread out as far as the eye could see.

As it turns out, the actual length of the highway was fifteen hundred miles, running all the way to the top of Mount Zion. The masterpiece before him was also only one such highway. There were twelve in total, one running upwards to Mount Zion from each of the twelve gateways leading into the city.

The sight of all that gold was absolutely intoxicating.

"Melanie, the streets of gold are real! They're real! I'm walking on streets of gold!"

Melanie laughed out loud at the sight of Ben jumping into the air and clicking his heels in some sort of a poorly executed Irish jig.

Everyone around them also laughed at the newcomer, drunk with the joy of dancing on streets of gold.

They had all seen this kind of exuberance before but it was always a delight to see it again and again each time someone new walked through the gate. It was something everyone had experienced and no one forgot.

Ben knew something of the characteristics of gold. He knew that in its purest form, it was actually transparent.

Sure enough, what they were walking on was shiny, thick, jaw-dropping, see-through gold, a chunk of which could make a man on earth both crazy and extremely rich.

What a contrast, Ben thought. *On earth, men would sell their mothers and kill each other for one square foot of this stuff that was being used here as pavement.*

Ben couldn't stop thinking about the obvious symbolism portrayed in the image of the streets of gold. On earth, it was everything; here it was nothing. On earth it symbolized the god of wealth, materialism and power. Not so here.

Ben thought about how the pursuit of money had consumed mankind, and driven millions away from the one true God. He now realized that those who pursued the LORD on earth were now blessed with the riches of knowing Him here, and throughout eternity.

This, Ben had come to realize, was real wealth. The irony was unmistakable.

Chapter Twenty

As stunning as the streets of gold were, running a close second were the twelve crystal-clear rivers, one of which ran down the center of each of the twelve streets of gold. Each river flowed fifteen hundred miles from its origin at the top of Mount Zion all the way to one of the city's twelve gates.

The river of the Water of Life, as it was sometimes called, was the mother of the twelve rivers. It began from beneath the very throne of God and cascaded down the mountain, dividing its course into the twelve rivers that flowed throughout the New Jerusalem.

On each side of the riverbank grew Trees of Life, bearing twelve crops of fruit, a different kind for each month. These trees became a main food source in heaven, and their leaves would eventually be used as medicine to heal the nations loyal to Christ when the New Jerusalem took up permanent residence on earth—the time of which no man knew for sure.

The crowd of well-wishers had stopped for a brief rest en route to Harmony and the party to follow.

One of the sure things in heaven was the fact that no one there was in a hurry. Why should they be, when all of eternity lay at their feet? Then again, there was not a lazy person in all of heaven. Everyone here was hard working but never in a rush. Stress, one of modern man's worst enemies on earth, had been replaced with God's peace.

Ben was not a shy person, but neither could it be said that he had a bubbly, outgoing personality, something he wished he did have, in order to handle the people that kept coming up to him and telling him how much they loved him and how much Melanie meant to them. Some he knew once they told him who they were, some he didn't. Some he recognized, though they were much older when he knew them on earth. Some had lived on earth several hundred years ago, relatives he had never met. *How weird*, he thought.

Ben wished Melanie, much more the talker than he, could stay closer to him, but it wasn't possible as one person after another would take one of them by the arm and go off into the crowd to meet yet another person.

Ben spotted Melanie talking to a man who turned out to be his grandfather. How strange, he thought, looking at this man he hadn't really known on earth.

As a boy, he remembered his parents never wanting to go and visit. He recalled the unkind words his mother would quite often say, "We're not going over there. Your grandfather has gotten religious and we don't want you going around any of that foolishness."

Now here, in this place, Ben knew that when the time was right, he and his grandfather would become great friends and make up for lost time.

The young professor paused for a moment to think about how good it was to once again be united with Melanie. They knew each other so well that they could communicate by just a glance, a certain smile.

Their marriage was indeed precious and close, a closeness Ben was beginning to see emerge as a theme in heaven that defined God and His people.

He would soon find out that things were much different here. There was no politics, no elected officials, no democracy. God reigned supreme and His subjects were all one with Him. Neither was there any rebellion, not because God had turned everyone into robots, but because they had so melded together with their Maker that the two had become one.

Was there the ability to rebel?

Of course there was. God would not be God if He didn't leave the door open a crack for rebellion. With God, there is always a choice, but no one who was here in their heavenly bodies, no one who had come from a life of hell on earth, was interested in abandoning their eternal paradise.

Melanie's happy band of friends and relatives were not the only ones creating a buzz on the golden boulevard. A mass of spirit people like themselves joined angels of all sizes and shapes in a bonanza of activity.

The crowds, ever jostling, moved along slowly. No one pushed, no one yelled, no one complained. The setting was much like a carnival stripped of anything gaudy, crude, or obscene.

Ben soon realized something else. There were a lot of people here saying "thank you."

The young professor hadn't noticed at first that he was a member of the "thank you" tradition, not until he suddenly found himself leaving the group and bolting toward a man he at first thought was a total stranger.

Reaching out, he grabbed the man's hand and shook it vigorously.

"Sir, you prayed for me at a very crucial time in my life and I just want to say thank you very much."

Ben was shocked over his sudden burst of boldness. Getting over it, he proceeded to tell the man the exact details of the prayer and the results as they unfolded at a particular time in his earthly journey.

The stranger, who had suddenly became his latest best friend, was glad Ben had stopped to share the story. He was grateful because he knew his prayer would mean an added blessing for his faithfulness.

The whole scene brought home the fact that knowledge in heaven was off the charts in comparison to the limitations on earth. The things he now knew were mind boggling. He would soon find out that they were also just the tip of the iceberg.

It took some time for all of heaven's newcomers to realize their powers and potential, to realize their intelligence was now operating at 100 percent rather than the mere 10 percent used by the smartest of the smart on earth.

Next to Mount Zion itself, the most happening places in heaven were the twelve boulevards leading ever upwards to the magnificent throne of God.

There were no towns per se inside the walls of the city of gold. The massive area was made up of regions, much like bedroom communities, clusters of individual mansions tailored to the tastes of their owners and set in the midst of breathtaking surroundings.

The focus of heaven was always Mount Zion and the world of worship that made up the lifeline of this incredible place.

Thus the majority of activity in the New Jerusalem had its genesis in God's mighty throne and the boulevards that brought people to and from the hallowed centerpiece of heaven—the dwelling place of the Most High God.

Melanie's party of a few hundred people made their way off the boulevard about five miles from the main gate they had entered.

It was impossible to find a happier, friendlier lot than heaven's occupants.

Like sheep following a shepherd, they meandered off the boulevard and onto a well-worn road that wound its way to a small branch of the mighty crystal river that flowed through the city from their gate of entry.

Before stepping onto the eastward-leading road, several stopped to wave good-bye to new friends they had met on their journey to the turnoff.

With farewells complete and laughter still ringing in the air, they made their way toward the river.

Ben caught up to Melanie, who was chattering away to a relative or friend—he wasn't sure which. He reached down and took her hand. Both shared an ear-to-ear smile that expressed a love hard to miss by those around them.

The countryside between the boulevard and the branch river was absolutely stunning.

The tree-lined roadway wound its way downward through meadows of flowers, whose fragrances blended with fruit blossoms, to produce smells only heaven could lay claim to. Overpowering the scene were the majestic mountain ranges that filled the landscape in the distance.

Ben guessed that he and Melanie were about midway in the pack approaching the river. There were no boats, no bridge in the distance, just the glistening, still water of the river which appeared at that point to be about half a city block across.

Of the many people in their group, it appeared only Ben was at all shocked, as he suddenly witnessed those in front of him step onto the river and begin to walk across, chatting as they went.

As he abruptly came to a halt, two people directly behind bumped into him, apologized, smiled, and walked around him.

Melanie giggled as she reached out to rescue her husband.

As she took him by the arm, Ben realized others around them were now laughing as well. It turns out the joke was a common one played on all newcomers, and who better than family and friends to pull it off?

So there he stood at the water's edge, feeling like a nervous child about to dive into the pool for the first time.

By now, the hundred or so spirit people in front of him had stopped pretending they didn't know about the joke. Each one turned from atop the water and joined those behind him for a chuckle at the newcomer's expense.

Enough is enough, thought Ben.

He boldly put his right foot forward and started to walk across the water. A chorus of clapping broke forth from the peanut gallery of friends and relatives, most of whom were now seated along the riverbank.

Gingerly, slowly, he walked till his confidence grew.

Such were the things that quite often caught you off guard in this place, things that had become natural for heaven's occupants, but not so for those who had just arrived.

As the remainder of the group laughed and walked across the peaceful expanse, it was impossible not to notice its clarity. Looking down, one could see all the way to the bottom. Fish and creatures of all shapes, colors and sizes, swam by at various depths beneath their feet.

Watching them was off the fascination charts, especially when you thought about the fact your view was not from the inside of a glass-bottom boat, but from the vantage point of actually standing on the water.

"Come along, Ben, we have to hurry or the others will get there before us."

Ben hadn't realized the crowd had moved on. What he did know was that being overwhelmed here was becoming quite common.

"I'll be right there," he shouted back to Melanie. "Just give me one more minute."

After all, he thought to himself, *it wasn't every day you got to walk on water and watch the fish swim beneath your feet.*

Chapter Twenty-One

Melanie's place was indeed a mansion in every sense of the word.

Ben's jaw dropped at the sight of it.

Only he fully understood his wife's love for anything southern, anything to do with the deep south of the United States.

The truth be known, Melanie could trace her ancestry back to the Cajuns of Louisiana, descendants of the Acadians who were expelled from Nova Scotia in the great expulsion of 1755. Melanie's mother was a LeBlanc, a proud French name with roots deeply imbedded in both Louisiana and in Acadian pockets throughout Nova Scotia.

Ben stood speechless on the mansion grounds and gawked at the magnificent estate that stretched out before him. He knew exactly what it reminded him of, though what he saw before his eyes was much more grandiose.

Gone With The Wind was Melanie's favorite movie. The mansion bore an amazing resemblance to Scarlett's beloved Tara estate, replete with the white pillars, fine furnishings, and elaborate grounds.

As he stood there, his mind flashed back to Melanie's words about having such a mansion when she got to heaven.

He'd always just smile whenever she would repeat her claim. As a matter of fact, she had said those very words just a few days before she died.

So there Ben stood, feeling a little sheepish at having not really believed his beloved wife. *So much to learn*, he thought. He was glad the Master Architect had not let her down.

The crowd, still talking up a storm, had dispersed across the mansion grounds awaiting an invitation, a signal from Melanie to enter her home.

Melanie ran over to Ben, took his hand, and hurriedly made her way up the stone walkway and the first of several steps leading to the landing.

Just as their feet touched the first step, out dashed Mosoo followed by Malak and an entire host of other angels.

Mosoo giggled as she announced to Melanie that everything was ready.

Ben laughed as well to see the pair of angelic beings working together again. He chose to savor the moment and not dwell on the hell he found himself in the last time he saw them.

Inlaid pure gold panels decorated the two huge double doors at the main entrance to Melanie's mansion. A jewel-framed plaque on the left door bore the name "Melanie MacDonald Jacobs" in large letters.

As Ben stopped to admire the beautifully scrolled letters, he suddenly jumped back, shocked by what he saw appearing right before his eyes.

As he stared at the plaque, these words, one letter at a time, began to appear: *"And her beloved husband, Ben T. Jacobs."*

"Melanie, Melanie," shouted Ben, his voice choked with emotion. "Did you see that? Did you know about this?"

"No," said Melanie. "This is the Lord and His goodness speaking to the both of us."

"What do you mean?" Ben asked.

"What He is saying is that He is now officially turning this mansion over to the both of us. It is no longer mine; it's ours. More importantly, He is approving of and blessing our continued marriage here in heaven, something He doesn't always do."

Those passing through the huge doors all knew what was happening and what a special moment this was. A wide berth was given the teary-eyed couple, as relatives and friends walked by in silence, speaking only in smiles.

Ben and Melanie were the last to walk through the entrance and into the large foyer. As they did, at least fifty or so children between four and eight years of age, yelled "Surprise!" in unison as they jumped and ran giggling, arms waving in the air toward Melanie and Ben.

Ben thought to himself how he had never seen such beautiful and happy children.

Squeals of "Hi, Miss Melanie," resounded throughout the foyer as the sea of kids mobbed the excited hostess.

It was quite the scene, especially when you added the interaction of a couple of hundred relatives, friends, and twenty-five or so servant angels moving about in the background, all slowly nudging their way toward the large dining room down the end of the first hallway on the left.

The children closest to Melanie hugged her neck. Others kissed her, as the remainder continued jostling and jumping up and down, trying to get closer.

"Children, children, I had no idea you were coming. Welcome, welcome. I'm so glad you're here!"

"Who are all these children?" Ben asked, shocked by their numbers and touched by their affection for Melanie.

"These are my students," she beamed.

"But who are they? And where did they come from?" asked a curious Ben.

"They are the innocents," remarked Melanie, as she gently lowered one youngster to the floor, only to pick up another whose arms extended lovingly toward her.

"They are a few of the children of earth, a small number of the millions discarded year after year through abortion, disease, murder, and accidental death.

They come here and the LORD assigns and oversees teachers who nurture them until the age of reasoning and choice. At that point they decide their ultimate fate, which is always to follow Him and do His work. He shows them so much love that none ever want to do anything else."

By now, only Melanie, the child in her arms, and Ben, were still in the foyer. Everyone else had moved into the large dining hall.

Chatter turned to thunderous applause as Melanie and Ben entered the room.

Ben was finding the whole thing overwhelming. As always, he found the fuss over him quite puzzling. It's not that he wasn't grateful; he just couldn't quite grasp the reception he was receiving.

Without much ado, and with a child about four still clinging to her neck, Melanie welcomed her guests.

"It's quite an honor to have all of you here today at this homecoming. As each of you know, these are such delightful times provided to us on occasion by our precious LORD and Savior. Please stay as many days as you want until all of you have renewed acquaintances, met new relatives and friends, and, most of all, made my beloved Ben *your* beloved Ben. Enjoy the feast and the fellowship, and thanks for blessing this home with your presence."

With the official welcome over, Melanie directed Ben to the head table, which faced one of the four long tables designed to comfortably sit approximately one hundred guests each.

Someone he didn't know said a lovely grace, and the feast began.

Ben was feeling a bit of déjà vu as he looked around the room at the beautifully adorned tables, overflowing with foods of every sort.

He thought of the spread the LORD had prepared for him in the midst of hell. There were definite similarities, the most notable being the abundance of so many things gold, and the sparkle they produced.

Though the LORD did not attend the banquet in person, the light of His presence was evident everywhere. He was indeed the focus of the entire planet, right down to all things before them in Melanie's master dining room.

Four enormous crystal chandeliers adorned the room as show pieces. Each hung equidistant from meticulously decorated high ceilings. Light filtered through each, and bounced around the room, sparkling and dancing in spectacular patterns, as it came in contact with the gold plates, dishes, and cutlery.

Huge arrangements of breathtaking flowers were artistically placed on the tables and throughout the room.

Magnificent embroidered ceiling-to-floor draperies were everywhere, each with a slightly different intricate pattern displayed in rich colors. The brilliant hues seemed to reach out and welcome guests into their beauty.

All of the splendor aside, perhaps nothing could match the richness in the abundance of stories people began to share with each other, about the goodness of the LORD.

It wasn't long before it was understood who was who and how so and so knew someone else, or was related.

Laughter could be heard everywhere; its sweetness melded with the joy of fellowship as it filled the room.

Malak, with a tray of food straddled on each arm, made his way toward Ben's table.

Winking as he approached, he leaned over and asked Ben how he liked the meal and what he saw thus far of the mansion.

"Everything is just fine; thank you, Malak. I was sitting here thinking how everything is out of this world."

Malak laughed at Ben's remark.

"Glad to see your sense of humor is still intact, Professor. Enjoy your meal."

Ben got serious for a moment.

"I will, Malak, and by the way, thanks for taking care of me and for being such a good friend."

Ben never realized angels could blush, at least not until he saw the redness in Malak's face as he acknowledged the compliment.

Chapter Twenty-Two

Melanie's secret note of approval was pure gold for Matt and Sarah, a gift they wasted little time putting to good use.

Being in their thirties, it was easy for the two of them to draw the conclusion that since true love had come knocking, and they weren't getting any younger, they had best get a move on.

To prove their point, they chalked up nineteen dates in the short while since Sarah read her mother's letter.

"Sarah, if I had known what was in that letter, I would have given it to you five years ago," teased Matt as he continued swinging the mop across the lobby floor.

It was Saturday morning. Sarah and the children had come over to help him catch up with this week's chores at the apartment building.

The kids loved Matt, and he certainly seemed to love them—something that brought Sarah great joy. He definitely had a way with them.

For one thing, he could get them to do loads of work by making the task at hand seem like fun. Sarah had to admit that she wasn't as good or creative in that department as he was.

Today's reward for completed chores was a trip for the four of them to Huskies stadium for a two o'clock football game.

It was almost noon. Matt thanked his crew of co-workers profusely. He ordered two pizzas for the hungry lot, still busy putting away the cleaning supplies.

The timing was perfect.

Just as the last items were tucked neatly away, the pizza arrived at the front door. Shouts and clapping filled the air, not only from the children, but a hungry Sarah and Matt, as well.

The kids ran skipping down the hall to Matt's apartment with Matt, Sarah, and the hot pizza in pursuit.

It didn't take long for the boxes to be opened, the pop unscrewed, the grace said, and the pizza eaten. The whole ordeal was over in twenty minutes.

Now it was time to head for Saint Mary's and walk off the pizza on the way.

It was a beautiful November day in Halifax, the kind of day it felt good to be alive.

Cold but sunny with cloudy intervals and a chance of flurries, is how the weatherman had forecast the day. He would probably be somewhat correct, at least on a few of his predictions.

The funny thing about Nova Scotia weather is its unpredictability. The joke is always that if you don't like the weather, wait five minutes and it will surely change.

For now, the sun was warming the faces of the foursome as they walked down Robie Street en route to the stadium, hot chocolate and extra blankets in hand.

It was one o'clock when they arrived at the Tower sports complex. The game didn't start for an hour, but arriving early was a must if you wanted a good seat.

Already the pregame hoopla was in full swing. Cheerleaders were on the field practicing their routines, much to the delight of a group of young males who obviously had too much to drink and too much to say.

The bleachers were already half full with quite the mix of enthusiastic fans. Not only did the students show up in great numbers, but the majority of the faculty and their families did so as well. Many of the alumni, some from 35 and 40 years ago, joined in the pre-game revelry. A few of the old-time diehards could be seen here and there, squeezed with pride into their faded Saint Mary's leather jackets.

Matt spotted some excellent seats half way up the left bleachers and near the fifty yard line.

The adults had decided to get seats first and go for the popcorn later, a decision contested slightly by Esther and Joshua, who fought the tempting smell as it wafted through the tower and chased them onto the field.

"Hey, Sarah. Up here."

It was Professor Hanrahan and his wife Alice sitting right alongside the very seats they had their eye on. The little troupe had been so intent on the seats that they hadn't realized they knew the couple sitting alongside them.

A round of smiles and inquisitive glances broke out as they climbed the steps and made their way into the empty spot.

"It's so good to see you Sarah. And, of course, you too, Matt," said the professor.

"I didn't know you two knew each other. Do sit down and tell us the juicy story," smirked the professor.

"And this can't be Esther and Joshua. Has it been that long since I've seen them?"

"Elliott, stop talking long enough to let someone answer," said Alice.

Elliott and Alice had been close friends with Sarah's mom and dad for over thirty years. The professor and her dad were also colleagues, and each other's closest friend, not to mention good hunting and fishing buddies. Only God knew how much those two loved to hunt and fish.

Sarah sensed they would get around to talking about her dad, but for now it was a relief that the focus was on the obvious romance between her and Matt. She figured Professor Hanrahan already knew about the two of them and was just being polite in pretending he didn't.

If the professor and Alice really didn't know, Sarah was sure they were the only two on the entire campus who hadn't heard the news.

Sarah knew Matt. She knew he was in a hurry to make sure everyone in Halifax had heard about them being an item.

The chatter and focus on all the pregame excitement had eaten away at the clock. Sarah continued chatting up a storm with Alice.

Matt tapped his watch and rubbed his stomach while rising from his seat as he pointed toward the confection stand. She knew it was his way of telling her he was going to take the children to get popcorn.

She nodded approval. Elliott tagged along.

The popcorn seekers had just reached the bottom of the bleachers when Alice placed a serious grip on Sarah's arm. The squeezing and look of fear in her eyes caught Sarah off guard.

"Oh, Sarah, I've got to talk to you. I know it's not a coincidence we've met here today. I'm so scared."

"Alice, Alice, what on earth is the matter?" said a puzzled Sarah. "What's going on? What's wrong?"

"It's Elliott, he's been absolutely strange since Ben's heart attack. It's like he's losing his mind."

Sarah found Alice's revelations startling, to say the least. She could tell by the look in her eyes that she wasn't fooling.

"But Alice, he seems his usual jovial self."

"It's all an act, Sarah—all an act."

For the next twenty minutes, Alice piled on one bizarre piece of the nightmare after another, as she unburdened the strange story to a shocked Sarah.

Apparently, the usually mild-mannered family friend and confidant of her dad, had been under a heavy spiritual attack since almost the same day her father suffered his heart attack.

"Sarah, you wouldn't believe the horrible nightmares he's been having," Alice blurted out between the sobs and whimpers that she couldn't control.

"Apparently, in his dreams, he's being attacked by a horde of devils led by some creature by the name of Zadar."

Up the steps of the bleachers came the popcorn seekers.

Alice quickly stopped talking, thanked Sarah for listening, and in a quivering voice asked if they could resume their conversation at another time, perhaps on the phone.

"Sure," replied Sarah, still reeling from what she had just heard.

Saint Mary's won the coin toss and chose to kick the ball to their opponents.

Not a human soul on the planet, except Elliott and Alice, knew that cold November day what the significance would be to a nerve-wracked professor and his wife, as the ball soared into the air.

All eyes were on the pigskin, especially the receivers who focused intensely as they aligned themselves to receive the ball.

But where was the ball?

It quickly became the question on everybody's mind as outstretched arms awaited a ball that never fell, a ball that literally disappeared.

An official scratched his head as he threw a flag on the play, but without a clue as to what the call would be.

Stunned players stood still on the field. Many of them threw their hands up in the air in a gesture of bewilderment.

A time out was finally called, and both teams retreated to their opposing benches.

Fans, throughout the bleachers continued looking skywards.

Journalists and cameramen joined in the hysteria over what was quickly becoming the strangest day in the history of SMU sports.

Herald reporter Aaron Cummings, Ben's former student, was there in the mix, unaware that what was taking place would soon send his career skyrocketing. It would also force him out of his shell and shed light on why he kept so much to himself.

Two questions occupied everyone's mind: What had happened to the ball? And what was anyone going to do about it?

The truth was: What could be done about it?

What exactly do you do when a football literally vanishes into thin air in front of an entire stadium of fans, officials and the media?

Finally, the frantic conversations and the scratching of heads came to an end, with the decision to bring out another ball and start the game over.

Up went the ball and down came nothing.

The reaction the second time around was much the same as the first. About the only difference was the quiet hush that fell over the stadium, a silence more still and eerie than a graveyard on a moonlit night.

Without fanfare, the stands began to empty in an orderly fashion. It became quite obvious that no one was interested in a confused announcement, aimed at keeping the people from leaving.

The media, in days to follow, would have a field day talking about the unprecedented crazy events surrounding the disappearing football, and the cancelled SMU game.

Of all the witnesses to the strange phenomenon, two in particular were more bewildered than anyone else. The shock came not because of what they saw, but because of what they knew.

Elliott and Alice Hanrahan recalled a mocking statement the professor had once made in a private conversation with Ben and Melanie: "The likelihood of God being concerned about the daily lives of people, is about as probable as me attending a football game in which the ball was kicked into the air and then disappeared in front of my eyes."

A shaken professor and his wife blended insignificantly into the exiting crowd.

Neither spoke as each tried in silence to piece together what had just taken place.

Chapter Twenty-Three

At first glance, it appeared heaven's saints had hollow legs. One could base the conclusion on the nonstop feasting going on at Melanie's mansion.

Ben was quite taken up with it all. He guessed that at least a full day of eating and fellowship had gone by. There were no clocks to know what time it was, and no calendars to tell the day, month, or year.

Ben paused to recheck his thinking.

He had to remind himself that this was heaven, not earth. Obviously there were no clocks, no calendars, and no rising or setting of the sun. Here, the glory of the LORD, the light emanating from His throne, was the source of all illumination.

As he looked around the room, Ben wondered if anyone ever got tired and went to bed. Leaning forward, he whispered in Melanie's ear: "Is anyone ever going home? When do we turn in? If it's not soon, I'm going to yawn myself under the table."

Melanie chuckled at her hubby's last remark.

Standing to attention, she tapped her fork on a gold goblet and announced their intention to call it a day, a night, or whatever it was that best described the eternal moment.

All in the room clapped. Most smiled.

When Melanie stood up, Ben expected others would follow, putting into motion the dispersion of guests. No one moved.

Melanie pulled Ben towards her and whispered in his ear. "Ben, no one is ready to go home just yet. A few will begin to leave over the next while, and probably return later. It's unlikely everyone will leave for at least a week or two."

A look of shock registered on Ben's face. "Yes, they get tired, but tired here is not like tired there. People rest here for relaxation and pleasure, not because their bodies demand it. There is no break down of the body here, no ageing."

Being a practical man, Ben had another question for Melanie, one he asked as they proceeded up the stairway: "And who gets to do all the dishes when the party is over?"

"Ben, Ben," she laughed as she squeezed his hand.

"You will find here that most things are taken care of by servant angels," she said as they climbed the long, winding stairway.

By now the pair had reached the landing on the second floor.

As Ben looked around, he saw Melanie in everything his eyes beheld. Paintings, seemingly so real you could walk into them, were everywhere.

The second floor landing took on the appearance of an art gallery in which each painting seemed to capture the essence of who Melanie was, and the things she loved.

One gigantic work in particular caught his attention.

In the painting, two young lovers walked hand in hand at sunset, along a sandy beach, their bare feet kissed by rippling waves at the water's edge.

"Isn't it beautiful?" beamed Melanie, her smile revealing those big dimples that Ben loved so much.

"It sure is," said Ben.

"It reminds me of the weekend we spent at Ingonish beach that first year we were married."

"It is, and that's us," laughed Melanie. "Would you like to go back there?"

"Melanie, stop your joking."

A smiling Melanie took him by the hand and walked toward the painting.

The next thing Ben remembered was hearing the gentle crash of waves and the sensation of walking on wet sand. He remembered wondering why he couldn't see anything and then chuckling when he realized his eyes were closed.

Melanie was by his side, holding his hand, just like in the painting, and, sure enough, here they were back on the shores of their favorite Nova Scotia beach.

The sun had begun to head slowly toward the horizon, spreading luscious shades of orange and red across the landscape.

"Is this real?" asked Ben, his bewilderment captured in the stunned look on his face.

"Indeed it is, darling. And check out that incredible sunset. Isn't it amazing?"

Ben couldn't get over Melanie's matter-of-factness about where they were and how they got there.

She didn't seem at all concerned that his brain was doing cartwheels, as he once again tried to fathom what was going on.

"Relax, Ben, I'll explain everything later. For now, let's just enjoy our time in this beautiful place. Look, there's a sand dollar, and another," said Melanie, squealing and jumping like a schoolgirl at recess.

For what Ben guessed was at least an hour, Melanie ran from one sea treasure to the next, as he tried his best to keep up with her.

Shells by the fistful, smooth rocks, and pieces of driftwood soon filled a wooden crate that had become part of the treasure collection.

In the midst of the excitement, Ben had noticed clams here and there, their presence made known by the squirts of water from holes beneath the sand.

Ben suggested they dig a few, make a fire, and cook them on the beach before the light of the setting sun got away from them.

Melanie didn't have to be asked twice.

"Oh, Ben, that's a great idea."

In one motion, she put down her box of treasures, picked up a shovel and pail, and began to dig.

"Melanie, where did you get the pail and shovel?" Ben asked.

He was especially curious because he was sure he hadn't seen them there a second ago. Her explanation was quite matter-of-fact.

"Ben, you will soon learn that part of being a heavenly being is walking in the knowledge that the LORD knows what we have need of, even before we ask."

Without skipping a beat, she turned over a large mound of wet sand, pulled it apart with her hands, and threw the first of several fat clams into her pail.

Ben wasn't quite sure he was totally satisfied with her answer.

"But how did the items get here at the exact time they were needed?" he asked.

"Hold that thought for just a minute, Ben. Oh, my goodness, this one is the size of my fist."

Melanie, Ben realized, would not be denied her enthusiasm. She was obviously more focused on the clams than minor items that appeared out of nowhere.

Ben wisely decided to leave the questioning alone and join in the fun.

"Here, let me help you," he said, smiling to himself as he cleared the wet sand from yet another spitting shellfish.

With the task complete, and the bucket full, Ben looked around for some dry wood to burn, realizing at the same moment that he didn't have matches to start the fire.

He said nothing of the dilemma to Melanie. Instead, he lowered his head—Melanie hadn't noticed the gesture—and asked the LORD to supply his need.

Nothing happened.

Was the LORD somewhere nearby laughing at him? This wasn't the case and Ben knew it. He thought of how the LORD had so mercifully rescued him from the horrors of hell, and taken him to heaven and Melanie.

As he glanced down at his feet, the matches were there. Ben smiled, picked them up, and wished he hadn't doubted.

"Ben, my love, I think you should get that fire started."

"Aye, aye, captain Melanie," answered Ben. Both chuckled and continued preparations for the clam feast.

A good-sized rock formation a short distance ahead looked like just the right sheltered spot to perch.

Gathering up the treasures, wood, and clams, the lovebirds headed for their destination.

A surprise, tucked behind the tallest of the rocks, awaited them.

Ben was the first to notice the bright-colored streamers blowing in the wind from atop a fairly large tent, replete with an off-the-ground bed inside, lanterns, and an array of breads, sweets, fruit and juices on a table tucked just inside the door. A large pot of water sat on a metal tripod a few feet from the door outside their cozy digs.

"Well, I'll be," said Ben as he placed his armload of items on the ground.

"Did you know anything about this, Melanie?"

One glance at her girlish smile told him she did.

"Well, maybe just a little," she giggled.

Ben slowly, but surely, was catching on.

"You asked the Lord to put the tent and the food here, didn't you?"

"Yes," she replied.

"Well, aren't you something now Mrs. Jacobs," teased Ben, as he turned back the flap of the tent for a closer look inside.

"I ask for matches, and you ask and get all of this."

Ben marveled at the instant accommodations and clung to the joy he felt as he pondered sharing them with Melanie.

The clam boil came and went quickly, but not before bringing great satisfaction, and full stomachs to the participants.

The fire by now had lost its crackle. Only a few red embers remained. Each birthed thin trails of smoke that wafted upwards, disappearing into the dark of a cool, moonlit summer's night.

Suddenly, without fanfare or notice, the serenity of the night was broken by the faint sound of dogs barking, a sound that quickly grew louder and louder.

The light of the full moon revealed more details as the source of the commotion advanced toward them.

A pair of large frenzied dogs pulled their drunken and profane-tongued owners closer and closer to the tent.

Giggling, and staggering a short distance behind, were two obnoxious girls trying their best to prove they were just as foul-mouthed as their male companions.

Instantly, out of nowhere, two large angels, swords drawn, appeared in front of the tent lighting up the surroundings with the glow of their presence.

Yelping dogs and drunken companions immediately took flight in the opposite direction.

All that was left was the overturned remnants of a case of beer, dropped by one of them as they ran from the scene. Also gone were the heavenly warriors.

Ben, who had been quite startled only moments before, now laughed at the fleeing foursome and their high-tailing, four-legged friends.

Melanie hadn't flinched throughout the ordeal. She showed no outward signs of being upset. With the calamity over, Ben and Melanie entered the tent, closed the flap, and prepared to turn in.

Silence took charge of the night, except for the low, rushing sound of waves breaking softly on the shore.

At last they were alone, locked in each other's arms, locked in private conversations that meant so much to each of them, conversations that would last well into the night.

Chapter Twenty-Four

Ben awoke shortly after dawn, startled but not surprised.

Not only was there no ocean to greet him, but there was no tent, and worst of all, no Melanie.

He rubbed his eyes several times hoping that perhaps everything that had disappeared, would somehow reappear. Deep inside he knew it wouldn't, but why not try?

Where was he? Where was Melanie?

Bright flashes of brilliant light emanating from the gold boulevard blurred his vision, causing him to squint. Though unsure as to how he got there, there was no doubt as to where he was.

Stretched out behind him was one of heaven's twelve pearl gates shooting magnificent soft colors in all directions. A flurry of angels could be seen coming and going in the expanse above the gate, a distance he judged to be about a mile away.

Extreme busyness best described what his eyes beheld around him.

Men, women, families, and angels of various heights and sizes, some with wings, some without, moved and crisscrossed the crowded street, all intent on achieving their goals.

Ben couldn't help but think how earth's views of this place were so off the mark.

He saw no idleness and no chubby-cheeked cherubs playing harps as they floated by on fluffy clouds. Heaven was definitely not an old folks' home.

The heavenly newcomer found himself turning the knob on a small shop door. He couldn't remember if there was any signage on the storefront window, nor why he felt compelled to enter this particular shop.

The door opened, and a bedazzled Ben walked inside.

What he saw was breathtaking.

Large, colorful bolts of the richest, finest fabrics he had ever seen, adorned the walls from floor to ceiling.

Their beauty paled in comparison to display after display of jewels of every sort imaginable. Some had been crafted into jewelry, but most just lay there in their natural state, unprotected on shelves. Some of the samples were bigger than a man's fist.

Ben stood in silence taking it all in.

"I'm so glad to see you," said a friendly voice behind him.

Ben turned to observe a tall, rather stout, impeccably dressed shopkeeper, standing before him.

Thick, black eyebrows and matching mustache dominated his facial features. He wore a sharp red fez, complete with black tassel, and ornamented with several jewels around its circumference.

The man's brilliantly white, collarless shirt, with its wide flowing sleeves, caught Ben's attention. The material was of the finest, smoothest silk he had ever seen. Bell-bottomed trousers of a similar, but heavier material, brown in color, covered his legs. Both shirt and pants were sewn with gold stitching. Finely crafted brown leather shoes that came to a point, completed his apparel.

"Do you know me?" Ben asked.

"Oh, yes, sir! Many of us on this route have been told you would be coming."

"And who might you be?" asked a puzzled Ben.

"My name is Karli Hakan and I am one of the Master's chosen, plucked from the jaws of hell at Antioch in 52 a.d. under the teaching of the great apostle Paul."

Ben was taken aback, not so much by the stand-at-attention, matter-of fact statement, but by the enormous broad smile on the shopkeeper's face, a grin that matched the brightness of the jewels and fabric in the room.

Ben wasn't quite sure if he heard the man correctly.

"Do you mean to say you knew the apostle Paul and that you've been here for nearly two thousand years?"

"Yes, sir, that is correct."

He went on to tell how Paul and his team had come to their region, in what is now modern Turkey, during a missionary campaign conducted in the years 47–57 a.d.

The jubilant shopkeeper's voice went up a notch with excitement as his story continued.

"I was a wealthy merchant who made my fortune in jewels and fine cloth. Despite my riches, I was not satisfied with my life. I felt empty inside, miserable, unfulfilled. My money bought me anything I wanted, but it could not buy me happiness, peace, or joy."

A frown broke out on the shopkeeper's face as he told of a wife who left him and of their childless marriage.

It took only a matter of seconds for his beaming smile to return, followed by laughter as his conversation turned back to Paul, whom he referred to as "the little man with the big Gospel."

"When I understood what the Lord had done for me and how his shed blood bought me eternal life, I knew this was what I had been missing. I was converted the first time I heard the Gospel," said a still-smiling Karli Hakan.

"What did you do then?" Ben asked.

I continued in my business and gave everything, except what I needed to live on, to Paul and the others to spread the Gospel.

He went on to tell story after story of how Paul and members of his team would come over to his house to break bread and have fellowship.

"I died in fifty-seven a.d.," said Karli bluntly.

"Never in my wildest dreams did I think my heavenly reward would be so great for my simple acts of kindness."

With his chest puffed slightly and a look of pride on his face, he proclaimed: "Why I've been allowed by the LORD Himself to design crowns, rewards, gowns, and outfits for literally thousands of saints who have come here over the years.

"If you meet Paul while you're here, check out the crown he wears. I designed it," said a beaming Karli.

"Well, well, if that isn't something," said Ben, surprised but not surprised. He thought for a moment about how he was talking to a merchant nearly two thousand years old, and how anything here was no more out of place than any of the other strange things he'd run into.

"Come with me," said an anxious Karli, tugging insistently at his shirtsleeve as he led him toward a door at the back of the shop.

To Ben's amazement the door led into a very large warehouse that dwarfed Karli's tiny shop entrance.

Within a minute of both men entering the large space, an estimated two hundred workers stopped what they were doing, rose to their feet, and turned toward them.

In one accord, the smiling staff proclaimed: "Welcome, Mr. Ben," and immediately turned back to their business. Their smiles and warm friendly greeting impressed a puzzled Ben who shyly mumbled a "thank you" half under his breath.

"What do you think?" asked Karli.

"I really don't know what to think," replied Ben as he looked around the warehouse, a veritable gold mine of fine fabrics and glittering jewels of all sizes, colors and shapes.

"How do these people know me?"

Karli smiled.

"An angel named Malak came by and told us you would come here. He gave us an order to fill and left."

"Malak! Do you know Malak?"

"I didn't until he came into my shop. He spoke very highly of you and told us what you would need," said Karli.

"What I would need? What was he talking about?"

Karli laughed. "Mr. Ben, come over here with me for a minute." Karli led him to a large gold-edged mirror that held the answer.

Ben had almost forgotten that other than a quick, somewhat-distorted reflection of himself in the angel Michael's sword, he had no idea what he looked like since his journey began. The truth be known, he had paid no attention whatsoever to his apparel. All he could concentrate on at the time was the fact he was thirty to forty years younger. His actual appearance wasn't on his priority list.

Ben stepped toward the mirror and took a look. Shock registered on his face. Tattered, torn, soiled, and blackened remnants of what used to be clothing, hung shabbily from his frame.

The first thing he thought about, as he beheld the disheveled mess before him, was Melanie's homecoming banquet. He felt his face flush as he thought of how he must have been perceived by all the guests.

Then he thought again of how welcomed he was and how loved he felt.

"Of course you were loved, Mr. Ben. You were also greatly respected and honored," said Karli.

Ben was still in awe over how he could have spent all that time in Melanie's presence, all that time with heavenly friends, without someone having mentioned how awful he looked.

He quickly grabbed the torn pocket of his shirt and smelled it several times.

Well, at least I don't stink, he thought to himself.

"That's right, you don't," said a smiling Karli. "Nothing in heaven smells offensive, looks offensive, or is offensive."

"But Karli, look at me. Look how utterly despicable I am."

Again Karli laughed.

"Mr. Ben, you are still thinking like an earthling. Heaven pays little attention to such things. It is the farthest thing from anyone's mind. No one is judged on outward appearance. All here look at the heart."

Ben was glad to be reminded of the news he should have known. He relaxed a little, but still shook his head over the mess revealed in the mirror. He kept thinking back to the banquet. How could he have sat so long and not even realized his tattered sleeves, the rips in his pants, his whole chaotic appearance?

Karli must be right, he thought.

He felt better when he realized he couldn't recall the clothing worn by the guests, that is, except Melanie. He could describe every detail about her smile, her hair, and everything she wore.

"So I'm standing here, not to be humiliated, but to understand a heavenly principle. Is that correct, my merchant friend?"

"Sort of," Karli replied.

"It is not by chance that you stand before the mirror feeling humiliated. Here, in heaven, we continue to learn as we did on earth, and, as it is there, the choice to do so lies with us. The reason you didn't see yourself in rags is that God did not allow you to do so. What He's asking now is whether or not you could mature if you had to stay in such a ruffled mess for eternity?"

Ben hung his head, too embarrassed to answer. He stood perfectly still for what seemed a long time, pierced by the words of a humble merchant spouting the wisdom of Solomon.

Karli broke the silence.

"Cheer up my friend, your heart has answered the question."

Without fuss or fanfare, Karli motioned to two of his craftsmen who immediately began to wheel a large, magnificent, very ornate armoire in their direction. Both workers smiled and left.

"Go ahead, Ben, open it up and take a look."

Ben opened the doors and was instantly overwhelmed by what he saw inside.

A rough count revealed close to one hundred finely crafted outfits, most embroidered with jewels. All were stitched in gold and woven from the finest of fabrics. The majority of the full-length pieces were white or off-white and made of silk.

The remaining pieces, especially the more casual ones, were crafted from the most incredible linens he had ever come across. Each was soft, durable and extremely light weight. The majority of those were of the deepest and richest colors one could imagine.

Jeweled belts of fine, soft leathers joined at least twenty pairs of sandals and shoes, all hand-stitched.

But as stunning as the wardrobe was, nothing held a candle to the armoire's dazzling centerpiece—a sparkling jeweled crown just sitting there radiating its beauty atop a velvet-covered stand.

"These are all yours; try some on," said an obviously proud Karli.

A shocked Ben reached over and felt the sleeve of the garment closest to him.

"These are amazing," marveled Ben as he fumbled through one garment after another, all the while offering praise and thanks to Karli and his team of artisans for their creations.

"But what would I do with all these? How would I ever know what to wear and when to wear it?"

"Time will let you know," answered Karli. "All of them are individually crafted for you, and bear your name. They not only tell who you are, but remain always yours and yours alone."

Karli went on to explain that no two people in heaven wear the exact same clothing.

"You're kidding, aren't you?" said Ben as he continued his perusal, his eyes lighting up like a kid in a candy store.

"Heaven," said Karli, is a place of order, a place of rank, and a place of position. These garments and all of the accessories, right down to the embroidery and stitching, tell the story of Ben. T. Jacobs."

"Grab a few and try them on," said Karli.

An armload later, a very excited Ben headed toward a dressing room, his master craftsman following a few steps behind.

Chapter Twenty-Five

Elliott Hanrahan couldn't sleep.

Tiptoeing down the hall, he made his way to his favorite chair in the living room. It was three in the morning, according to the clock on the DVR.

Elliott had decided not to turn on any lights and to try his best to be quiet for fear of waking Alice.

God knows, he thought to himself, *if I can't sleep, at least someone should in this crazy house.*

Crazy best described the strange, continual state of crisis they seemed to find themselves in since Ben had his heart attack.

"Will it never end?" he shouted from his curled position in the green leather chair.

Elliott composed himself, realizing his loud comment had caused Alice to stir. Since their home was a split-entry and his study was downstairs, he decided to retreat to his sanctum in the basement. At least down there Alice wouldn't hear his laments.

Not sleeping was becoming routine for Elliott. The latest disruption came with the disappearing football incident two weeks earlier when he and Alice had met up with young Matt and Sarah. For Elliott, the incident had compounded fears of any hope of a return to normalcy.

In the last two weeks, Elliott had even taken to blaming the young couple for his mounting problems.

Alice had tried to tell her husband that the ball incident was a sign from God.

"A sign from God, really?" he mumbled to himself as he turned on the light to his study, his voice riddled with sarcasm and ready to explode with anger.

Elliott's stature as an academic wouldn't allow him to hear of such things, and his oversized ego held him in check from seeing anything her way.

Little did Elliott know that he was not alone when he flicked on the light.

His books and papers were piled in a mess atop his cherished antique oak desk. His degrees and awards hung silent on the wall.

About the only thing that looked out of place was a giant, fifty-inch Plasma HD TV that seemed to take up the greater portion of an entire wall.

Alice tried to talk him out of buying it. She told him how ridiculous and out of place it looked, but he wouldn't listen.

She had told him many times that he was turning away from being an avid reader and was becoming a TV addict. Elliott poured himself a Scotch, settled into his leather recliner, and reached for the remote.

Unknown to the professor, three pairs of eyes watched his every move.

The angelic messengers had been sent to the Hanrahan household in response to the unrelenting prayers of a worried Alice.

Elliot didn't really care about her conversion. He knew her closeness to Melanie Jacobs would eventually rub off one day, and it did. The only thing he appreciated about her changed life these past seven years was the fact that she was never openly pushy about trying to convert him.

Meanwhile, the three members of the heavenly host hovered near the ceiling, moving slowly back and forth, anxiously anticipating the completion of their mission.

On Streets of Gold

Seconds before Elliott's finger touched the power button on the remote, the TV came on by itself. It happened so fast he never really got a chance to react. Before he knew it, a drama began to unfold on the screen, one he would soon recognize, one that would leave him glued to the TV, riveted to his chair in disbelief.

A young boy about six or seven, obviously frightened, lay shivering in his bed. It was difficult to make out his face because he kept pulling the covers up over his head.

Elliott took another gulp of Scotch, not exactly sure why he was so fascinated by what he was seeing.

Within seconds, he had his answer.

The boy in the scene pulled the covers down far enough to reveal his face. The lad was none other than Elliott himself.

His latest sip of Scotch sprayed across the room, as a shocked Elliott realized he was watching himself on the screen.

Elliott's immediate reaction was to see what channel he was watching. Flick as he may, none of the buttons on the remote had any effect whatsoever on the television.

Whatever was powering the TV was not of this world, and Elliott knew it—he knew it from the chilling of his body and the goose bumps that began to travel up his arms.

Spooked, he scanned the ceiling, the floor, and the walls for some hint of explanation.

For the next two hours Elliott sat glued to scenes and events, so personal, so gut wrenching, they seemed impossible to fathom.

He knew only God Himself had the power to reveal such intimate details about his private life, about every hurt he'd ever had as a child from as long ago as he could remember, right up to the present time in his adult life.

This stuff was powerful and haunting, gripping Elliott down to the very core of who he was.

Being a man of reason, Elliott knew the value of observing patterns.

In the case of the most difficult times in his life, the times when he secretly cried out for help, he noticed there were always three angels sent in answer to his awkward prayer.

Why three? He didn't know. What he did know, from the scenes of his life flashing before him, was that they always did show up.

Because he could never see them, he automatically assumed that asking for help from any kind of a god was useless. Elliott's conclusion had always been that God didn't care, that no one cared about him, or what mattered most in his life. What he hadn't seen until now, was that just the opposite had been the case.

The LORD also revealed to the shocked professor the circumstances leading up to his greatest moment of shame, his attack on Ben, his best friend and cherished colleague.

Chills ran up Elliott's spine as the tell-all scenes showed him standing alone at Ben's hospital bedside with a pillow in his hand. It showed a close-up of his bulging eyes, full of hate, as he brought the pillow closer and closer to Ben's face.

Just as he began to apply the pressure, he realized what it was that made him stop.

In the natural, he credited himself with merely coming to his senses seconds before he killed his best friend.

On the screen, he saw the real answer. God pulled back the veil of the supernatural to reveal an angel's hand under the pillow keeping it from touching Ben's mouth.

Two other angels, one placed at each of Elliott's shoulders, gently pulled him back and away from Ben's bedside.

Elliott recalled having stood there in shock, thinking he had calmed down on his own, and had made a rational decision not to commit such a hideous act.

Details on the screen showed what really happened.

Elliott was unaware that a fight of great proportions had broken out just prior to the attack on Ben.

Clashes of swords rang out in the night sky above the hospital.

A large force of Zadar's goons had rushed the hospital in a frenzied attempt to finish Ben off, only to be met by a band of warring angels sent into action by the incessant prayers of a desperate Alice.

Elliott had no choice but to accept, with shame, what he was watching on the screen. It kept flashing the story of what really happened, not only that night, but the weeks and months leading up to the clash of the spiritual titans battling it out in the night sky.

Elliott, who thought perhaps he had been losing his mind, had no idea of Zadar's grooming to take over his thinking, and convince him to try and kill Ben.

Behind the scenes, the old beanbag warrior was doing his best to destroy Ben and his family as well as his circle of friends, including Elliott. The claws of this formidable foe had begun to sink deeper into the university world, a world extremely important to Halifax and Zadar's base in the Atlantic region. Elliott's TV spewed out only a capsule version of events, but he saw enough to realize what a pawn and fool he had been, in a deadly game played out by players he hadn't even realized existed.

At one point in the showdown, it looked like all would be lost.

Zadar himself appeared on the scene and reached a vulgar, hairy hand right through the roof and clawed at the numb brain of Elliott as he stood there over a comatose Ben.

The angels in the room joined those on the rooftop in pushing and pulling him back and out of the reach of Ben.

Alice, who had been fasting and praying for her husband, had also been joined by Matt and Sarah, as well as other prayer warriors from their church. Their efforts provided the angels of God with the necessary heavenly power to persevere and secure a victory in the battle for Ben's life.

Elliott, via his glaring plasma TV, was also given a glimpse of the power of prayer as it relates to spiritual warfare.

A shaken Elliott Hanrahan had seen enough. Tears flooded uncontrollably down his face. There was no sense in trying to regain his composure. He had simply lost it, filled to overflowing with remorse concerning what he had done, and at the same time empowered with an intense desire to make it right.

All Elliott could think of was the love God had for him in spite of everything he had messed up, and all the people he had hurt.

Suddenly, as quickly as it had turned itself on, the TV went blank, silent. When it did, the three angels in the room made themselves visible to Elliott. Rather than being shocked, he half grinned, obviously glad to see them.

Neither they, nor Elliott, spoke a word.

At that moment, words didn't really mean a lot. The radiance of the glory of the LORD was all over the three previously hidden angelic beings. Each approached Elliott, put their arms around a broken man, and welcomed him into the family of God.

The repentance of Elliott's heart gave rise to jubilation and rejoicing on the part of the angels in the room, on the rooftop, and in heaven above.

It wasn't long before the room emptied, and Elliott found himself alone with his thoughts and an incredible peace, the likes of which he had never known before.

Dawn was about to usher in a brand new day.

Meanwhile, a brand new Elliott sat smiling in what was left of the dark, anxiously awaiting first light and a chance to tell Alice what had happened.

Chapter Twenty-Six

Ben sat by the riverside dressed in one of his Karli-made casual outfits.

He had to admit he loved them all, especially the less decorative, brightly colored ones designed for the outdoors. The one he was wearing was so comfortable it felt like a second skin.

A grove of fruit trees bent their lush, fruit-laden branches gently toward the water's edge. All was well, yet he felt somewhat strange, somehow a bit unsettled in his spirit.

He knew such feelings were unusual in this place, perhaps unheard of.

After all, he thought, *I'm on my way to Zion, the very throne of God Himself. What could be more exciting than visiting the very place where God dwells?*

All of heaven's occupants visited the throne on a continual basis to worship the Master. Ben had been told by Karli that he too would go several times, but he would always remember his first visit as the best.

So what were these feelings?

For the first time since he came here, he began to seriously think of things on planet earth. *But why bother?* he thought. *Who in their right mind would want to think of that place after having been shown a glimpse of heaven?*

Within seconds, Ben had the answer.

His thoughts went back to some of his first encounters with the Lord. He remembered being told that He had work for him to do, work that would take place on earth, not here in heaven. He also remembered, only too well, Satan's anger over his being allowed to come here, and then being sent back to earth to tell others what heaven was really like.

Ben's thoughts and uneasy feelings were suddenly interrupted by a majestic white dove, gliding to a landing not more than two feet in front of him. As soon as it touched the ground, it began to preen the soft feathers beneath its beak.

The bird was like no other he had ever seen.

Oh, he had seen plenty of doves before, but this one was quite different. Though its beauty left you spellbound, it took second place to an aura of comfort that seemed to radiate outwards from it in all directions.

"Come with me and I will show you things you have not seen."

Ben turned quickly to see who was speaking. There was no one in sight. The sounds were coming from the dove.

"Did you just speak to me?" asked a startled Ben.

"Yes, I did," said the dove, not missing a beat as it continued fussing and preening its glistening white coat.

"Do you find it strange that I am talking to you?" asked the dove, this time staring straight ahead in Ben's direction. Eye contact with this incredible creature had an instant calming effect.

Within seconds, Ben felt he could throw in his lot with this bird, fly into the forest, and never return. The dove indeed commanded instant respect.

"Who are you?" Ben asked.

"You can call me Paraclete," said the dove.

"Come and let us explore what you haven't seen of heaven."

A loud, whirling, flapping noise immediately erupted as Ben took a step toward Paraclete.

Just like the pumpkin became Cinderella's coach, the bird instantly morphed into a creature large enough to climb aboard.

With no hesitation whatsoever, this mighty man of science, who once questioned everything, now found himself gently placing his arms around the dove's neck. He swung his leg over its back, and tucked his feet under its wings.

Off they flew.

Their flight was slow and smooth. Man and beast glided as one just above the tree level, close enough to still smell the amazing fragrances wafting upwards from the orchards and flower gardens below.

The buildings, the river, and the incredible streets of gold seemed so much more intense from their vantage point.

From where he sat, Ben couldn't see anyone pointing upwards or staring at them. He guessed a man riding a giant dove wasn't such a big deal to the hundreds of heavenly beings moving about below. Then again, Ben had long since given up on anything seeming strange in heaven—new maybe, but not strange.

"Where are we going?" asked Ben.

"On this route, we are not far from the region's Valley of Precious Stones. We will go there first," said Paraclete.

"Okay by me," nodded Ben.

Where they were going didn't really matter to Ben. He was too caught up with the magnificent scenery and his ride on a dove taxi to register what his pilot was saying.

Ben estimated they had traveled about one hundred miles over absolutely stunning countryside by the time they approached their first stop on the other side of the valley.

The low-level flight was the first time Ben had a chance to see any significant piece of heaven's landscape.

What he saw from above was a patchwork of orchards, fields, streams, and mountains, with lush valleys in between.

There seemed to be no heavy concentration of large towns; rather, cluster after cluster of huge mansions, some still under construction. All were positioned to take advantage of panoramic views.

From what he could tell as they flew over, nothing on earth compared to the type of architecture, or structure design of the mansions he saw.

Many of the small regions he observed appeared to be thematic. That assumption would later turn out to be correct.

Ben remembered seeing one particular region whose focus was obviously raising horses.

Ranch after ranch, all quite large, filled the landscape below. Each contained plenty of wide, open range, where some of the most beautiful horses he had ever seen roamed and frolicked in the sweet fresh air.

Ben wondered, as he soaked in their beauty, where the larger breed of white horses lived, the ones he remembered being ridden by heaven's contingents of warring angels.

In particular, he wondered about the enormous white steed he rode on with the archangel Michael.

Paraclete and Ben flew over the length of the valley before landing.

It didn't take long to realize how aptly named the valley was.

From one end to the other, there were stark evidences of rich deposits of precious minerals, the likes of which no one from earth could even begin to imagine.

The bright, shiny, yellow gold, so evident just about everywhere in heaven, came from valley regions just like the one they flew over.

For miles and miles, bulging seams of yellow gold deposits could be seen in the foothills, interspersed with the greens of the forest. The contrast was breathtaking.

Ben was beginning to understand something of the commerce of heaven.

One thing he noted was that everything done here was in stark contrast to the ways of earth.

There were no massive cities of concrete and steel, no large industrial towns with smokestacks spewing waste into the atmosphere, no cars or airplanes to pollute the air.

The countryside beyond the golden boulevards, at least the little of it he had seen thus far, was similar to parts of mountainous valley areas he knew from regions on the earth.

There was however, an incredible difference, an abrupt contrast in the way things were conducted here in heaven.

Commerce on the golden planet was not money driven. Nothing was fueled by greed.

Therein lay the secret, Ben thought. With money, power and drive for possessions taken out of the equation, gone also was deception, killing, and wars. Love replaced hatred. Peace had done away with turmoil.

The whole thing was so simple that it was profound.

Ben wondered why he hadn't put it together before. Probably, he thought, it was because there were so many new things to see and ponder.

His journey over the Valley of Precious Stones made him realize that people here toiled for pleasure, and worked only at what they loved and were gifted to do.

"Wow! What a concept," Ben murmured to himself.

"It is quite amazing, isn't it?" piped up a flapping Paraclete.

Ben, engrossed in his thinking, forgot for a moment that he was flying above the trees on a giant bird. He deduced it was probably his new heavenly friend, and not his own intuition, that helped him reach his conclusions.

"Everything has been provided, including mansions to live in, and purpose for living, throughout eternity," added Paraclete.

"Such is the generosity and love your God has for you."

Faint sounds of shouting, and what sounded like cheering, could be heard above the treetops as the flying duo winged its way past the valley's last outcrop of thick forest. So much for thinking no one had noticed them.

Coming into focus below was an estimated two thousand valley residents jostling, gazing, and pointing upwards at the approaching guests.

Lower and lower they descended, the faces of the people now visible.

A huge platform at the end of a lush green field also came into view. Surrounding its perimeter were at least fifty huge angel guards standing still, expressionless.

A hush fell over the crowd as Paraclete and Ben descended to the center of the platform. The sound of trumpets filled the air as all present bowed their heads and fell to their knees.

A confused Ben knelt as well, but had no idea what was going on.

Chapter Twenty-Seven

Sarah didn't want to answer the phone.

She could see from caller ID that it was Alice Hanrahan and decided not to pick up.

The truth be known, as much as she loved Alice, she was growing weary of getting nowhere each time she reached out to help her. But, as the seconds ticked away, conviction won out and she reached for the phone.

"Sarah, Sarah, is that you?" asked Alice, her voice over the top with emotion. "It's Alice!"

"Are you okay, Alice? What is it?" asked Sarah.

"Oh, my Lord, oh dear God, Sarah, it's Elliott. For the past three hours he's been crying and telling me of an encounter he's had with the Lord. Sarah, it's a miracle, an absolute miracle," said Alice between sobs and gasps to catch her breath.

If either woman could have seen the other, they would have laughed. Both were simultaneously jumping and squealing ecstatically as each new piece of information about Elliott unfolded.

Alice's amazing story of Elliott's supernatural encounter sent shivers up and down Sarah's spine.

Not only was every tidbit amazing, but it was also spiritually sobering as Sarah thought about the goodness of the Lord, and how He always answers prayer, sometimes not on our timetable, but always on His.

She thought also about what a doubting Thomas she had been, in regards to believing God would actually be able to straighten out the mess Alice and Elliott found themselves in.

Some say bad news travels fast, but in this case it was good news that stole the show, producing a domino effect as it moved faster than lightning across the phone lines of the city.

Sarah's first call, after hanging up from Alice, was to Matt. He called everybody he knew. She called everybody she knew.

Before long there was hardly a soul in their circle of colleagues, friends and church family, who had not heard the news. Everywhere, someone was calling someone else about what had happened.

Tom Mont, the pastor at Crossroads Christian Assembly, wasted little time extending an invitation to Elliott to speak on Sunday morning. Elliott, never shy when it came to public speaking, was only too glad to tell his story to the congregation at Alice and Sarah's church.

So it began.

In a matter of days, a ball that seemed to take years and years of prayer to get rolling was now moving faster than a freight train.

Other events, in what would become a widening outbreak of revival, slowly began to unfold.

Sarah's beloved children, for the past month, had been experiencing unusual and increasing supernatural visitations from angels, most often in the nighttime while they were sleeping.

In the bedrooms of their tiny Fairview home, they began to experience visits from a host of heavenly messengers. Each one shared details of the part the children would be asked to play in a citywide visitation of God.

Sarah often thought of the prophet Joel's prophecy of how the LORD would pour out His Spirit upon all flesh in the end times. In nighttime dreams and visions, that she too began to take part in, it became crystal clear Halifax, at the very least, was about to experience a time of refreshing, a time of revival never seen before in this part of the world.

Sarah was told that God's choice of who would spark the revival, was about to shock a lot of religious people.

One angel visitor, in particular, informed her that Christian leaders with more of a love of money than their flock, preachers preaching under their own steam, and pastors laden down, hamstrung by barren programs, weren't on His priority list to lead the charge.

Sarah was told that young children, whom the LORD spoke of so often in the scriptures, were about to be brought to the forefront of the action.

When she asked why this would be the case, one heavenly visitor replied, "Their obvious innocence, lack of questioning of God's Word, lack of stiff-necked traditions, and their penchant for earnestly praying and believing God are the things about to be anointed with power."

The angel continued, "The opposition to children playing a major role in church affairs will be fierce. Learned men, who do not manifest the heart of a child, have always been a stumbling block to any move of God. This one won't be any different."

Sarah and the other parents involved in the visitations knew that the uproar that would ensue would be a monumental task to overcome. The angels themselves would have to deal with a multitude of bruised egos that arose in the ranks of the church, and gave enemy forces of darkness, more fuel for the fire.

Satan, everyone involved in the visitations knew, was not about to stand still and watch God's plan unfold right before his eyes.

The forces of darkness over Halifax had already intensified in the past few months. Many a battle had broken out in the skies over the city, as the enemy got wind of what God was doing and tried to counter His every move.

Things were happening.

Slowly, bits and pieces of the puzzle began to fit.

Why a non-church man like Ben T. Jacobs was taken to heaven on such a monumental spiritual journey, and why Elliott Hanrahan was suddenly a believer, began to slowly make sense.

Time would prove that both of these men would be instrumental in the move of God, not because they were anyone of great importance, but more so, because they would allow themselves to be men of childlike faith, men willing to listen to God and His plans, rather than winging it with their own.

Chapter Twenty-Eight

Heaven's glow is what Ben liked to call it.

Everywhere on the planet, the presence of the Lord cast an incredibly soft light, most often shades of the color of jasper and clear as crystal. As he opened his eyes on the platform, he realized the light had intensified.

No longer soft, the colors were much brighter, intense. The entire atmosphere was charged with a presence so powerful, so gripping, it felt like your feet were cast in cement, unable to move.

Ben slowly lifted his head and opened his eyes just in time to witness Paraclete ascending upwards amidst light brighter and stronger than the noonday sun.

The gasps of the crowd grew louder, as everywhere people broke out in anthems of praise.

All hands were raised in adoration as the Spirit's ascent suddenly slowed and He began to speak. Every particle of the air was charged with glory. No one moved a muscle.

"Continue your work and honor your Lord Jesus with the fruit of your labors. He is worthy to receive honor and glory and praise. Love Him. Praise His name."

With those words, the ascent was complete, and Paraclete was gone.

Ben was more than puzzled about what had just happened, exactly who Paraclete was, and where he had gone.

"Have you never heard of the Third Person of the trinity? You just rode into the valley on His back."

The voice, the quickness, and the sharpness of the tones, were all too familiar. Turning to his left, he locked eyes with none other than Malak.

"How's it going, Professor?"

"Malak! I'm so glad to see you, my friend."

At Malak's beckoning, man and angel stepped from the platform and began to weave a path through the crowd.

The throngs of people who had come out to see Paraclete were not disappointed. Though the visit was short, no one seemed to mind. Whispers of praise were on just about everyone's lips as the crowds slowly began to disperse.

Ben was relieved to see Malak again. It seemed each time they met their bond grew stronger.

He still didn't know all he wanted to about Malak, but he was definitely becoming more comfortable around him. One of the things he liked most was getting straight, frank answers to his questions.

And it certainly seemed the longer the heavenly journey continued, the higher his pile of questions rose.

The object of his next query was certainly nothing new to his angel friend.

"Malak, can you tell me where Melanie is?" Ben's voice gave away just a slight tinge of anxiety.

"Relax," said Malak, sporting his familiar broad grin and that twinkle in his eye.

"When she's not at home, she's tending to children in the Valley of Innocence. We'll be going there soon," said Malak matter-of-factly.

A sense of euphoria swept over Ben at the thoughts of seeing Melanie again. Her last abrupt departure left him a bit frustrated, though not worried. He knew nothing harmful or mean was possible in heaven's realm. Each new experience in this place stirred up a lot of questions, but never doubts about intentions.

Speaking of questions, Ben couldn't resist asking Malak what the sudden disappearance of Paraclete was all about. He was indeed in awe over the fact that he had come in such close contact with someone so important. Nevertheless, he was under the impression their tour was to have been a lot more extensive.

"Yes it was," said Malak.

"I don't know the details, but usually when that happens, something major is going on. I can tell you one thing; you are indeed blessed to have even come near Paraclete."

The conversation between Malak and Ben was interrupted by someone shouting and waving their hands.

"Mr. Ben, Mr. Ben, you look stunning in that outfit. Who crafted such a fine garment for you?"

Laughter, and an extended hand of greeting, followed the comment.

Ben smiled and hugged his enthusiastic jeweler and tailor now standing before him.

"Great job on the outfit," was Malak's opening remark.

"Thank you, sir," Karli replied. "Now, come with me for dinner. I insist."

Ben looked to Malak for confirmation.

"Sure, why not? We appreciate the invitation," said Malak.

The scenery at the mouth of the valley was breathtaking. Ben would have preferred to walk and take it all in, but where Karli lived sort of put a damper on walking.

His mansion, as it turned out, literally extended out over the edge of a mountain summit visible in the distance. One look made you realize you would have to be a mountain goat to get there.

All three did an instant transport instead. More accurately put, Malak and Karli did; Ben had just gone along for the ride. All he really knew was that in an instant they had gone from the floor of the valley to the sprawling property of Karli's mansion.

Ben, the physics professor, wasn't so sure how this instant transportation system worked. He knew from his studies of metaphysics that there were more than the three dimensions of height, length, and width known on earth.

He knew scientists had figured out that there were at least eleven dimensions that existed, though they couldn't figure out how to access them.

Ben wasn't sure, but believed that in heaven there were probably a whole lot more than the eleven known to the scientific world on planet earth.

The ins and outs of the transport system definitely piqued his curiosity. For now, however, such thoughts were quickly replaced by a shock factor brought on by the intense beauty of Karli's place.

A virtual mountaintop, Masada-like resort stood before them, arresting the senses with its panoramic view of the valley floor—a regular visual feast to the eyes.

The trio stood atop a huge patio, surfaced with an array of hand-crafted marble tiles, which extended in one direction to meet a long set of five stairs, leading up to a wrap-around veranda, which led into Karli's two-storey mansion. The size of the mansion and its colonnade proved to be larger and more stunning than anything he had seen thus far.

In the opposite direction, the patio, complimented by a fountain at its center and surrounded by an array of trees, shrubs, and flowers, led to what appeared to be, at first glance, the edge of infinity. A railing hemmed in the sheer drop into the valley below but could not be detected with the naked eye. Ben was unsure what exactly the transparent material was made of; all he knew was that from a distance, it looked like it wasn't there.

Four or five servants, one of whom had wings, came bounding out to meet them.

"Please come in; everything is ready," said the winged servant, all the while smiling from ear to ear.

All three went inside for what would turn into a three-hour feast of fine food and fellowship, the likes of which Ben wouldn't soon forget.

Chapter Twenty-Nine

Soft, fluffy snow continued its gentle descent.

After three hours of unrelenting snowfall, Sarah's lawn resembled a winter wonderland. The white stuff covered every bush and shrub, now bent low to the ground.

Matt and the children, only a week before, had dressed the greenery in bright lights. There would be no prize for symmetry, but the trio didn't really care. At the time, they were having too much fun to worry about how well their masterpieces were strung.

Now the lights were covered by at least three inches of snow that turned the branches into a soft glow of bright colors blending together under their white blanket.

Sarah kept going to the window to look for Matt.

It was Christmas Eve, her absolute favorite day of the year. Ever since she was a little girl, she had always loved anything and everything to do with Christmas.

She had been taught her addiction well. Her mother Melanie was the same way.

This Christmas would prove bittersweet for Sarah. It would indeed be a most blessed and happy Christmas because Matt was in her life. But it would also be sad because her father still remained in a coma.

This was the first Christmas in her entire life that she would not be able to interact in a meaningful way with her dad. Now, four months after falling into a coma, he was being moved from the hospital to a long-term care facility.

One lone tear moistened her cheek as she stood once again by the window. She quickly wiped it away, and allowed herself a tiny grin, as she thought of how it would be better in one sense: the new facility was in Fairview and only a few blocks away.

And besides, Sarah assured herself, she could cling to the Lord's promise to bring him around. She believed the Lord, but had to admit that sometimes the sting of the wait was hard to bear.

"Mom, Mom, when will Matt get here?" asked a fidgeting Joshua, who came bounding into the living room from the kitchen, obviously on a sugar high from the homemade cookies that he and his sister were supposed to have only "a few" of.

Esther, who had already consumed her share, had just returned from the attic, where she had once again been searching for her favorite ornament that had somehow gone missing. The tree had been up for over a week, but the ornament was nowhere to be found.

Sarah let out a sigh of relief as the headlights of Matt's old car finally turned into the driveway.

"Children, Matt's here."

A loud "yeah" arose simultaneously from the kids, as Sarah went to the door to let him in.

"Merry Christmas," shouted Matt loudly, even before the door was fully opened.

Sarah leaned over to plant a kiss on his cheek and in the process almost knocked the parcels out of his arms.

"I'm sorry I'm late; I couldn't get the old clunker to start."

"What's in that one?" squealed Esther.

"Who's that one for?" asked Joshua.

"Children, where are your manners?" Sarah half chuckled.

"Let him at least get his coat off. The two of you are going to have to settle down, she said sternly. "You're acting like a pair of jumping beans."

Sarah burst out laughing. She knew no one, including herself, could take the comment too seriously.

Matt finally managed to park his coat in the front hall closet and find a spot on the sofa, not an easy task, as he fought his way through scattered piles of gifts that hadn't yet found their way under the tree.

The presents for Sarah and the children sat in a neat pile on the coffee table.

"Why don't you put your gifts under the tree, Matt?"

"Great idea," said Matt, his ear-to-ear smile giving away his absolute excitement about spending Christmas with the three people he loved most in the world.

Matt placed his awkwardly wrapped gifts under the tree, returned to the sofa, and once again took up sipping an eggnog-laced coffee Esther had handed him the minute he sat down.

"Sarah, the tree and the house decorations really look nice."

"Well, Matt, you had a part in it too."

Matt smiled.

All he had really done was put the tree in its stand and place a few ornaments here and there. He noticed the few he had hung were moved around by Sarah after he had gone home. Getting all the decorations just right was Sarah's domain, a job passed down to her from her mother.

Esther and Joshua, who had been sitting on the floor, practically under the tree, continued to stare and whisper about the new additions Matt had just added to the pile.

Joshua, when he was sure no one was looking, bent back a loosely taped corner of his present from Matt. He was sure his mother hadn't seen him until he heard her voice.

"Shame on you two, get away from those presents," Sarah said firmly.

"Oh, Sarah, let them be; it's Christmas Eve. They're just making sure they know exactly which present to open before they go to bed."

It had always been a tradition in both families to open one present before midnight on Christmas Eve.

"Okay, you're right, Mr. Smarty Pants. By the way, is there one there for the special lady in your life?"

"Could be," blushed Matt, who changed the subject, choosing to speak about the progress of the pies baking in the oven.

The aroma of two apple pies cooling on the kitchen counter had captured Matt's attention. Two rabbit pies, still cooking in the oven, competed for control of his sense of smell.

"Why don't you children go up and get ready for bed, and when you come downstairs we'll start the games."

Esther and Joshua knew the routine and were glad the clock was ticking down to present-opening time. Before the chosen gift was opened, there would be an hour or so of games, the reading of the Christmas story from Luke Chapter two, and the eating of the pies.

Two very anxious children didn't have to be told twice. Away they flew, their feet hardly touching the stairs.

Sarah joined Matt on the sofa, leaned forward and put her head on his shoulder. A warm smile broke out on Matt's face as he placed his arm around her and gave her a gentle hug, followed by a soft kiss on the forehead.

"Matt MacKeen, we are actually spending our first Christmas together. What do you think of that?"

"What do I think of that? Well, I keep thinking someone is going to pinch me and I'll wake up and realize the past few months have only been a dream."

Sarah reached down and pinched Matt on the leg.

"There, I'm still here and you're still here, so it can't be a dream," teased Sarah.

"You're right," said Matt, "and I'm sure enjoying getting used to it."

At that moment the timer dinged, a reminder to take the remaining pies out of the oven.

Excusing herself, Sarah darted for the kitchen. When she did, Matt put his plan in motion.

Ever since he secretly bought her diamond three weeks earlier, he plotted how and when he would ask her to marry him.

Since Christmas meant so much to her, and because he was going crazy over wanting to make things official, he had decided Christmas Eve would be the time to make his move.

Matt, at the exact moment that Sarah had darted to the kitchen, dashed to the hall closet, reached into his coat pocket, and retrieved a small, red velvet bag, closed snugly at the top with a gold-corded drawstring.

Quick as a flash, he placed it on a branch of the tree toward the back that was not easily visible from any angle in the living room.

Matt plunked himself on the sofa just moments before Sarah came back into the room.

Another kiss, this one firmly on the lips, took up the next few moments, abruptly interrupted by the sound of the children running and pushing their way down the stairs.

"I finished first."

"No, I did."

"Children, children, did I just see the two of you shoving each other coming down the stairs?"

"Sorry, Mom," said Esther.

"Sorry, Mom," echoed Joshua.

"My, my, you would think it was Christmas Eve around here."

Sarah's comment drew a round of laughter.

"Okay, who's up for a few games of Junior Scrabble?"

A resounding "yeah" rang out simultaneously from Esther, Joshua, and Matt. All three had their hands raised in the air as a sign of affirmation. Sarah laughed to herself at Matt's enthusiasm. She often referred to him as her third child.

Esther cleared the kitchen table, Joshua got the game, and Matt poured everyone a glass of root beer. Sarah shook half a bag of chips into a large mixing bowl and placed it on the table.

Approximately an hour later the games were over. A round of teasing was in order as Esther had won the first game and Joshua the second. The children were quick to lovingly point out that Sarah and Matt weren't much of a challenge.

At Sarah's request, the gang retreated to the living room for the reading of the Christmas story.

"Matt, would you be so kind as to read the story for us?"

The broad grin on Matt's face gave away his delight in being asked.

The old familiar story never sounded so fresh and new and so full of meaning. An actual presence of the LORD could be felt in the room as both adults and children reflected on the powerful message that so transformed the world.

"That was beautiful, Matt. Thank you."

Matt, always shy about receiving praise, acknowledged the compliment with a smile and a nod.

"Well gang, who saith we eat?"

An instant exodus to the kitchen erupted the very moment Sarah's words left her lips.

A Christmas-print tablecloth was quickly spread. The sound of dishes being plunked on the table joined the clinking of silverware. In less than three minutes, the hungry brood was seated at their familiar spots.

Esther said the grace, and each of the four quickly devoured most of the rabbit pies, followed in short order by the apple.

Then it was off to the living room, and for the children, the best time of all—the opening of that one chosen present that for days had particularly piqued their curiosity.

Esther, being the oldest child, was allowed to go first.

She chose a gift signed jointly by Sarah and Matt. Inside was an entire twelve-volume set of pioneer books for children written by her favorite Christian author. Esther's squeal said it all. She had asked for one of the books and was overwhelmed to receive all twelve.

Joshua, the family Lego genius, received one of the latest editions to add to his collection of the prized creative toy. His gift was also from both Sarah and Matt.

Sarah asked Matt to go next.

"No, no, you go next, Sarah."

Because she wouldn't listen, Matt complied and began to open a brightly wrapped gift that he knew was from her.

An audible gasp could be heard when Matt opened the present. Professionally framed, in an expensive gold-plated frame, was Melanie's letter to Sarah about him, the one that he had secretly kept for so long.

A speechless Matt fought back tears and the redness in his face, but to no avail.

A gift to her from Matt was opened last. Sarah said nothing about her suspicions. She unwrapped the tiny box that turned out not to be what she thought, though it was a beautiful and touching gift just the same.

Matt had bought her a pair of very expensive silver earrings in the shape of a heart with a tiny gold cross in the center.

After the excitement over the gifts had settled down, prayers were said kneeling at the sofa, and it was off to bed for Esther and Joshua.

All was quiet and picturesque as Matt and Sarah sat together on the sofa and stared at the twinkling lights of the Christmas tree.

"I don't remember that ornament, Sarah."

"What ornament, Matt?"

"The one in the red velvet pouch near the top, on the left hand side of the tree. Come over here and look. You can just barely see it."

Sarah's curiosity jumped into high gear. She couldn't figure out why Matt, who didn't seem to take much interest in ornaments, was now so interested in this particular one.

Sarah stood to her feet, went to the tree, and took the ornament off the branch.

"I really don't know what that is, or who put it there, Matt."

"Well, maybe you should just take a look inside, Miss Sarah."

Sarah's heart began to pound. Could it be what she was thinking? Inside was indeed a tiny, square-shaped, velvet box.

Taking a deep breath, she opened it and let out a scream.

"Do you like it?" asked Matt, who was now down on one knee at Sarah's feet.

"Like it? I love it," squealed Sarah.

"Will you marry me?"

"Will I? Try and stop me," she said between hugs, kisses and pirouettes around the living room.

Chapter Thirty

The Valley of Innocence was a most intriguing place, a place filled with so many children, so much laughter.

Ben wasn't sure how he and Malak arrived here. He vaguely remembered saying good-bye to Karli, and then presto, here they were in these new and strange surroundings.

He recalled thinking for a moment how Alice must have felt when she first arrived in Wonderland. But this was so much more than Wonderland. A better name, he thought, would be the Magnificent Land of Smiling, Happy Children.

An outbreak of joy and laughter filled the air—obvious byproducts of the happiness etched on the faces and demeanor of the children.

Everywhere you looked there were small, orderly groups of smiling kids. At the side of each was a teacher, or guardian. Most of the leaders were women, some were men, and others were angels, easily detected by their radiance. Some had wings, some did not.

"What and where is this place?" Ben asked Malak.

"This is the Valley of Innocence I told you about earlier. It is actually one of twelve such valleys. There is one on each of the twelve boulevards that wind their way to the throne."

"What happens here, Malak? What is the purpose of this place? Why are there so many children here?"

Ben was obviously overwhelmed by the thousands of little people of all sizes, shapes, and colors weaving their way through this delightful place.

Malak explained that where they were standing was in essence one gigantic fun park for the children to come and unwind.

Ben, dazzled by his surroundings, thought about how Disney World had nothing on this place. As a matter of fact, as Malak would explain, each Valley of Innocence, only on a larger scale, somewhat mirrored the theme park concept of the famous Florida attraction.

The park they were standing in was amazing in that it was created by the LORD for the pure enjoyment and fun of the kids, and that's exactly what everyone here was having, as children and guardians jostled about trying to decide which attraction to visit next.

There was also a nature park replete with every flower, tree, fish, mammal, reptile, and creepy crawly thing the Creator had ever called into existence.

Another park was made up strictly of conference centers, schools, and libraries, all set in picturesque village surroundings, replete with manicured gardens and grounds.

A plethora of shops spread out before them in all directions. Each appealed specifically to the needs of the children. The most popular were those offering every type of delicious fruit, sweet, and candy imaginable.

Ben's curiosity kept getting the best of him.

"But who are these children? Where do they come from and where are their parents?"

"These are the precious, innocent babes of earth, the unwanted, those who have been killed or died in their mother's womb, those who have been murdered, those who have died prematurely, victims of accidents, starvation, or disease," said Malak.

The corners of his mouth were drawn downwards, as were his eyes. It was a look Ben rarely saw on the face of his angel friend. "They are the flowers plucked too early, who did not have a chance to bloom. They have been gathered by the angels from all ages since time began, and brought here to be cared for and taught, under the watchful eye of the LORD Himself."

"Do they always remain as little children?" Ben asked.

"All the children who have ever come here are taught and nurtured until they are adults. When they reach adulthood, they must decide for themselves if they want to continue in the LORD, or choose banishment for their rebellion."

Ben was amazed at what he was hearing.

"Has anyone ever chosen to walk away from all this?"

Malak hesitated for a moment before answering.

"No," said Malak.

Ben figured the short pause gave Malak the few seconds he needed to put his computer-like brain into gear and scan the centuries back to the beginning of mankind.

"There has never been such a rebellion, at least not that I have ever seen, or been told about."

Something else puzzled Ben.

"Are these children aware of any other choices besides what they know?"

"Oh, yes, of course," said Malak.

"A large part of their studies has focused on the behavior of man in relation to God, going back to the beginning of time. Each has seen how God has always loved His creation, and how man has forever been given free choice to choose or reject God's love."

"When they become adults, they use the knowledge of earth's history to make their own decision about their future."

Malak continued, "God has appointed teachers, those from every century on earth, those who have a special gift, and who truly love children. Here in heaven, these teachers fulfill their calling by teaching the little ones who come here."

Ben was impressed. He remembered thinking such a task would be a good fit for Melanie.

Wait a minute, he thought, his mind racing as he picked up on something he'd forgot. *Isn't this what Melanie does here in heaven?*

Ben had become so caught up in his surroundings that he had totally pushed aside the fact that Malak had already told him they would come to this valley, and that Melanie would be here.

"So Malak, where is Melanie?" asked Ben, his eyes scanning the flowing crowds, hoping to spot his beloved wife.

Malak chuckled. "Something told me you wouldn't forget my words about Melanie. Come with me."

It seemed funny at the time. There sat the pair, angel, and man on a bright colored monorail, gliding slowly across the wonderland below.

"Where are we going, Malak?" Ben asked. "And by the way, isn't a monorail a strange mode of travel for you?"

Malak laughed.

"The longer you stay here, the sooner you will discover that the Master is an incredible God, a God of magnificence and incomprehensible variety. Sometimes He simply chooses to allow us to slow down the pace and take time to smell the flowers and enjoy the ride."

Good answer, thought Ben.

Their mode of travel certainly allowed for close-up views of the park, and a greater chance for observance and interaction with the children and their guardians, as they jostled on and off at the various stops along the winding route.

The faces of the children said it all, as did their behavior.

It was impossible to miss how happy, well-behaved, and polite each of them were, as they munched and shared their treats. All sat quietly, without screaming or being mean to each other, or their teachers. Also noteworthy, was the fact no one was shoving, squirming, or climbing the walls inside the rail car.

Ben hadn't noticed the attractive lady in the red, gold-fringed shawl enter the rail car.

She and her twelve students sat near the front. Ben and Malak, when they first got on, had positioned themselves in the back row in the last two seats on the right hand side.

About three minutes into the ride, the teacher turned to point out something of interest to the children. When she did, Ben realized the lady in the red shawl was none other than his beloved Melanie.

"Melanie! Melanie!" he yelled out from the back of the rail car as he arose to go to her. As he did, he felt Malak's firm hand holding him back.

"She can't hear you, nor can she see you, Ben."

"What do you mean? Why not? What are you talking about Malak?"

Ben wasn't angry. It was next to impossible to get angry in this place. He was more taken aback than anything else.

Malak went on to explain.

"My orders are to not allow you to interact with Melanie, at least not for the time being."

"Your orders? What do you mean your orders?"

"Ben, I know we've become close, but you must always remember that I am, and always will remain, an angel on assignment. Whatever God says, I do."

"What exactly do you mean?" Ben asked.

"Let me explain it this way. Throughout the centuries, angels have cared for and watched over the affairs of man, especially those who have come to know and love the Lord as their Savior. If there is one thing above all else that we have detected as a weakness of man, it is his inability to trust God for the things he cannot see or cannot understand."

"This weakness gets him into trouble time and time again," explained Malak.

"Angels don't have this flaw. Because of a superior knowledge and an eternity of watching a trustworthy God never break His word, we know what He says is always right and part of a solid plan for good. Thus we carry out everything He says without ever questioning Him."

Ben knew what Malak was saying was true. A lump in his throat and a tug at his heart bore it out.

The next stop was ice cream alley. Melanie gathered the children and headed for the exit.

Though she hadn't, Ben was sure she looked directly at him and smiled as she and the children got off.

She was gone.

The whole heart-pulsing scenario played out in a matter of fifteen minutes. Ben kept trying to convince himself that God's reasoning was always the best.

He pressed his nose against the window and watched as long as he could until Melanie was out of sight.

He had to admit he wasn't finding the lesson an easy one to learn.

Chapter Thirty-One

Something was eating at Elliott Hanrahan.

It had only been a week since his conversion, but what a week it was. Joy unspeakable had been his portion for seven days and seven nights, ever since the visit of the three angels to his study.

Elliott had truly, and deeply, felt the power of God's forgiveness. He loved what he felt and never wanted the feelings, or the truth behind them, to stop.

A standing ovation followed yesterday's testimony at Crossroads Christian Assembly. No one in the congregation had ever heard anyone speak so eloquently, so powerfully, and with so much passion.

For the record, the applause and the accolades weren't about to swell Elliott's head. After all, his speaking abilities had been the talk of the university for decades. He was indeed a communicator, and now, with God's anointing, he was about to enter a new arena, as a chosen vessel to carry His message to the masses. Elliott didn't know all of this just yet, but he soon would.

So why was something bothering him, to the point that he took a day off from lecturing and sequestered himself in his study, alone with his thoughts?

The answer to the question could be summed up in one three-letter word: Ben.

Elliott was beside himself with feelings of guilt about what he had almost done to his best friend. He had mentioned these feelings to

Alice, feelings he felt were holding him back, trying to belittle his conversion, and make him feel he didn't deserve God's love and forgiveness.

Her answer had been swift and to the point.

He could hear her words ringing in his ears, as he sat in his study staring at the monster TV that he had vowed to remove. A glass of his favorite soda sat on the table beside him, a reminder of his instant deliverance from what had been a growing dependence on the Scotch that had befriended him.

"Mr. Hanrahan," she told him in a firm voice, "you, like every other Christian, has an enemy that will hound you till the day you die. Your job is to defeat him with the Word of God and your testimony. Speak the Word against him, resist him, and he will flee from you."

Elliott so appreciated Alice by his side. He knew that in the weeks, months, and years that lay ahead, she would help him, she would be his teacher, his professor of the Word, his confidante, and his friend.

As for what to do about Ben, God himself settled the matter.

"Go to him and make it right, not for his sake, but for yours."

The voice, not what you would call audible, though crystal clear, was soft, commanding, encouraging. Elliott knew it was the voice of the Lord, a voice he would become quite adept at discerning as time went on.

"I want you to learn a lesson about forgiveness. At some point, I will teach the same lesson to Ben. At the appointed time, he will forgive you."

Elliott listened intently, motionless in his leather chair.

Suddenly, before him, he saw a picture, somewhere in what he guessed must be the recesses of his mind, almost as if on a movie screen, though none was present.

He saw a tap with water running out of it. A hand was controlling the water and the force of its flow.

The voice continued.

"The water flowing from the tap is my forgiveness. I provide the forgiveness that you can't. But the hand in the picture is yours. You control the opening of the tap and how much is let out."

Elliott, in a way, now felt worse for what he had done to Ben, but at the same time was overjoyed by God's promise that his old friend would be willing to forgive him.

He also felt very humbled. After all, the Creator of the universe was teaching him a lesson. How incredible was that?

On the surface, the lesson appeared quite simple, but when unwrapped, it became something incredibly profound.

Elliott thought for a moment of the many times he, and probably millions of others, had imitated true repentance and forgiveness with a glib and hollow apology, that didn't really mean anything.

When the vision lifted, Elliott felt enraptured by a peace that flowed over him like a warm, sweet honey. It moved down his body, starting at the top of his head, and ending at the tips of his toes. It then seemed to roll gently across the floor and vanish through the walls of his study.

Elliott knew he had been in the presence of the LORD.

He also knew, and accepted, that he would never again be secure in his former world of all things rational, and all things scientifically proven.

It was only fifteen minutes by car to the villa. Elliott could honestly say he didn't remember getting into the car and heading toward the Fairview facility. Now here he was in the parking lot.

Sheepish, scared, embarrassed, and ashamed, were only four of the many feelings the professor felt as he walked nervously toward the front door.

The nurse behind the desk offered up a broad smile.

"Hello, may I help you?"

"Yes, I'm here to see Ben Jacobs."

"Are you a member of the family?" the nurse asked. Her smile had disappeared. Her eyes squinted slightly.

"No, I'm a former colleague of his, from the university. My name is Elliott Hanrahan."

"Mr. Hanrahan, you do realize Mr. Jacobs's condition?" Her voice changed. Gone was its friendly tones.

"Yes. I know he's in a coma. I just want to see him and stand at his bedside for a short while."

"Sir, if you'll be so kind as to have a seat for a moment, I'll contact his daughter to see if he's allowed visitors."

Elliott complied, though not quite sure what was going on.

A few minutes later the nurse returned.

"Sir, his daughter gave permission for the visit and told me to thank you for coming over. Come with me and I'll take you to his room."

Elliott was obviously unaware that Sarah had asked for a description of what he looked like before granting her permission. She knew, of course, what her good family friend, and now brother in the Lord, looked like, but she had to know for sure if this was really him visiting her dad.

In the past month several threatening phone calls had come into the villa regarding Ben. The staff were all put on alert and told to keep a watchful eye on his room, and not to allow any visitors if they weren't absolutely sure who they were.

It turns out Ben's room was only two doors down from the central desk, a perfect setup for the staff to screen who entered his room.

Elliott nodded at the two strikingly handsome young men standing on either side of the door to Ben's room.

"Good day gentlemen."

His greeting drew a strange look from the nurse who turned around to see who Elliott was talking to. She, of course, couldn't see the two guards, and was oblivious to the three warring angels inside the room.

Elliott walked into the room behind the nurse who promptly did her checks and left.

Slowly, he inched his way toward Ben's bed, his feet seemingly weighed down in shoes of lead.

Suddenly, something changed. A definite peace filled the room, taking the edge off a nervous Elliott. There he stood, perfectly still, engulfed in the warm, friendly feelings that had taken over the room.

The repentant professor soaked in the atmosphere, as he stared intensely at his friend, hooked up to tubes, wires, and the machines that had become his lifeline.

Finally, he moved closer, right up to the edge of the bed.

When he last saw Ben, his friend was extremely thin, almost gaunt. Now his once ashen-faced colleague seemed to have a little color in his cheeks. He even looked as if he may have put on a pound or two.

Was this wishful thinking? Was he letting his imagination run wild? Was he just hoping beyond hope?

The visitor cleared his throat.

"Well, Ben, I don't know if you can hear me or not. I've got something to say that's extremely difficult for me," said Elliott, his voice cracking with emotion.

"I am the one who slipped into your room and tried to smother you with a pillow. I confess this before Almighty God, and beg your forgiveness for such a horrible thing."

There was no movement or sign from Ben.

Elliott continued.

"I have since become a Christian, and am slowly realizing that God has forgiven me."

By now, the tears had begun to flow down Elliott's face, quickly turning to sobs, as he stood there alongside his old friend.

Perhaps his emotions were getting the best of him. Surely he must be imagining what he began to see through his tears.

As he fully opened his eyes, Elliott saw Ben's left hand slowly but surely inch toward his. Ben's fingers, and the palm of his hand, fumbled atop Elliott's.

Though the patient's eyes remained tightly closed, a definite, gentle squeeze had taken place—a squeeze that spoke volumes between two old friends.

No other human being saw the exchange, but three white-robed angels looked at each other, nodded, and smiled.

Chapter Thirty-Two

What happened in the Valley of Innocence had been a shocker to Ben.

Malak's powers made it easy to discern Ben's hurt. Besides, he had been with him and knew firsthand what he was going through. He understood his mixed feelings about his love for God, and his love for Melanie. He knew that Ben was troubled over seeing Melanie on the monorail and not even being allowed to say hello.

"My friend, it's time."

Ben glanced inquisitively at Malak.

"What do you mean? It's time for what?"

"It's time for a visit to the throne, to the very place where the Godhead dwells."

Ben, who had been sitting somewhat slumped on a bench next to Malak, now sat straight up.

"There were other places along the journey that we were to visit first, but I think it is best that we go there now," said Malak.

Ben nodded his approval.

It was beyond his comprehension to understand what Malak was thinking or what his intentions were.

Malak was good at what he did. He was good at taking care of his charge. He knew his job well. He knew how to keep one ear on Ben and his thoughts, and his second ear on what the Master was saying about the task at hand.

Malak knew that the more Ben saw of heaven, the more he was trying to define it around Melanie, as if they were merely living on earth in some version of utopia.

This wouldn't do. Malak would see to it.

He also knew that a visit now to the throne would be the tonic Ben would need to make him think clearly and understand the task that lay before him.

Malak had grown fond of Ben. Because of the fondness and his complete loyalty to the Father, Malak vowed to do his utmost to make sure nothing stood in the way of fulfilling God's best for his friend.

Ben wasn't sure how far they had traveled on their 1500-mile journey, from where they entered a gate of pearl to where they would arrive at the actual throne. He wasn't even sure which of the twelve boulevards they were traveling on to get there.

On earth, any such lack of knowledge usually sends the average person into a tizzy. Such was never the case in heaven.

He had to admit he was getting quite the kick out of not knowing what was going to happen next. An even greater thrill was having such a peace that he really didn't care.

As a matter of fact, he was never quite sure who would be crossing his path next, or even what happened to his traveling companions.

Malak was a case in point. Minutes ago they were sitting together on a bench. Now he was nowhere in sight.

Who did show up out of nowhere, immaculately dressed and grinning from ear to ear, was his new friend Karli.

An entourage of artisans and tailors followed close behind, trying to catch up with him. With that bushy mustache and matching eyebrows, you couldn't miss him bouncing through the crowd toward Ben.

"Ah, Mr. Ben, there you are."

"I heard you were going to the throne, so I came immediately," he said, huffing and puffing as he tried to catch his breath.

"We've brought five of your finest outfits, all suitable for visiting the throne, along with matching sandals and accessories. We will go with you to ensure the fittings are proper and that you understand the protocol of your first visit."

An ecstatic Karli had spoken so fast that Ben could barely make him out.

"Protocol, outfits, accessories?"

Ben tried his best to understand him, but the tailor's words kept getting drowned out in the mounting noise of the crowd.

One thing he knew for sure, Karli would have him up to speed and decked out in proper attire by the time they got there.

Thousands upon thousands of people had crowded the boulevard heading north. Hundreds more could be seen picnicking in the fields, flower gardens, and fruit-tree groves that dotted the landscape along the riverbank.

The massive crowd of throne seekers ebbed and flowed, back and forth, with an intensity that reminded him of the Bay of Fundy tides of Nova Scotia. Excited worshippers returning from the throne constantly mixed with those en route. Often a round of shouts and hugs would break out, as one group would run into someone in another whom they recognized from their region.

The mood, as always, was ever festive, jubilant, reverential.

As far as the eye could see, the bustling boulevard was bursting with the excitement of the masses, moving ever onward in the glow of the golden thoroughfare.

Ben picked up on many of the conversations along the way.

All of them seemed to focus on one thing—seeing the Glory of God on His majestic throne.

Ben began to notice something unusual was occurring the farther north they traveled. It didn't happen suddenly; it was more of a gradual process.

At first, he wasn't exactly sure what it was.

If their journey was on earth, one might deduce the air was thinning as they reached higher heights, making them lightheaded, even giddy.

In a sense, the air was changing, but it wasn't that it was thinning. The farther north they went, the greater the atmosphere was affected by the Glory of the LORD—a glory that filtered down through everything in heaven. It was obviously intensifying the closer they got to the throne.

The next thing he began to notice was the change in the richness of the colors.

As the light from the throne grew brighter, so did the colors. Everything in their path was being cast in a deeper richness, a richness producing hues impossible to describe.

Each mile they walked, the intensity grew.

Ben was also aware that neither he, nor anyone around him, had a clue about time. No one seemed to know whether they had been traveling for a day, a week, or a month.

Also, the light of heaven continually energized its occupants, to the point they never got overly tired from their journey.

Traveling great distances on foot, without even a hint of exhaustion, became the norm. Resting did occur, and sometimes sleeping, but both were undertaken by choice, not out of necessity.

So on they trod, laughing, fellowshipping, having fun, each one enraptured in an air of expectancy.

Chapter Thirty-Three

Melanie knew Ben was still in heaven.

There wasn't a day that went by that she didn't think about him. As a matter of fact, she knew a whole lot more about him, his whereabouts, and his mission than one would have thought.

The source of her information was two-fold.

Heaven's residents, Melanie included, were a gifted lot. It was estimated that mankind on earth only used approximately one tenth of his brain power, the other nine tenths having been lost at the time of the fall. The restoration in heaven of that missing nine tenths made for an obvious world of difference.

Melanie had the benefit of being heavenly working on her behalf. She also had the presence of the Lord and His wisdom to tap into.

The Lord, in His kindness and mercy, had visited her during that amazing and delightful night spent with Ben at Ingonish Beach.

She would never forget that wonderful time they had digging clams and cooking them on the beach as the waves serenaded them in the background.

Of course, the nighttime spent tenting under the stars, wrapped in each others arms, was the best part of all.

Incessant conversation with the man she had spent her entire adult life with on earth was a pleasure she would tuck away forever.

In a way, she felt bad for Ben, though she knew she shouldn't.

She remembered back to that Ingonish night, when the Lord had appeared to her as they slept. He had laid out the whole plan of Ben's visit, and she knew that it was not only a good one, but it was also the best one.

She had to admit, however, that there were some parts of the plan she would like to have seen carried out a little bit differently. Then again, she knew quite well that her motives and her heart were at loggerheads with what was best.

Melanie wanted to see more of Ben. Above all else, she wanted him to know that it wasn't her choice to spend so much time apart while he was here in heaven.

She was also a bit upset about her abrupt departure, a parting that took place without even as much as a proper good-bye.

All these things she pondered in her heart as she sat sipping her morning tea on the sprawling balcony just off the master bedroom.

Five years in heaven had taught Melanie many things. One of them was to not question the Lord. An even more difficult task was learning to grasp the Father's love, to marvel at its depth, to understand His trustworthiness.

Learning not to question the Lord was certainly not because He was a hard taskmaster. To the contrary, the tenderness and love shown her and the millions who shared this city, this planet, was unfathomable.

Melanie's thoughts were interrupted by movement she caught out of the corner of her eye.

"Will there be anything else, Miss Melanie?"

"No thanks, Mosoo," replied Melanie, as she smiled at her angel friend and servant.

She laughed out loud at Mosoo, who curtsied in jest, returned the smile, and waved as she left the room.

Melanie returned to her inner thoughts.

She reflected on how the greatest example of the Father's love was ever present, ever around them, ever intertwined in their daily lives. It was found in none other than Jesus, the only begotten son of the Father.

One look into those loving eyes, and everything vague became instantly plain.

His wonderful presence was no farther away then a prayer on the lips of his children. Jesus was certainly not literally by her side every day, but He always did come at times when she needed Him the most.

"I'm sorry Lord for not fully trusting you."

Melanie had uttered the words aloud in response to an incredible jolt of peace that came over her. At the same time, she felt an arm gently placed across her shoulder.

There was no visible, physical presence of the Lord on her balcony, but she knew it was Him and that He was there.

"Thank you, Lord, for the precious reminder of who you are, and how much you love me."

Melanie finished her tea, concluded her praise time, and walked back inside.

The Lord's gentle nudge of assurance was certainly appreciated and just the boost she needed to put her concerns about Ben to rest.

It was not that she thought for a moment that Ben was being treated unfairly. To the contrary, she knew he was having the time of his life. What she also knew was how much more there was to enjoy here if he were a full-fledged resident.

She found herself smiling dreamy-eyed into her dresser mirror about the prospects of an eternity spent here with Ben. This mansion was, after all, not just hers, but theirs. Both their names were inscribed on the door.

She had to confess that because they were, she had indeed tried to push herself into an early start on a heavenly, permanent relationship, one the Lord had not yet sanctioned.

She now knew that the LORD's assurance, given to her on the balcony, would sustain her until all the pieces of the puzzle were in place.

Melanie finished brushing her hair, now glistening in the soft hues that flooded her room. Putting down her gold, pearl-handled brush, she let out a yell.

"Yes!" she shouted loudly, throwing both hands into the air.

The ecstatic gesture was over her renewed realization that Ben was saved, that he, like she, had the assurance of eternal salvation because of what her precious LORD had accomplished on earth's horrible cross.

Her mind flashed back to the tears and the years she had spent on earth praying for her wayward husband to accept the LORD as his personal Savior.

Still sitting at the dresser, she bowed her head and asked once again for forgiveness. This time it was for allowing herself to get tangled up in the details while forgetting what God had achieved in the big picture.

She was quite aware that Ben didn't yet have all the freedoms and perks she was afforded in heaven. For starters, he couldn't, as she could, instantly transport himself anywhere he chose.

But, she resolved that one day he would, and she was now finally willing to wait for that day to come.

Getting up from the dresser, she went to her closet, chose one of her favorite outfits for school, and continued getting ready for another day doing what she loved best—teaching the precious little ones in her charge about the magnificence and majesty of a God who loves them.

Chapter Thirty-Four

Michael commanded the respect of millions of angels, and rightly so.

His presence was a force to be reckoned with, respected, and revered, whether in a war room at Angelica, or off somewhere battling warring forces.

Today was no different.

More than fifty thousand angels, give or take a few, had gathered at his palace to prepare for war and to receive their instructions.

Some had never fought under one as great as Michael. Incessant chatter about what they could expect, and about how nervous they were, filled the camp. The entire place was abuzz with talk of war.

A sea of white tents, row on row, dotted the landscape as far as the eye could see in every direction around the palace. Hundreds of bright colored victory pennants flapped in the breeze above poles that surrounded a large war-room tent at the centre of the mass of dwellings.

The sounds and smells of neighing, snorting horses filled the air. Many of the majestic beasts were brightly adorned with jeweled bridles and matching braided manes and tails.

Swords and golden trumpets glistened in the brilliant light that shone around them. The sounds and preparations for battle were everywhere.

The upcoming campaign would focus on an earthly mission, fought over the Atlantic region of Canada—more specifically, the city of Halifax.

Most of the force called to Michael's side had never heard of Halifax, but they soon would.

Loud trumpet blasts from atop the high walls of the palace brought a hush over the encampment that only moments before had been charged with excitement.

The quiet gave way to the audible sound of approaching hoof beats, as a large contingent of horsemen began their descent toward the camp.

Michael led the troop, followed close behind by a band of elite generals.

When the faces of the riders came into view, there was Malak, riding high and proud on a stunning steed at Michael's side.

Such was heaven—never able to be more than remotely understood by outsiders, and always a marvel to even those who live here. Where else could an angel rise in one day, from the ranks of a humble servant, to Michael's top general in a war campaign?

One thing must be understood regarding all things heavenly. As great a commander as Michael was, not a jot, nor tittle, ever got a green light in heaven without a thorough consultation between him and the Godhead.

The meeting between the L{{ord}} and Michael had already taken place. Details would now be shared down throughout the chain of command. What would follow was cast in stone.

Angelica, land of the angels, was a place like no other.

Non-stop drama was the bedrock of this incredible region, an area roughly the size of earth's continent of Africa, and located approximately a thousand miles east of the great city.

It was here in the region of Michael's home base, a virtual military pentagon for warring angels, that most of Angelica's activity unfolded.

Though not many of the Angelica warriors had heard of the upcoming Atlantic campaign, it didn't stop the beehive of speculation over who would be chosen to fight at Michael's side.

As far as those in the know went, Malak definitely wasn't on any short list of candidates guessed to be in the running. Then again, in defense of right decisions, no one knew what Michael and the Lord had discussed behind closed doors.

Malak was certainly now aware, and was quite surprised by the Lord's request. He had thought for sure that his job was only to befriend, guide, and protect Ben and others like him—end of story. How wrong he was.

Now he was being thrust into the role of a general on a campaign that he knew was developing all around him, but one in which he had no previous knowledge that he would play such a high profile role.

Malak hoped he would get the chance to explain to Ben that he had not abandoned him. He wanted him to know that he simply had new orders, and a new hat to wear in this ever-widening arena.

Meanwhile, Michael and his generals quickly dismounted amidst shouts of praise from the warriors, who had scurried to the scene to get a glimpse of him and his entourage. Within minutes, the brains of the upcoming campaign had disappeared inside the war-room tent.

This session of generals would last for three hours.

First and foremost, were reports from the field about the amount of prayer support that had risen from the Atlantic region.

Two senior recording angels were called into the meeting to report on statistics gathered and recorded in heaven by those in charge of books and records. The numbers and volume recorded on prayer was impressive, but well below what would be necessary.

Malak thought about how earth seldom gets it when it comes to prayer. It is on this one single score that the most feathers are ruffled on the wings of heaven's angels.

Man's lack of understanding of how prayer moves the hand of God, was a sore spot with Malak. Every force of angels who ever gathered to move against the forces of darkness plaguing the earth, came up against the same problem.

The frustration inside the tent became evident the longer the meeting went on. Most of the generals in the room wanted to proceed based on the stats thus far.

Michael vetoed any attempt to begin the campaign without the necessary authority and shield of prayer.

"My fellow generals, let us remember who's in charge," said Michael, his booming voice resonating across the room. "This is not our campaign; it is the Lord's. When the prayer build up is sufficient, we will move. Until then, we sit and plan."

The discussion on that particular issue was over. The bowed heads and sheepish grins left no doubt that the subject wouldn't be brought up again, at least not for the time being.

Malak, though still in the war room, let his thoughts drift far from what the speakers were saying and onto the campaign and what would happen next.

A meeting of war generals, of an angelic kind, is certainly not conducted as it might be among generals of an earthly army, Malak mused to himself. *There is no CNN, no plethora of media trucks salivating outside the tent waiting to pounce. There are no press conferences to report half-truths about strategy.*

Malak thought about how heaven could be a strange place if one's mind was set only on how such things were carried out on earth.

In this place, he knew that the Lord and His will were always the focus, always the centerpiece. There were no super egos, and no political agendas fueling a heavenly war campaign.

Throw in the fact that angels were created beings that never died, and you had some interesting scenarios that unfolded as they did God's bidding, whether it was serving in a kitchen or wielding a sword on the battlefield.

I'm a good example of that, Malak thought.

The fact that angels are so advanced in intelligence and so able to move rapidly and undetected between the worlds of heaven and earth, is beyond an earthling's imagination, but nonetheless a truth that has flown under the radar of man's reasoning since the beginning of time.

Malak knew that it was not so much that man has never been told, or that the evidence for such a host of beings was not there.

To the contrary, it was unequivocally recorded throughout the Bible and evidenced time and time again by those who have witnessed angels firsthand.

It was always God's angels, especially those who went to war and fought battles to defend God's interests regarding mankind, that had the hardest time understanding mans' problem, which they knew to be one of unbelief and lack of prayer.

Malak's musings continued.

Angels see man as somewhat of a spoiled child who is continually being a brat to a dad who loves him, Malak thought.

That dad, to the angels, was everything. He was total, unconditional love; he was their master, the focus of their affection, the creator of their being. How Malak wished he could drive that point home to those he served.

And because God was so forgiving and wanting the best for mankind, so did the angels. But, because they could serve God by serving mankind, they had become totally loyal to a creature that remained a puzzle to them.

From heaven's viewpoint, it was easy to understand the frustration and anxiety that unfolded inside Michael's war tent, and Malak's heart.

More meetings would be necessary and would be scheduled soon.

For now, the meeting was over. Before they got up from the table, Michael gave out specific orders on how to encourage the saints of the Atlantic region to get more involved in the battle of their knees, the battle for more intense prayer to cover what lie ahead.

One of the things that would be used, as an enticement toward greater prayer, was the LORD's granting of an increase in visible angel sightings, mostly in the night, and at times of prayer.

The winged creatures were also about to show up with more frequency in some of the oddest places imaginable.

The spiritual war plans were taking shape.

The pot had begun to stir.

Chapter Thirty-Five

The bear hug was enough to make a grown man cry.

A gasping Matt became the recipient the instant Sarah hung up the phone after talking to Elliott Hanrahan.

"Matt! Matt!" she blurted out, between sobs and attempts to catch her breath.

"What is it?"

"It's dad! It's dad! He squeezed Elliott's hand."

"He did what?"

"He squeezed Elliott's hand! He squeezed his hand!"

"You're kidding!"

Sarah released her grip on Matt and threw her hands up in the air.

"I don't think the nurses believe Elliott," she kept repeating, "but I know he did. I know dad squeezed his hand. Elliott wouldn't lie about such a thing."

"Grab your coat; we've got to get over there."

Matt tried to be calm, but couldn't find his car keys. He finally found them right under his nose on the kitchen table, after a frantic look around the house.

Both darted for the door, their coats half dragging on the floor.

It wasn't long before a cold blanket fell on the excitement.

As a matter of fact, things had already begun to chill by the time Sarah and Matt reached the front desk of the villa.

It's not that the staff didn't believe Elliott, but, as usual, there was some skepticism.

"Sarah, let me say up front that we're excited, but we haven't really seen any change in your dad," said head nurse Sue Blakely.

"What exactly do you mean?" asked Sarah.

"Well, to be truthful, it's only been an hour since Mr. Hanrahan reported that your dad squeezed his hand, but he hasn't responded in such a way since, and he has not regained consciousness. We're sending him to the hospital in an hour or so for some tests, to see if they can figure out what's going on."

Sarah just smiled, said thank you, and headed into her father's room. Matt followed close behind.

Her dad certainly didn't appear any different, at least outwardly. He just lay there as usual, his eyes tightly closed. But, if there was such a thing as a glow meter, he was off the charts, and much improved.

Sarah, by now, could easily discern things of a heavenly nature, things easily detected in the room by those in tune with the LORD.

She knew that she knew, down deep inside, that her dad had responded to Elliott with a squeeze of his hand, and no one would be able to convince her otherwise.

Sarah and Matt expressed to Ben how delighted they were about what Elliott had told them on the phone. They each gave him a kiss on the cheek, said a short prayer, and left.

The news about her dad was great as far as she was concerned. It was right up there on the good news scale with their wedding announcement she and Matt had made public the week before.

February fourteenth would be their day of bliss.

It was actually Matt who came up with the date. He knew what a hopeless romantic Sarah was, and how a Valentine's Day wedding would send her over the edge of all things wonderful. And besides, it fell this year on a Saturday. Surely that was a sign.

Matt loved Sarah so very much, but on the practical side of things, he was the first to admit he had no idea what was in store when he proposed on Christmas Eve. All he knew was that he seemed to be on a merry-go-round since getting down on one knee in Sarah's living room.

Like most men, he couldn't fathom what would be involved in planning a wedding. His only solace was that Sarah certainly seemed to know. Because she did, he was more than willing to stand back and let her do whatever it took to pull it off.

The latest thing was the dress.

In the hunt thereof, Matt soon displayed to the world what most men know about the wedding dress, or for that matter, a wedding—nothing.

Matt was indeed interested, but failed to realize that it was more complicated than going to a store and grabbing the first long, white gown off the rack.

How well he was learning his lesson.

It was Saturday, a clear, crisp winter's day in the first week of January. He and Sarah had just stepped out of a coffee shop on Spring Garden Road and were headed across the street, in the direction of yet another store, to look at dresses. This would be their third of the day, and it was still only mid-morning.

Matt's only plan was to just keep smiling until his bubbling fiancée found that just right masterpiece that she was sure would make her the prettiest bride to ever walk down the aisle of a church.

By three o'clock that same day, Sarah had her dress.

The yell she let out was louder than the noonday cannon on Citadel Hill. Matt was glad; she was glad; eventually, everyone she phoned that day would be glad.

But now it was on to other things pertaining to the big day.

Matt was delighted that they found the dress. He figured the rest of the planning would be a piece of cake.

A silly Matt soon found out differently.

They now had to find dresses for the others in the party, including Esther, who was almost as excited about the wedding as her mother. She had been asked by her mom to be her junior bridesmaid. You would have thought by her enthusiasm that she had been asked to escort the Queen of England on a royal tour.

Joshua would be a junior groomsman, and was indeed up for the task, though he was not quite as enthusiastic as Esther (dressing up was not his cup of tea). The children were ecstatic over the whole idea of their mother marrying Matt. As far as both were concerned, they were an instant family the first day their mom and Matt started to date. Making it official, would be the frosting on the cake.

And, as Matt would soon find out, dresses were not the only thing on the mind of Sarah the wedding planner. There were also the invitations, the church hall to decorate, the rings, the license, the cake, and the nailing down of the food preparations.

The wedding would take place at Crossroads, their home church, an assembly that had truly become a warm and welcoming beacon to Sarah, Matt, and the children.

The only ticklish spot in all the planning was the question of who would walk Sarah down the aisle. Her Celtic temper flared anytime there was even a hint of anyone, other than her dad being there to carry out the task.

Every time the subject came up, she insisted that her father would be the one walking by her side. There would be no substitutes and no discussions to the contrary.

Matt, being of a more gentle and quiet nature than Sarah, gave his fiancée a wide berth in the matter and convinced anyone connected with the wedding to do the same.

What he did do, however, and swore him to secrecy, was to ask Elliott to be a stand-in for Ben, just in case.

Chapter Thirty-Six

Calls to the *Halifax Herald* about yet another unexplained supernatural event, were becoming eerily commonplace.

This one was turned over to seasoned reporter Aaron Cummings.

The assignment editor's decision to give this latest story to Aaron was not a surprise to anyone in the newsroom.

Aaron had aced his piece on the disappearing football at Huskies Stadium, a story he turned into a four-part series that landed on the front page of the *Herald*. Hits on the paper's website had been off the chart.

More important to his career, was the nomination the series received for an Atlantic Journalism Award, the coveted prize sought after by every eager reporter and photographer in the region.

For some reason, the story had piqued the curiosity of news gatherers clear across the country. Newspapers from coast to coast began to pick it up and run it on their front page.

Aaron figured it was the curiosity about the unexplained that had fueled its popularity.

The twenty-seven-year-old journalist had been like a dog with a bone on the story, and it paid off.

Only Aaron knew how much he needed some good news coming his way.

The husky, strikingly handsome newshound, had lately been running out of money and time to pay his bills.

A magazine had offered him five thousand dollars for a fresh story on the supernatural happenings in Halifax. They would even supply their own photographer to follow him around and get the shots for the feature.

With the state he was in, five thousand dollars was much needed cash he could use to stave off the bill collectors. The truth be known, he was two months behind on his rent and three on his car loan.

Only one person at the *Herald* knew the mess he was in. That one person in his corner was his managing editor, Bill Jackson.

He and Aaron knew each other from the same small town in northern New Brunswick, though Bill was ten years his senior.

The newspaper business was in the Jackson's blood. Their dad had made his living in the business, and had obviously instilled a love of journalism in his kids.

Aaron guessed that if he only had one good friend, it might as well be someone with some clout. He would never misuse their knowing each other, or look for special favors. He had too much integrity to go that route.

At the *Herald*, Aaron's co-workers had great respect for their colleague, but could never figure out why he was so withdrawn, and such a loner.

The truth is, Aaron Cummings had a secret, one that he buried down deep inside.

Only Bill Jackson knew what it was, and because of it, tried to help him whenever he could.

Aaron was engaged during college to none other than Bill's younger sister, Anna.

Theirs was an incredible story of romance. It seems they had known each other forever. Neither could remember a time when they were not in love.

The romantic duo grew up only two blocks from each other and had gone all through school together.

When it came time to go to college, it seemed an obvious fit to come to Halifax and enroll in journalism at the University of King's College.

Both Aaron and Anna had their career choice sealed after being seriously bitten by the journalism bug in high school. Together they ran the newspaper with a dogged determination to make it the best school paper in the province.

So off to Halifax they came, both infused with a desire to study hard and go on to a successful career doing what they loved best.

They became engaged to be married in the middle of their final year. Both families gave their blessing, although each secretly wished they would consider a longer engagement, at least until they had completed their degrees and had good paying jobs.

All was going well, too well.

The first hint of a flaw in their Camelot relationship came with Anna's announcement that she had joined an astrology club that met on Friday nights in one of the dorms.

It seemed innocent enough at first.

Aaron worked at a grocery store near the campus on most Thursday and Friday nights, and all day Saturday. He felt it would give her a chance to do something while he was working. She could get her mind off the books, and it sure seemed less harmful than wasting time and money wallowing in Halifax's rowdy, downtown bar scene.

It turns out, the bar scene may have proved the lesser of two evils.

Within six months, Anna not only became someone he didn't know, but someone he hardly even recognized, someone who threatened to kill him, someone who attacked the policemen who tried to arrest her.

It seems a whole dark, seedy world had come crashing in on her, a world seldom understood by those caught up in it, those unaware of the powerful forces behind its grip.

It was a mess, an ugly, painful mess.

Anna's transformation, like any transformation, started out slowly, but quickly progressed.

Aaron began noticing little things that were out of character for her. She started acting different, looking different, talking different.

It was no more than three weeks after her first astrology meeting, that he woke up to the shock that his darling fiancée—the same woman with the strikingly beautiful, long, strawberry-blonde hair—now had short, jet-black hair with a pink stripe down the middle.

Apparently, at two o'clock in the morning, she had gotten out of bed, gone to the bathroom, and come back sometime later with a brand-new hairdo.

Two weeks later, she came home from classes proudly displaying a lip and matching tongue ring.

The frosting on the cake came a month later when she took off her sweater to reveal a not-so-pretty skull and crossbones tattooed on her right shoulder. Also, her clothes were suddenly black and nothing but black. She said it was the only color that went well with her silver chains and studded leather bracelets she began to wear.

Upon investigation, it turned out she had met some rather unsavory characters at the astrology club who were into a whole lot more than who was born under what planet.

A profound dislike for anything to do with God was another thing he noticed happening to his precious Cinderella, the girl who was quickly morphing into someone Aaron figured must be a distant relative of Attila the Hun.

The anti-God thing was indeed strange, considering neither he, nor Anna, had ever been what might be called "religious."

It took several months for the puzzle pieces to fit. Answers finally began to flow when he discovered and began to read a Satanic bible he found hidden under her side of the mattress.

Over the period of six months, and just before the final collapse of their relationship, Anna slowly but surely stopped talking to him. She began to treat him not as her closest friend, but rather as an "enemy of the cause."

What the cause was, he wasn't quite sure.

Aaron was more angry than sad about the whole affair, and he took that anger out by diving into what he did best—investigative research.

Research became his best and only friend. Unfortunately, things he found out were discovered too late to help his beloved Anna.

Perhaps it was the hallucinogens she was experimenting with, or maybe the occult practices she fell into, or just, in general, the overall influences of the wrong crowd.

Maybe it was a combination of all of the above.

The day their house of cards finally fell was devastating to Aaron.

He came home that afternoon from class to find a note pinned to the door of their tiny residence apartment. It was short and to the point: "Anna has been arrested and taken to the police station."

No one was around. The halls were empty. It seems those who were behind closed doors didn't want to get involved with the ugly mess that occurred when they came to get her.

Apparently, Anna had taken some sort of a mental breakdown. She started smashing everything in the apartment, and screaming to the top of her lungs.

When the police broke down the door, they found her huddling in the corner with a kitchen knife in her hand.

It took two burly police officers and two campus cops to subdue her. Before they did, she had lunged at one of them and cut him on the forearm.

Five years can slip by pretty quickly.

As Aaron sat at his desk on the third floor of the newsroom, he looked out the window and paused to reflect on his latest assignment.

There wasn't a day that went by that he didn't think about Anna. No one knew, but he also visited her two or three times a week, even though she didn't seem to ever make much progress. The authorities had told him there wasn't much use in visiting, but he refused to listen.

Anna had been arrested on that horrible day five years earlier and charged with assaulting a police officer. The case, however, never went to trial, because she was found mentally incompetent and sent to an institution for an indefinite period of time.

Aaron now dedicated his entire life to finding a way to help Anna escape from her lost world, a world he vowed he would find his way into and bring her back.

Though a difficult task, Aaron completed his final year and received his journalism degree.

He started at the *Herald* two weeks after he graduated, and although a bit of a social misfit, he had proven in the past five years to be a highly skilled and invaluable reporter.

As he continued staring out the window, he wondered if somehow the type of stories he was being pitched lately had a connection to Anna. Maybe it was a stretch, maybe not.

"You ready, Aaron?"

It was Blair, the photographer sent to accompany him on his latest assignment, this one over at the Metro Centre.

He grabbed his coat, notebook, tape recorder, and coffee, catching up with Blair just as the elevator door opened.

Chapter Thirty-Seven

Ben, always the lover of knowledge, was quick to pick up on the fact that not all angels are created equal.

Since his arrival, he had learned that they are a company, not a race. They do not procreate, and because they do not die, their numbers always remain the same, numbers that literally run into the millions upon millions, all of them grouped together by task and rank, most serving in a constant run between heaven and earth, others more strictly concerned with duties around the throne.

Karli—his tailor, jeweler, and growing friend—seemed to be an authority on them. Ben guessed that since Karli had been here for nearly two thousand years, he obviously had gained considerable insight into the subject.

These fascinating creatures had become an increasing source of both curiosity and amazement to Ben.

The farther he and his troupe journeyed on their street of gold, the more of them he saw.

Many of the ones he was now coming in contact with, were in stark contrast to any angel he had seen since his arrival in heaven.

Seven or eight flitted by, seemingly oblivious to Ben, Karli and the others. They were obviously too intent on their task ahead, to pay much attention to them.

Their peculiar brilliance caught Ben completely off guard. Never could he ever have imagined such creatures.

"Karli, what were they?"

"They are cherubim," was Karli's answer. "Aren't they beautiful?"

Beautiful could not describe what his eyes beheld.

As they moved quickly past, Ben's first impression was that they looked like giant, pirouetting ballerinas. Each of them had many faces, all aglow, each radiating a look of inquisitive wonderment, like a deer caught at night in the headlights of a car.

Each had wings, feet, hands, and a great many eyes, all of which seemed to capture, in an instant, the thoughts and movement of anything, and everyone, in their path.

Though their rotating glances were short, lasting probably no more than a minute, the intensity on their faces as they stared back at Ben and the others made the encounter seem much longer.

Then they were gone.

"They'll be back. Before long, you'll see thousands of them," said an obviously excited Karli.

"Aren't they beautiful? Aren't they beautiful?" Karli kept repeating, his chin slightly dropped, his mouth wide open, and his eyes the size of saucers.

"Every time I come here, I am amazed at how intense these creatures are about magnifying and glorifying the LORD they love so dearly."

Ben was moved by Karli's intensity.

One thing was for sure: the portion of glory emanating from the cherubim was beyond anything he had felt surrounding any spirit or creature in heaven, excluding the LORD, or Paraclete.

Karli explained that their throne service, their working in such close proximity to the Godhead, couldn't help but rub off on them.

The light show intensified as Ben and his merry band of anxious saints drew closer to the base of Mount Zion. Earth's aurora borealis paled in comparison to anything they were seeing as they approached the last leg of their journey to the throne.

In a sense, it seemed hard to believe they had traveled so many miles on foot to reach this mysterious pinnacle he had heard so much about. But here they were, and with no one tuckered out.

Such was the stamina of heaven's occupants, a spirit people constantly rejuvenated by the waves of the Lord's glory that permeated this place, especially as they drew closer to the throne.

Wave after wave of glorious, heavenly music and songs of praise now wafted over the top of the last series of foothills.

The sweetness and intoxicating power of the praises left listeners in a state of awe, almost too enraptured to walk.

Many of the thousands of people, now choking movement on the boulevard and jamming the river bank and meadows in between, fell down on their knees and lifted their hands in praise toward the throne that lie just over the next ridge.

The whole scene left Ben and his troupe, like all of the others, speechless.

An indescribable desire to worship had engulfed the throngs of saints, now visible all around them.

Suddenly, and without warning, Ben felt himself being lifted upwards above the crowds.

Within seconds, the throne came into view, a visual feast too magnificent for words to properly describe.

Ben had no idea who or what had a hold of him. It didn't really matter; he was too busy trying to get his eyes to take in what his mind was having difficulty trying to register.

Higher and higher they soared to a height where it was possible to view the entire throne.

Below were hundreds of surrounding structures that made up what seemed to be a city unto itself, one that he would come to understand existed solely to meet the needs of the Godhead, display its glory, and execute judgment.

The River of Life, massive and stunning to look at, gushed noisily from the top of the mountain and flowed through and under the throne. As it did, it divided into the twelve smaller rivers that followed the path of the twelve golden boulevards winding their way toward the gates of the city.

The main throne was enormous.

Ben was not sure how, but it became apparent from high above that it fronted on all twelve boulevards at the same time, giving the millions who came here on a continual basis, a clear view of its magnificence from any of the twelve approaches.

A permanent rainbow, breathtaking in its vivid colors, encircled the throne shooting colorful beams of light in all directions.

Suddenly, Ben and his escort made a rapid descent. He had guessed right; they were flying in for a closer look.

As they moved around the base of the mountain, Ben counted twenty-four smaller thrones, each with twenty-four attendants. *Elders* is what his guide called them. All had on white gowns and wore crowns of gold.

Surrounding the main throne, on all sides, were thousands upon thousands of cherubim flying and flitting about, tending to and glorifying the Godhead with loud praises and shouts of adoration.

Above the throne was yet another breed of creature that Ben was seeing for the first time.

"We are the seraphim," boomed a loud voice.

These six-winged angels also numbered in the thousands. They formed an impenetrable mighty host, an army hovering, jostling, shouting praises to the LORD of LORDS, the Father, and the Spirit.

Ben observed that with two wings they covered their face, with two others their feet, and with the remaining pair, they flew. He guessed that their faces were often covered to withstand the intense glory experienced the closer they came to a member of the Godhead on the throne.

Ben now realized his escort was one of these angelic beings, this particular one having been sent to the outskirts, to bring him up higher for a panoramic view of what was going on below.

Of the millions who came to the glorious throne of Mount Zion, no one could ever, or would ever, return to their portion of heaven without a deeper, more heartfelt appreciation for their Master, for the One whose sacrifice gave them eternal life, and its abundance of blessings that go with it.

Ben joined the masses that made up the enormous sea of people worshipping before the throne.

As he did, he began to experience a whole new world unfolding before him. Its purpose, its focus, was the Godhead, and the Godhead alone.

No one conversed.

No one even looked from side to side at the person next to them. There was no interest in doing so. All eyes were on the throne and the One who gave His life for all before Him.

It's quite a thing to hear thousands upon thousands of worshippers break forth in the same words of worship, hour after hour. There was no pause until the next phrase of adoration replaced the last, as the crowds lifted their voices over and over again in perfect unison.

One phrase in particular seemed a favorite with Ben's newfound massive choir.

They kept repeating the words, "Alleluia; salvation, and glory, and honor, and power, unto the LORD our God."

Chapter Thirty-Eight

One look in the direction of the Godhead instantly let you know what all the praise was about.

God the Father sat on the throne, robed in splendor deserving of His presence.

But how does one describe such a being?

Ben, the man of science, was completely baffled.

He saw what he saw before him, but was having difficulty formulating thoughts that could explain what his eyes beheld.

He wasn't seeing the semblance of a wise old man in a long, white gown and matching beard. Yet he was.

He wasn't even seeing the semblance of any figure of a man before him, yet he was.

It is said that the eyes are the window to the soul. Perhaps it is only in such a thought, that description finds meaning.

To begin with, looking at the Father was like looking through a large, beautiful diamond too massive to even imagine. The glances from His eyes filtered through the stone and mixed with the abundance of colors from the rainbow.

The effect was astonishing.

It wasn't, however, the effect, but rather the substance beaming from His eyes that told the story.

In the Father's eyes was everything good and decent.

In them was mercy. In them was love, compassion, understanding, and kindness. Everything about those eyes gave a sense of a God who is all-knowing, all-caring, all-encompassing.

As He looked out over the sea of adoring people, each and every person before Him knew how special they were. His eyes, those penetrating, loving eyes said so.

They also told a story of deep compassion.

Without saying a word, the thousands upon thousands of saints before Him knew that they knew how glad He was that they were there, safe in His arms of love, safe under His wings of protection.

They also saw the love of a father for his only son. It was plain. It was everywhere. It was tangible enough to reach out and touch.

Ben's thoughts, affected by the pure, transforming power of God's love, were in themselves changed.

He could now sense more deeply, and understand more clearly, the pain of the Father, who willingly sent His only begotten Son to the cross to redeem mankind from the clutches of sin.

As one stood there captured in a web of gratitude, something else became crystal clear.

Flashing before his mind, and he guessed everyone else's, was an awareness of the sin each human being had committed on earth that caused the Father the pain of sending Jesus to the cross.

The awareness did not come from a guilt imposed by the Father.

Instead, its genesis, the very reason it was allowed, came from the Godhead's desire to reveal a glimpse of the kind of love that forgives rather than condemns.

Looking at Jesus, seated at the right hand of His Father, was something else again.

To see the Father is to see the Son.

To see the Son is to see the Father.

Everyone in heaven knew this truth.

Ben, in the several months he had been here, had overheard many a conversation expressing the great hope that more people on earth would come to a fuller understanding of it.

Jesus, several times during His earthly ministry, told those He came in contact with that He and the Father were one. To know one was to know the other.

There was no place like heaven to bring home this truth.

Ben focused on, and beheld the glory of God's Son, seated at the right hand of His Father.

Though their two hearts beat as one, there was one major difference that became clear when the two were observed side by side.

It wasn't His gold embroidered gown of fine white linen, nor the several bejeweled crowns He wore on His head, that caught Ben's eye and stood out. Nor was it His face like lightning, nor His eyes like flaming torches. Rather, it was the clearly visible nail-scarred hands that caught the attention of those who beheld Him.

All who worshipped here knew the significance of the scars.

They knew only too well that they were the only thing in all of heaven that was manmade.

An awestruck Ben continued taking in his surroundings.

As he did, an incessant, loud cry of worship resonated from the throne. Saints and creatures alike could be heard repeatedly shouting: "Holy, holy, holy is the LORD God Almighty, who was, and is, and is to come."

His attention now shifted to the third person of the trinity, the Holy Spirit.

He could hardly believe his eyes. There right before him was his friend Paraclete.

But a bird He wasn't.

Herein lay part of the difficulty of fully understanding the Godhead. Even heaven dwellers never entirely grasped the deepest of mysteries surrounding the threesome.

Of the three persons who made up the trinity, the most intense amount of mystery and symbolism surrounded the Holy Spirit.

The truth of the Scriptures was vividly enriched within Ben, the neophyte, as he stood there before the throne.

Standing in the presence of the Holy Spirit enabled him to recall the many times the third person of the trinity had appeared in different forms.

One was His appearance as tongues of fire on the day of Pentecost. Another was when He showed up as a dove when Jesus was baptized in the River Jordan.

He has also appeared to mankind as a mighty, rushing wind, as the oil of anointing, and as the comforter, when Jesus ascended into heaven after His earthly ministry.

These truths raced through Ben's mind, the result of an anointed understanding of the Third Person, whom he previously knew only as Paraclete, the name Jesus used when He referred to the Holy Spirit.

For Ben, the many changes of the Spirit were not new. After all, it was he who had ridden into the Valley of Precious Stones on the back of a gigantic dove.

What he now saw before him, in the brilliance of heaven's display of the spectacular, was not a giant bird, but rather a giant spirit, not visible in physical form, but in the magnificence of the attributes of the LORD.

Ben had no idea how long his understanding of the Holy Spirit would last. All he knew for sure was that the deep things being poured into him, were indeed, quite humbling.

He didn't know if the thousands of worshippers all around him were being blessed with such knowledge and understanding.

All he knew for sure was that his whole being shook with a powerful intensity, with a deep knowledge of his God, with an understanding of His power and goodness that moved him to his very core.

So if the Holy Spirit was a spirit with no physical form, why was he given the ride of his life on a giant bird?

He had no sooner formed the question when the voice of the Spirit gave him the answer.

"Peace, love, and purity are symbolized in the dove. They are attributes of your Savior. I allowed you to get that close to me so that you could feel that close to Him."

In an instant, Ben was aware of how precious and driven the Holy Spirit was. He now understood the singular purpose of this magnificent being, whose sole intent was to show the world, and heaven, how much they are loved and forgiven by their Savior.

Something else, now embedded in Ben's mind, was the fact that the Holy Spirit was a person, the third person of the trinity. He was not some mysterious, ghostly puff of air that could not be touched or understood by humanity.

He was an equal partner of the Godhead, a partner with emotions, feelings, immense compassion, and a job to do.

He realized these things as he stood gazing at the lamps of fire burning before the throne. Each one stood for an attribute of this amazing member of the Godhead.

The attributes that particularly caught his eye were the wisdom of God, His understanding, His counsel, His might and His knowledge. Ben could actually see how each of these worked and were embodied in the Holy Spirit.

The Spirit of Knowledge was the one Ben found the most fascinating.

He half chuckled to himself as he thought how he would like to do a paper on the subject and send it back to earth. *But on second thought, who would read it? And if they did, who would believe what I wrote?*

It was not a mistake that the Holy Spirit was not depicted as a visible person in a long gown. Rather, it was an act of deliberate design.

Ben reflected on what he was hearing.

It was so true what the Spirit was telling him.

He couldn't remember the last time he had heard someone on earth comment about so and so being "handsome" in understanding. *Sadly, we only think of "handsome" in terms of looks*, he mused.

Ben was entirely grateful to have had the Spirit made so real to him, thanks to the magnification of his spiritual eyes.

As he continued to drink in the wonders of the throne, he hoped beyond hope that this incredible experience would never end.

Chapter Thirty-Nine

It seems strange that a ten-year-old kid, and her eight-year-old brother, would be key drawing cards to fill the Halifax Metro Centre.

Esther and Joshua Jacobs were two of several main speakers for the three-day Gospel festival being conducted under the banner: *Bring Back the King*.

The event was big, really big, and the first of its kind ever held in Atlantic Canada. More than one hundred fifty of the region's largest churches were on board as organizers of the mega event.

The enthusiasm and excitement for the festival was over the top. Never in the Atlantic region could anyone ever recall such a genuine push, to not only reach the lost and fire up the saints, but to also bring down a piece of heaven through praise and worship.

What was the genesis of all the enthusiasm?

It had all started several months earlier when the supernatural began to invade the natural.

It began with the unusual happenings in Halifax, and pushed out to other Atlantic cities and towns, like ripples invading the still waters of a pond.

Prayer had become the engine driving the chugging revival.

Lately, the chugging was being replaced by a steady, consistent rate of speed, as more and more supernatural shockers began to pop up in the region. Sightings of angelic beings increased rapidly, disturbing the unbelieving minds of thousands of people, from all walks of life.

It was ironic to see the media becoming one of the biggest and brightest lights of the supernatural bonanza.

It all started with Aaron Cummings and his stories on the unexplained events surrounding the disappearing football at Saint Mary's.

It was now just five days before Friday night's festival opening. Aaron had agreed to do an advance article on the event, complemented by photographs of some of the key speakers and organizers. Just as he entered the main foyer of the Metro Centre, he spotted Elliott Hanrahan, the festival coordinator.

This was not the first time they had met.

Elliott had been the subject of one of Aaron's more recent assignments.

The popular Saint Mary's professor was not only causing quite the buzz on campus, but he was also becoming the talk of the town, after allowing the story of his conversion and friendship with a comatose Ben T. Jacobs out of the bag and onto the front page of *The Chronicle Herald*.

A great many church people were finding all the attention quite amusing.

It seemed for years they had to scratch and fight for even a paragraph on the religion page. Now they were being hounded for stories about what was supernaturally going on in their towns and cities, stories editors kept putting on the front page without even being asked.

The latest story on Elliott, especially the part about Ben's daughter claiming her father would come out of a coma and live to tell of stories from beyond the grave, had definitely sent *Herald* subscribers into a reading frenzy.

The growing hysteria was also beginning to bring in a few of the big TV media outlets from far and wide to scout out what was going on. It had been rumored, that someone from the popular news giant CNN, might be coming this way to check things out.

Aaron was impressed with the efficiency of the team of organizers scurrying about the Metro Centre, putting up huge banners, and checking everything from lighting and stage equipment to final details about programs and seating arrangements. Nothing was left to chance.

The young reporter didn't know what it was that he was feeling in the building. To him, there seemed to be some sort of a super, electrical charge running through the entire place.

He mentioned what he felt to Elliott, as they settled into two seats in the upper bowl for the interview.

Elliott was quite frank.

He explained the feeling, as the presence of the Holy Spirit beginning to fill the place, in answer to all the prayer offered up by Christians across the Atlantic region.

Aaron heard what he said but didn't acknowledge the words he had spoken. Instead, he quickly changed the subject.

As much as he liked Professor Hanrahan, Aaron had to admit he felt nervous in his presence.

The interview lasted two long hours.

Every minute that passed, a fidgety Aaron kept repeating his questions, all the while crossing and uncrossing his legs, ad infinitum.

Finally, Elliott asked him what was wrong.

Aaron was quick to tell the professor that he was fine and that nothing was bothering him.

Elliott stared at his interviewer with raised eyebrows and a look that said he didn't believe the young reporter.

It seemed Elliott's testimony of conversion, and the fact Aaron lately found himself around Christians and stories of the supernatural, was breaking down the walls he had put up in his life, walls to keep others out, and to guard his secret about Anna.

Aaron's softening was far from dramatic, at least on the outside. As a matter of fact, he would continue to struggle for some time with the raw emotions he so desperately wanted to conceal.

"No offence, Professor Hanrahan, but I just can't see what happened to you, that is to say your conversion and all that stuff, ever happening to me."

"Are you trying to convince me, or yourself?" Elliott asked.

Aaron flashed a half smile, all the while wondering how the professor seemed to be reading his mind.

How he wanted to blurt out what was bothering him. How he wanted to trust this man with his inner most thoughts. How he desperately wanted to befriend him. But he couldn't. And he wouldn't, at least not now.

The interview ended with a handshake and a promise to meet again when the festival got under way.

Elliott said a silent prayer for Aaron, as he watched him disappear from the walkway separating the upper and lower bowls of the centre.

"Elliott, Elliot!"

The professor turned to see another festival organizer standing in the entrance to the foyer, beckoning him to come over and meet a reporter from the *Moncton Times & Transcript*.

Sharisse Brown apologized for not calling ahead for an interview. She had been in Halifax on another matter when her assignment editor called and told her to get over to the Metro Centre. He insisted she do a story on the upcoming festival.

Elliott looked at his watch, smiled, then told her she could have a half hour of his time before his next class at the university.

Chapter Forty

Ziggy was a most unusual demon.

She had once been, before the fall, very much a favorite angel in heaven.

Now she sat alone, on assignment at the bedside of a patient in a mental institution, a person who should never have fallen to such a low state but did.

Ziggy's cunning abilities saw to it.

It was Ziggy who set the trap Anna Cummings fell into.

A double insult unfolded in the drab, bleak room that was Anna's home. She was not only coming to grips with having to live here, but she also had to put up with taunts from Ziggy, taunts that went on day and night.

At times she could see her sitting there in the corner chair, mocking, telling her she would never get out of this horrible place.

Such was her life.

The only bright spot was Aaron and his faithful visits.

Aaron wouldn't give up on his beloved Anna and vowed to never stop fighting to get her back.

Anna, meanwhile, was ever so slowly beginning to realize more and more things about her plight.

When she first came here, she was heavily sedated and constrained in a straightjacket.

Though her first few days were a blur, occasionally bits and pieces fell into place regarding what had happened.

She remembered cowering in the corner when they came to the campus to take her away. She remembered the absolute fear that overcame her at that moment.

She could also recall a feeling of remorse for the policemen who came to get her, especially the one she remembered cutting with a knife.

Remorse was something the authorities said she lacked entirely, but that wasn't true.

Though she didn't speak a word for almost a month after they incarcerated her, some tiny semblance of her former self was still in there.

Perhaps it was only one lone ember, but it was that one ember that Aaron kept seeing and doing his best to fan into the person he once knew, loved, and desperately wanted back in his life.

The truth be known, had it not been for the persistence of Ziggy, combined with Aaron and Anna's ignorance of the supernatural world, her five years locked up in this place could have been over in five months.

All of Anna's problems could be traced back to Ziggy, but not the grotesque Ziggy who sat in sheer delight tantalizing her, all the while rocking and laughing hideously from her chair in the corner.

Anna first met Ziggy in a dream.

Her first impression was that she was the prettiest, most savvy individual she had ever encountered.

Anna was hooked the first time Ziggy spoke. That soft, assuring, hypnotic voice was too much for a neophyte like Anna, to resist.

Ziggy had that way about her.

She exuded a charm that almost instantly left victims paralyzed by the poison she inflicted on anyone drawn into her web.

Slowly, but surely, one dream at a time, night after night, Ziggy broke down Anna's ability to reason.

First she attacked her sense of respect for authority.

"Why should you listen to anything Aaron tells you? He only wants to control you, to tell you what to do, to make you subservient to his way of thinking."

The old adage about hearing a lie so often that it begins to sound like the truth, slowly but surely sank its teeth into Anna's thinking.

Once the poison set in, it was easy for the outward changes in appearance and behavior to take place. Anna's demonic attacker was well on the road to achieving all of her hateful objectives.

Ziggy's success at overpowering Anna didn't come about as the result of her subject being a total pushover. Though few and far between, there were some moments of resistance.

Any time Anna fought back, it was because of Aaron. Their lives together had been so special, so happy. How could everything she had known suddenly be so wrong for her?

Every time such a thought came to the surface, Ziggy countered with an antidote from her well-stocked bag of tricks and lies.

"Anna darling, you know there is no such thing as an absolute. Be your own person. Be free. Don't be held in the bonds of what society tells you about right and wrong. There is no right or wrong."

The rant never stopped.

Perhaps Anna's biggest problem, and Aaron's as well, was her lack of a grounded belief system that could counter what Ziggy kept feeding her.

Neither Anna nor Aaron knew of the power and authority the Christian had over demons.

Ziggy certainly knew about such power, a power that is the worst nightmare for every demon that slivers its way through the dark, unseen world.

Demons, including their master, are not all knowing, and they cannot be in two places at the same time.

Because of this fact, an overconfident Ziggy, began to make mistakes in her assignment to totally destroy Anna Cummings by eventually getting her to commit suicide.

Part of the problem with demons is that most of them have egos bigger than their ability to follow orders.

In other words, they don't like to be told what to do.

Ziggy wasn't any different.

Beanbag Zadar, Ziggy's boss, had given her orders to destroy the lives of both Anna and Aaron simultaneously, and at a set time that he would give her.

She was to put an equal amount of effort into bringing down Aaron, as she did Anna.

Ziggy didn't listen.

A rosy picture had been painted in her weekly reports to Zadar's second in command. As far as he knew, the plug could soon be pulled on both of them, at a time chosen by Zadar, to bring the maximum benefit to the war effort over the Atlantic region.

But one prayer changed everything.

Elliott Hanrahan's prayer for Aaron as he walked away after the interview unleashed the warriors of heaven to surround him and protect him.

He was now not so easy a target.

Ziggy knew it, and shook at the thoughts of what her negligence might have unleashed.

Her only hope of avoiding being reprimanded or banished to a dirty, rotten job somewhere in the lower pits of hell was to lie, cheat, and do everything she could to keep the news from Zadar.

Unfortunately for Ziggy, her problems had just begun.

In Elliott's prayer time on the evening of the day he was interviewed by Aaron, he and his wife Alice bombarded heaven on Aaron's behalf.

Worse still for Ziggy was Elliott's obedience to the Holy Spirit to activate the prayer chain at Crossroads Christian Assembly.

Now there were at least fifty people praying for the young reporter and whatever he was hiding behind his mask of silence.

This new series of events had Ziggy in a tizzy.

The nervousness, the twitching, the drool on her froglike face, were telltales that made Anna sit up and take notice of the changes in her captor.

"What are you looking at, you pitiful creature?" barked a spitting Ziggy from across the room.

Rather than fear and trembling, the outburst brought wails of laughter, a rare response from Anna.

"My, my, Miss Ziggy, what has rattled your chain?"

The comment and the boldness behind it shocked Ziggy, and probably Anna as well.

Anna rarely spoke about anything. As a matter of fact, she rarely spoke at all.

Aaron's beloved Anna was totally unaware of the new changes that were taking place in her situation and on her behalf.

Prayer and more prayer kept turning circumstances upside down.

The Holy Spirit, who never shows up too early or too late, dropped a word of knowledge into Elliott's spirit about the secrets Aaron held onto so tightly.

Elliott, in a vision, saw the tormented situation Anna found herself in.

The insight gave him the direction he needed in prayer. The knowledge was not to be shared. It was to be used as a weapon against the forces of darkness trying to destroy the young couple.

The hell of the situation was now front and centre on heaven's radar.

Elliott, who loved to pray, vowed to never give up until all the chains that bound the couple were broken.

Chapter Forty-One

The gold of the boulevard offered up an unusually bright glitter as they walked along. Actually, they weren't really walking; it was more of a skipping, a leaping, a dancing, and a praising of the Lord.

A visit to the throne always sent one's senses whirling, carried to new heights by a cornucopia of emotions.

Unspeakable joy broke out in Ben's little group and in every other band of worshippers, as each slowly began their journey back to their mansions, lifestyles, and tasks in the city of gold.

It was Karli's husky voice cutting the pristine air that stirred Ben from deep thought.

Up to that point, he hadn't realized there were others around him.

"Mr. Ben, Mr. Ben, what did you think? Wasn't that something? Wasn't that something?"

Ben laughed at his very excited friend, a friend he had learned to appreciate dearly.

"Karli, what can I say? The throne is so much more incredible than anyone could ever express. It certainly takes your breath away."

Ben knew, as did all the others who went there, that one second before the throne was worth more than a hundred years of trouble-free life on earth.

On a strictly sensual level, Karli and the band found plenty to talk about. They always did each time they came here.

Sure they were excited about the worship and praise around the throne, but they also enjoyed talking on the way home about all the incidentals observed during the visit.

Who was wearing what garments? What jewels were in each crown? Who was wearing the best accessories? What were the patterns and stitching in the embroidery work? On and on it went. The list was endless, the chatter incessant.

Even Ben was complimented on the outfits he wore, all said to have been quite proper for the different places he stood and the hosts he saw.

Ben, still very much captured in the glow of his visit, was surprised at what he heard, as his mind began to register bits and pieces of their conversation.

A broad smile crossed his face.

The truth be known, he hadn't even realized he was wearing clothes, let alone accessories that matched. He had wisely allowed his appearance to be tied to his confidence in Karli, a superb craftsman who always took his work quite seriously.

One thing was for sure, Ben had absolutely no recollection of wardrobe changes, or even people being around him. It seemed everything simply faded into the background when he was in the presence of the Godhead.

It turns out there was something Karli and the others didn't know about.

None of them were aware of the private conversations and time Ben had spent with God the Father.

How it came about was not exactly clear to Ben.

To understand the mystery, it must first be understood that time does exist in heaven, but not like it does on earth.

No one watches clocks because there aren't any. There are, however, segments, portions of what we call time.

Ben actually spent one of these portions with the Father.

He was taken, during the segment, down a most unusual trail that started at the throne.

What is difficult to understand in heaven, but is nonetheless true, is that the Godhead is not only all powerful and all knowing, but it is also omnipresent. In other words, any member of the trinity can be in several different, or even all places, at the same time. Humans can't, and neither can angels.

The concept is mind-boggling, but as Ben often put it, what isn't in this most delightful and intriguing place?

So, as God the Father sits forever on His throne, in some form or another, He can also take a little side journey whenever He wants.

It was on one of these that Ben found himself a guest. How long it lasted, he didn't know.

The man of physics, who had long since given up on figuring things out, both stood in amazement with thousands of others at the foot of the throne, but also went somewhere else with none other than God the Father.

Ben remembered walking slowly down a long hallway, God the Father slightly ahead of him by a few steps. He remembered the glory, the power, the glow, the absolute radiance He projected.

Intricately designed, highly polished marble floors and gold furnishings added to the brightness.

They turned the corner to a much shorter hall with but one room at its end. Ben remembered wondering what was behind the large, double doors.

He soon found out.

As the intricately crafted doors swung open, everyone inside immediately knelt in adoration as God the Father entered the room.

"Please continue," was all He said, but it was the way He said it, in such a soft, loving, but yet authoritative voice.

"Welcome Master," proclaimed the occupants in unison.

"We welcome you also, Ben."

He recognized no one in the room, but they all seemed to know his name. Ben chalked it up as just part of the mysterious nature of heaven.

In an instant, probably because The Father had put the knowledge into his spirit, he knew he was in the presence of greatness.

Who were these men?

Ben didn't know.

What he did know, was that there were twelve of them.

Each stood to their feet, and took up positions across from each other, six on either side of a long, magnificent table made of a dark wood he didn't recognize, its beauty enhanced by hundreds of inlaid jewels.

The glowing masterpiece formed the focal point of the furniture in the room. The Father stood at the head of the table; Ben stood at the other end. Everyone waited, heads slightly lowered, for God the Father to say something. For a very nervous Ben, the wait seemed to go on forever.

"Please be seated."

"I won't be staying. I simply wanted to introduce you to Ben in person. He is to be shown how the plans are going, and to be given your advice on the matters I have discussed with each of you. He is a good man who has a very important job to fulfill when he returns to earth."

With those words spoken, God the Father nodded to the men in the room and disappeared.

Peter spoke first.

His loud, boisterous voice broke the silence, introducing laughter, and dispelling what was otherwise an awkward moment.

"So, my young professor, or should we call you an old professor, unfair a comment as it might seem, given the almost two thousand years each of us have been around."

The comment definitely struck the funny bone of everyone in the room.

Extending his hand toward Ben, the burly man with the ruddy complexion, stated his name.

"My name is Peter. I'm an original apostle of the Lamb. So too are all of my brothers in the room."

Ben, even if he stretched his imagination, couldn't proclaim to be a Bible scholar, but he definitely knew who the famed twelve apostles were.

He said nothing; his tongue was too tied up in knots to speak. He knew his jaw had dropped. He made a conscious effort to close his mouth and not appear so dazed.

One by one, the others left their positions to come to his. All shook his hand, hugged him, patted him on the back, and returned to their seats.

"Please feel at ease."

This time it was John—a tall, slender man with long, curly hair, a beard, and dark penetrating eyes—who spoke.

"All of us are simply mortal men who lived on earth like you. Someday you will be like us and take on permanent immortality, serving Him forever in a new heaven and a new earth."

Ben made a glib comment, something about never being able to achieve what the others in the room had achieved.

"You mustn't think like that," said John. "No man accomplishes anything except the LORD empowers him to do so. Your achievements will be no greater, or less, than ours should you choose to always be loyal and obedient to Him. God chooses different tasks for each of His servants. He esteems none any greater than any other. He simply looks at and rewards their obedience to the task and their love for Him."

His meeting with the apostles seemed like it went on for days, but could have lasted only hours. Ben wasn't sure.

On and on the conversations went, each spiced with equal doses of both laughter and seriousness.

A band of brothers they were indeed.

Ben was excited because he was made to feel like an equal, appreciated, and loved as much as any of the others in the room.

Rich spiritual and practical insight flowed like warm honey into Ben's spirit. Total confidence became his portion for the task he knew he would soon face.

Ben, deep inside, was totally aware that the Lord would help him accomplish every detail of his earthly mission.

For the first time, he felt equipped and ready to leave his paradise and return to earth.

Meanwhile, he intended to squeeze every second of enjoyment he could, out of each and every experience he was afforded in this place.

For the present, he particularly enjoyed hanging out with Karli and his artisans, one of whom he could hear calling his name in the background.

Hearing the sound of his friend's voice, made him aware that he was no longer in the presence of the apostles.

He couldn't say he felt sad about the meeting being over.

Pushing any such thought aside was easy, considering the pleasure and insight he had derived from being in the presence of these twelve great men. What he learned from each of them, would be invaluable for the journey set before him.

Chapter Forty-Two

Sarah seldom found herself with free time on her hands.

Today was one of those rare exceptions. Grabbing her Bible and a coffee, she made herself comfy in her favorite chair by the front room window.

The bright sun on the white snow forced her to squint as she glanced out at the wonderland that blanketed her lawn.

All the wedding plans were on schedule. Matt was home working on a serious university paper, and the two kids were down at the church helping with last minute preparations for the big festival.

She actually had some free time. How great was that?

Looking to the left at the big Scotch pine, she spied two sparrows pecking away at the feeder. The scene instantly made her think of how God cares for such tiny creatures, a sign that He certainly will take care of us.

Sarah's thoughts turned to her dad, as she randomly opened the Bible. Her eyes fell on a verse that made her heart jump and her body tremble.

There before her were the words: *"This sickness is not unto death, but for the glory of God, that the Son of God might be glorified thereby."*

Goosebumps ran up both arms.

She knew instantly that the verse was in reference to her dad.

The knowledge brought her great joy, as she thought of the LORD's kindness in speaking to her with a message from His written Word.

She tried to fight back tears but couldn't.

Sarah had always been confident in the dream the LORD had given her several months earlier about her dad.

Now she marveled at how God, the builder, kept building on the promise, how He kept finding ways to encourage her.

The encouragement meant a lot.

After almost six months, the long list of those who believed Ben would make it had pretty well dwindled down to her, Matt, the children, and a few close friends.

Sarah thought of how the little things, the little nuggets like this verse, always came just at the right time.

Her mind zeroed in for a moment on the many people she knew who would dismiss opening the Bible to that particular verse, as just a coincidence.

Sarah knew better but wouldn't tell anyone just now. The truth be known, she didn't want the hassle.

Her thoughts turned to Matt.

She began to dwell on the absolute blessing he had become to her and the children.

Matt was her knight in shining armor, her second chance to get it right.

Any time she felt overwhelmed by all that was happening lately, she thought back to Christmas Eve and ran the picture through her mind of a nervous Matt down on one knee, trying his best to graciously propose.

The scene made her giggle. It made her feel warm inside.

It seemed there was only one thing missing in the Cinderella story.

There was but one dot that didn't connect with all the others. That dot was her mom.

How she missed her. How she wished she could be here to help with all the wedding plans, to talk with her, to counsel her, to see the mature woman she had become.

Meanwhile, in the faraway world of heaven, Melanie was also deep in thought, that is until Mosoo came right through the wall.

She did that a lot, but Melanie, as usual, couldn't find it in her heart to scold her for not using the door and for not knocking.

Also, as usual, Mosoo was off the charts with excitement. The tips of her wings were moving so fast they had filled the room with a humming noise.

Melanie's facial expression turned from one of mild frustration, to laughter, as she focused on her servant-angel bouncing up and down, and looking as if she was about to burst.

"What is it, Mosoo?"

"It's a hand-delivered message from the Father," came a quick reply, followed by a rapid clapping of her hands.

"Thank you, Mosoo."

Mosoo wasn't leaving.

She just stood there, staring at the letter, her inquisitive dark eyes sparkling with curiosity.

"Thank you, Mosoo," Melanie said again.

"But, Miss Melanie, aren't you going to open it and see what it says?"

"I'd rather open it later."

Mosoo finally got the hint, offered half a curtsy, and left the room. This time she actually used the door, and even opened it before exiting.

Letters from the throne were always something special. A lot of people, including Melanie, stored them away as keepsakes. Each one was unique, each a work of art.

God, of course, didn't need to write letters. However, being who He is, He often chooses to do so. As all occupants of heaven soon find out, He is both caring and very personable.

Direct communication, mind to mind, is so much easier, but not as personal. Only an actual visit tops one of His letters.

Melanie sat alone in the giant parlor off the main foyer.

The letter, with her name beautifully scrolled just below the bright gold seal, lay unopened on her lap. There it would stay for quite some time.

She was in no hurry to open it.

Why should she be? Once opened, it would lose its sense of intrigue, its mystery, its mystique. She chose instead to savor its flavor until she was ready to take a look inside.

Besides, if her intuition was correct, she already knew its contents.

For quite some time, especially the last three weeks, Melanie's heavenly life was being bombarded by messages about her earthly family.

Specifically, Melanie was becoming more and more aware of something going on in Sarah's life.

Glimpses of the upcoming wedding had begun to fill her thoughts and dream patterns.

As a mother, was she sad to be missing her only daughter's wedding? Was she upset that she wasn't there to help her prepare for the big day?

Melanie continued to search her soul for answers.

She decided the answer was no to both questions.

To comprehend a no answer, one must fully understand what it means to be heavenly, to be caught up in a world so different from earth and all its cares.

Melanie was always an excellent mother while raising her only child on earth's distant shore. The bond between the two was unshakeable, solid, a relationship to be admired and envied by all who knew the Jacobs family.

But that was then, and this was now.

In heaven, it was not that you couldn't contact the other side, or that you didn't care about any one or any thing there. After all, since

Ben had arrived, she had already gone back once to spend that special night with her beloved husband at Ingonish beach.

Such visits, however, must always be viewed in context.

God is not in the habit of sending heaven's occupants back to earth. Melanie's visit was indeed the exception to the rule, and it was allowed for a specific purpose, decided upon by the Master.

The truth be known, no one ever wants to return, except to fulfill a specific desire that God puts into the heart of the person He sends back.

The average occupant of heaven, at all other times, hardly ever considers his or her former home.

You might call the whole thing a case of planetary amnesia.

In the glory land of heaven, there is no stress, no fear, no care, and no desire to invite any such things back into one's life.

Thus, the heaven dweller is an altogether different creature than an earthling.

To begin with, you might say their wiring is not the same.

They do not long for the unfinished business of earth, mainly because they are programmed with an exuberant desire to worship and please the Lord here in heaven.

The desire stems from a full-blown awareness of how much He loves them, and how much He sacrificed to purchase their eternal life.

Melanie knew all these things in her heart. She also knew any heaven dweller would go back in a flash if it meant helping with something the Lord was trying to accomplish through their return.

All these things had captured Melanie's thoughts as she stared at the letter sitting on her lap.

Her heart was telling her that an upcoming visit was probably in store. The feelings for her daughter and her upcoming marriage more or less confirmed her suspicions.

However, she still didn't want to open the letter.

Not just yet.

Chapter Forty-Three

Esther's room didn't look much different than that of any other ten-year-old girl.

In one corner, a large glass case proudly housed a doll collection. In another, a similar cabinet was home to at least forty toy horses of all shapes, colors, and sizes, each with a name and a unique personality, at least as far as Esther was concerned.

The pink spread on her canopy bed matched the wallpaper border, also pink and sporting a scene of galloping, wild horses.

A tall, white, five-drawer dresser with pink knobs, took up the lion's share of one wall. A large floor-to-ceiling bookcase, also white with pink shelves the same shade as the knobs on the dresser, dominated another.

Sound asleep, under the lace-draped canopy, was Halifax's tiny Cinderella, a quite ordinary child who was about to become a star attraction at tomorrow's quite extraordinary festival.

At the foot of her bed, as always, was a large, brown, stuffed horse, slightly bigger than a Border collie.

Esther's picture Bible, still opened, lay across her chest. It was her absolute favorite of the six Bibles she owned. Clearly visible were pictures depicting Daniel in the lion's den, the story she loved more than all the others.

One of the many things that set Esther apart from other kids her age was her insistence on going to bed as early as she could after the evening meal.

Most people who knew her found this odd. But Esther had her reasons.

Within a month or so of her grandfather falling into the coma, both she and her brother began to experience nighttime supernatural visitations.

It certainly wasn't every night, but there wasn't a two-week period that she didn't have at least one dream or an actual visitation from an angelic being. Sometimes the LORD Himself showed up.

This past month, the length and frequency of the dreams and visitations had increased dramatically—not as much for Joshua, but certainly for her.

Tonight she had helped her mother with the dishes, done her homework, prayed, grabbed her picture Bible, and was in bed by seven o'clock. Two fluffy pillows propped up her head, her face barely visible behind a mass of long, flowing curls.

She remembered looking at the clock on her wall just before she fell asleep. It read 7:28.

Esther very much enjoyed the times she spent during supernatural encounters. The incredible beings she met always made her feel like family.

It's not that Esther didn't love her own family. She actually adored them, especially her soon-to-be new dad, Matt.

Both she and Joshua couldn't wait to legally have their name changed to MacKeen, a process to begin as soon as possible after the wedding.

Esther, within seconds of falling asleep, found herself at the centre of a large platform, filled with hundreds of angels, most of them engaged in what appeared to be nervous conversation.

The majority kept peering out over the crowd below, glancing back and forth over their shoulders and sometimes straight up.

She kept wondering what they were so anxious about.

Four huge guards, at least twelve feet tall, and with swords drawn, stood at each corner of the stage, and peered into the crowd. For a ten-year-old only slightly familiar with the supernatural, this was quite a sight. She had never seen this many angels in one place.

Faces in the crowd were now visible. Hundreds of angelic beings hovered over the people. Some of them zoomed back and forth at incredible speeds.

Though it wasn't immediately known to Esther, there were also thousands more stationed above the building and across the city.

"Where am I?" she asked, not sure if she'd actually get an answer.

Suddenly, a man in an orange jacket, appeared out of nowhere, and began walking briskly across the stage toward her.

"You're here at the festival that starts tomorrow," came the answer.

"You're the man! You're the man!" Esther squealed, her utter surprise quite evident as the stranger's face came into view.

Esther, by now, was jumping up and down. The man, smiling broadly, stopped abruptly in front of her.

"So you do remember me?"

"Of course, I do. You're the man who saved my brother and me from those awful beasts that day on Citadel Hill, but you disappeared before we could thank you."

"Yes I am, and I'm sorry I had to rush off."

"Oh, that's okay, but who are you?"

"We were so scared and you made us all feel at ease. And how did you know so much about our grandfather? Oh, my dear, we were so terrified."

The man reached out his hand to shake hers, pausing for Esther to calm down and stop talking.

"I was assigned to you the day you were born."

"Cool!"

Esther smiled. Her next question shed light on what's important to a ten-year-old.

"Why do you always wear orange?"

"That's easy. It's because I like the color orange."

"Wow! So do I."

The theology on guardian angels might be of great interest to Christian thinkers around the world, but right now, the "cool" thing for Esther was the color orange.

With the matter of orange behind her, Esther unleashed a barrage or rapid-fire questions at her new angel friend.

"What is your name? Can you fly?"

The instant bond between the two, who were still standing to the side of the podium at center stage, was obvious by the outbursts of laughter they were sharing.

"Well, in answer to your questions, my name is Angelo, and yes I can fly."

"Wow! Cool! So your job is to take care of me? What about my brother Joshua?"

"Yes, he is my assignment as well."

"But, how can you take care of him if you are taking care of me?"

Angelo laughed aloud at the questions Esther kept asking.

"Here, let me show you."

In an instant, Esther, in her mind's eye, saw a man standing by the bedside of her snoring brother. The man was indeed Angelo, and yes, he was wearing his orange jacket.

For what seemed like two, maybe three hours, the pair talked and laughed their way into a deeper friendship as Angelo continued to explain his role in her life. He did so, all the while answering the never-ending questions Esther kept asking.

With the list seemingly exhausted, or at least slowing down, Angelo now turned the conversation toward the seriousness of their current situation, and where they were.

Up to this point in her life, Esther had considered her journeys into the supernatural world somewhat of a game.

Now for the first time, the game was taking on a more serious twist.

Esther tried her best to adjust to the change in demeanor, quite noticeable on Angelo's face.

She continued fidgeting with the colorful bands at the ends of her long pigtails as she listened intensely to everything Angelo was saying.

She did understand that they were standing on the stage of the Metro Centre a day before the festival was to begin, but she wasn't really sure why.

"Come with me," beckoned Angelo as he reached out and took Esther by the hand.

Somewhere in the skies above the city, Esther was allowed a glimpse into what exactly was going on.

What she saw shocked her.

Part of her childlike innocence was taken away that day, as the young evangelist witnessed the fierce battles occurring in the unseen world above her city.

Angelo, as he had been that day on Citadel Hill, was there to protect her, to guide her through the many disturbing events she was about to witness.

Drooling, violent, ugly beasts on horseback, too many to be numbered, were slowly advancing toward the outskirts of the city.

Frightened by what she saw, Esther buried her head in the soft, orange silk of Angelo's jacket as he zoomed in for an even closer look.

"Child, you must look up and witness what I am showing you."

Angelo's voice was compelling, firm.

Esther slowly opened one eye for a closer look.

Protecting her, on all sides, was a host of giant, angelic warriors glistening in the light that surrounded them.

Angelo's frightened young charge wasn't sure how they got there. She guessed they must have flown in while her eyes were shut.

A broad smile on her youthful face, gave away how glad she was to see her rescuers.

Esther felt herself being shaken but couldn't quite figure out what was going on.

In the distance, ever so faintly, she could hear someone calling her name for what seemed like at least ten minutes.

"Esther!"

"Esther!"

"It's your mother! Wake up! Wake up!"

Obviously startled, she sat straight up in bed, threw her arms around her mother, and immediately began to blurt out the details of her strange journey in the night.

Chapter Forty-Four

"Go!"

The one-word command was all it took to unleash the powerful forces under Michael's command.

The warriors under heaven's greatest commander had encountered incredible opposition to reach the outer fringes of the Atlantic provinces.

One battalion, in the past week, had won a major battle above the Tantramar marshes of Amherst, a historic town situated near the border of New Brunswick and Nova Scotia.

The push had not been easy.

The vast expanses of the country had become a war zone, from the coast of British Columbia in the west, to the frozen wilderness to the north, the United States border to the south, and the Atlantic Ocean to the east.

The amazing thing about the warfare above Canada's skies was that few Canadians in the towns and cities below were aware of the battles, nor the effects they were having on the citizens. Most knew a dark cloud of some sort had settled over the country, but few could put together what exactly was going on.

This was indeed the point.

Hell wanted to keep it that way and dreaded any sort of a revival breaking out in the eastern region of the country. The fear was that it would spread outwards and across the land.

Thus the opposition countrywide, though intense, proved to be minor in comparison to the bottleneck of furious clashes that intensified over the Atlantic region, a region in which hell's most fierce and determined forces, had decided to take a stand.

There was a reason for the intensity, one earth's human players in the region, knew little or nothing about.

Canada was long overdue for its first ever full-blown revival.

Hell knew this to be a fact, and was doing everything in its power to stop any breakout from becoming an all out disaster.

The unlikely Atlantic region, the poorest and least populated in the country, was quickly becoming ground zero. A bull's eye lay smack in the middle of Halifax.

Commander Zadar certainly knew how high the stakes were.

He had been called to hell just a week earlier, on the very day that Michael's forces had reached the outer fringe of the Atlantic region.

Satan's loud-and-clear message didn't leave any room for interpretation.

"Stop the revival in the region, or lose your command!"

The words were followed, in a flash, by a blow to Zadar's blubbery head, a blow that sent him flying almost a mile across the barren, blackened wasteland of hell's northern command headquarters.

The demoralized commander picked himself up and quickly returned to his earthly command, now more determined than ever to put a stop to any hopes of a pending revival. At least that was the impression he left with Satan's closest henchmen, and bodyguard of high-ranking goons.

Though he would keep his inner thoughts to himself, Zadar was beginning to realize how impossible it would be to carry out his master's orders.

Prayer, a sweet odor in God's nostrils, but a stench in Satan's, was breaking out all over the place. Its release kept multiplying and empowering Michael's forces.

As for Zadar, there was indeed a definite reason why he didn't dare tell his master what he was really thinking.

Losing his command was one thing. Losing his life as he knew it, and the probability of banishment to a menial task, perhaps tending stinking cells in hell, was another.

But whether he liked it or not, Zadar was being pushed into a corner faster than even he could have ever imagined.

Within the past twenty-four hours, on the very day of the festival's opening, Michael's forces had broken through to the skies over Halifax.

Perhaps it was because of the spike in prayer, the continued increase in angelic appearances among the people, the media blitz that followed, or all of the above.

Whatever it was, the city was abuzz, bursting at the seams with excitement and anticipation.

No one sensed what was in the air more than Bill Jackson, the *Halifax Herald's* managing editor.

Bill would be the first to tell you, that things had gotten so out of hand, that he had to cancel all requests for staff vacations, and days off, even if you were sick. He had made it known that even if you died, he still expected you to come to work.

Phones were ringing off the hook with citizens who felt they had a story that should be covered. Some of the requests were from crackpots, but most were legit.

Bill's biggest and constant problem was having too many good stories to cover and too few staff members to cover them.

How he wished he could clone Aaron Cummings, his star reporter. His second choice was to hire more staff, which he did.

After a lot of phone calls and the pulling of a few strings, he managed to convince five third-year journalism students from King's College to come and work for the *Herald*. He had to promise them the moon and a truckload of cash to do so, but it was all worth it to take some of the pressure off his staff.

But, even with the extra help, more stories continued to pour in than he had reporters to cover.

Stories about angel sightings had been on the front page for the past six days in a row. They were becoming as commonplace as the weather report.

Who would have thought?

Bill sat at his desk and recalled how six months ago, someone calling up about an angel sighting would have been dismissed as a kook. He certainly wouldn't have given a green light to cover such foolishness.

But that was then. This was now.

On the practical side of things, the accommodations crunch became a growing story that had to be continually updated.

The twin cities of Halifax and Dartmouth, and all the bedroom towns and communities surrounding metro, were bursting at the seams. For sure, there was no room at the inn; not at any inn.

In the church world, things had become even more chaotic, but in a joyful, exuberant kind of way.

Metro Christians were extremely ecstatic about what was happening.

For openers, you couldn't find a church in the city that wasn't packed, not only on Sundays, but for mid-week services as well.

Bible studies and prayer meetings, instead of being thought of as just one more thing piled onto an already-busy week, were now considered the-place-to-be events.

People were openly talking about the things of God. They were doing so on buses, at the grocery store, in the malls. And of course, they were asking where to go to find out more, thus the reason churches were filling up, and people were flocking to home fellowships.

The lid was clearly blown off a subject that had always been considered taboo, or, at the very least, not politically correct. Now everyone wanted to talk about what was going on. They wanted to discuss all things "religious."

For the Christian, every day was becoming a hallelujah day, a day that couldn't begin soon enough.

The days were also becoming somewhat like old home week.

Most Christian families in the metro area were getting calls from relatives and friends across the province, some even across the country. Most requests were the same: someone who knew someone who knew someone was seeking accommodations so they could make it to even one day of the festival.

As for the festival itself, it had become apparent shortly after booking the Metro Centre that the facility wouldn't hold the crowds.

Organizers had to scramble, but were successful in securing the old Forum in the city's north end, as well as the Dartmouth Sportsplex.

Nailing down the use of the additional venues, would give the overflow crowds a place to watch the event on the big screen, via satellite.

Color-coded, free tickets had been handed out for the past month at all metro churches.

Tickets for the Metro Centre venue were gone in a week. Seats for the other two venues were gobbled up in four days.

Chapter Forty-Five

The opening day of the festival was bitter cold.

Anyone brave enough to venture outdoors immediately saw their breath transformed into frigid puffs of air.

People were lined up at all three festival venues, some as early as six o'clock in the morning to get the best seats for the official ten o'clock opening.

Many of the early birds were being interviewed on the streets by hungry newshounds, curious about their willingness to brave the cold for three hours before the doors opened at nine o'clock.

The lineups themselves became somewhat of a church service, as shivering patrons shared their faith, sang praise songs, and sipped anything hot they could get their hands on.

Long lines snaked their way for several city blocks at all three locations.

Newspaper vending machines, placed at every corner in the vicinity, were empty within minutes of being filled. The *Herald* had even hired school kids to walk the lines and sell papers.

Also impossible to ignore was an army of TV and radio types.

A jumbled mass of trucks, wires, cables, and scurrying technicians filled the landscape around much of the Metro Centre perimeter. It seemed that every five minutes the excitement was ratcheting up another notch.

The frenzy flowed into the foyer and down the aisles, culminating in a sea of lights and sound system equipment, preparing to beam the live event across the country.

The Metro Centre was not the only beehive of excitement.

On a smaller scale, organized confusion was breaking out at Sarah's Fairview home.

Esther couldn't find her Bible. Neither could she find her favorite hair band. Joshua's pants to his only suit were at least an inch shorter than when he last had them on two months earlier—minor details to some, but major to a frenzied mother.

Sarah was trying her best to keep the lid on everything.

"Sarah, you're always calm, except when you're not calm."

Matt's remark drew giggles from Esther and Joshua; from Sarah it drew raised eyebrows and a smirk.

"Mr. MacKeen, if you think between this festival and a wedding in less than two weeks that I haven't got a lot to do, you are sadly mistaken."

Matt apologized for his last remark, headed out the door to warm up his excuse for a car, and scrape the frost off its windows.

Meanwhile, across town, two women were making their way into the backseat of a taxi. One said nothing, but the other started chattering the instant the cab drove off in the direction of downtown.

The younger of the two kept staring out the window and commenting on every single thing that went by. The older woman smiled and nodded at her companion, who seemed to be enjoying her ride with the enthusiasm of a young child.

Her inquisitiveness caught the eye of the cabbie, who every now and then glanced into his rearview mirror, trying to figure out what was so amusing.

Everything going on inside the car, however, paled in comparison to what was happening outside on the roof of the vehicle.

The whole scene would have been comical, if it wasn't for the serious nature of what was actually taking place.

Unbeknownst to the car's occupants, there, on the roof, was none other than a very distraught Ziggy, swaying back and forth and hanging on for dear life.

If, at that moment, the seen world could have tapped into the unseen world, it would have witnessed the bulging eyes and screaming voice of a frightened demon in its final throes of being dislodged forever from the life of Anna Cummings, who, by the way, continued to drive merrily along, enjoying her ride to the Metro Centre.

Her companion sitting next to her was her very prim and proper social worker, Ann Jones, who had also become somewhat of a friend.

Ziggy's head, as she bounced around on the roof, was obviously being yanked back and forth by none other than the heavenly warrior, Angelo, the man in the orange jacket.

It took no more than a few minutes for Angelo to dispose of Ziggy. One swish of his powerful sword ended her grip on the cab roof. In a single motion, Angelo had pierced her side with his blade, and at the same time flung her upwards, high into the sky and out of sight. A fading smoke trail was all that remained.

At the very moment the attack was over, a peaceful Anna looked up toward the ceiling of the cab. Though she couldn't see what had just happened, she was instantly aware that Ziggy's powerful grip on her life had somehow come to its final end.

Real peace, complete peace for the first time in a long, long time had totally replaced her torment. Tears of joy flowed down her cheeks and met at the corners of the wide smile on her face.

Ann looked over at her charge and smiled as well.

In all the years of counseling and helping others, she had never seen such a seemingly hopeless case as Anna's turn around so quickly.

Up until two weeks earlier, all of the staff at the institution had just about given up on her, that is, until that unforgettable day one of the workers walked into her room to witness an instant transformation.

Anna was sitting fully dressed in a chair by her bed. She was combing her hair and smiling, like the cat that swallowed the canary.

"Good morning," she proclaimed to the worker. "I love your hair, and adore that outfit you're wearing!"

The shocked staffer immediately left the room without saying a word. She ran as fast as she could down the hall to tell her superior what she had just witnessed.

Twenty minutes later, the head of psychiatry was on the phone calling the *Herald*. His message to Aaron Cummings was short and to the point: "Get over here right away; I think she's back!"

Aaron took his advice.

Within fifteen minutes, the young reporter was seen dashing down the hall, into Anna's room, and into the arms of the woman he loved.

Kisses, hugs, and tears flowed like an electric current, back and forth between them. The two had once again become one.

Doctors, nurses, a ward clerk, even a few of the cleaning staff had gathered outside Anna's closed door to listen and speculate on the joyful reunion going on inside.

It's not that they were being overly nosey. For most, it was more so a genuine interest in the young couple they had felt sorry for and had learned to love over the long course of Anna's illness.

If her situation was simple, Aaron would have walked out of the institution that day with Anna and drove home to begin the rest of their lives together.

But, alas, such was not the case.

There would be several months of interviews and evaluations in her immediate future.

Aaron was quite aware of how the system worked and how slowly the wheels of change did grind. However, before the day was over, they would concede that after five years of waiting to see her well, a few more months wouldn't make all that much difference.

The authorities at the institution would prove to be more than gracious, more than fair.

Already in just one week, they had allowed Anna's request to leave her once-locked room to attend a supervised visit to the much-talked-about Metro Centre festival.

It was nine o'clock.

The cab pulled up three blocks away from the Metro Centre, no longer able to fight the gridlock.

Anna and Ann stepped onto the curb, locked arms in the cold, crisp air, and joined the crowds slowly moving toward the front doors of the centre.

Chapter Forty-Six

Ben stood alone on the wall near the gate—the one that had been his point of entry when he first arrived. He wanted some time to himself, some time to think and reflect on his journey to this majestic place.

Atop the wall was one of the brightest and most enchanting locations he had seen in heaven—that is, except for the throne itself.

The colors from a thousand rainbows were no match for the magnificent hues that bounced off the jeweled walls, walls that were kissed by the glory of the Lord, a glory that permeated and defined everything in this place.

Below him, twelve angels could be seen flitting about at the gate, carrying out their daily business.

Ben liked to spend time at the entranceways, watching the faces of those entering their heavenly home. He particularly liked to see the joyful reunions that took place at each of the gates, as relatives were reunited with loved ones that had gone on before them.

From his vantage point, he could see the golden boulevard below, spread out as a tapestry—one that only God could weave.

Like an eagle scanning the countryside, he would watch the activities on the roadway, as it wound its way past grove after grove of sweet-smelling fruit trees that hugged the banks of the River of Life.

It was going to be difficult to leave this place.

How could it not be?

After all, his beloved Melanie was here. He thought back to how she had been the sole focus, his sole reason for wanting to get here.

Hadn't he accomplished his mission? Had he not seen her? Had he not been able to hold her in his arms again?

He knew the answer to his questions was a resounding "yes." Why then did he not feel totally satisfied? Why did he not feel totally at peace in this place of perfect peace?

Deep inside Ben knew the answers to his questions before he asked them. But he also knew there was therapy in the asking, therapy in the formulation of the questions, in the working through of the answers.

He also knew something else. He knew that since his journey began, he had been totally transformed. He was no longer the Ben he used to be.

Something in his heart now made him think of others more than himself. Something made him think constantly of his Lord and the sacrifice He had made for him.

But if he had the chance, wouldn't he still want to grab Melanie by the hand and jump back into the world they came from?

His answer, he concluded, was both yes and no.

Sure, in many ways he would like nothing better than to resume life back on earth with Melanie.

But this place, this joy, these people, this Godhead he had become so personal with, restrained him. He was indeed a man caught, a man torn in two different directions.

Then again, when he put the two options side by side, there was really only one path he could follow.

To stay here was the obvious choice, unless you were slightly insane.

The most important fact: Melanie was here, not back on earth.

Here, you were loved beyond measure. Here, you fully understood love itself, love in the form of a person, the second person of the Trinity, the one who gave His sinless life to redeem us.

Here, you were also "rich." Here, you were rich beyond measure; rich spiritually, emotionally, and physically.

Here, you lived forever in a mansion with no financial worries. Here, there were no health issues, and never would be. Here, there was never any fear of dying.

So, what would compel a man to return to earth?

Couldn't he just go and live forever in his mansion with Melanie? After all, he was co-owner of the heavenly real estate made just for them.

Two things played a role in Ben's dilemma.

One was free will.

It would be so easy, if God just said: "You're going back; get over it."

But he knew God wasn't, and isn't, like that.

Always He gives us a choice.

On earth, He woos us our entire life. He continually presents His only way to eternal life, through the shed blood of His Son.

Then He waits.

And He waits.

He waits a lifetime for us to drop all our ways to get to Him and choose His.

If we don't, we seal our own fate. If we do, heaven's arms open wide, and when our life on earth is finished, we end up here in this phenomenal place.

Part two of Ben's dilemma was trying to figure out what to do about this great love he had been shown and so freely given.

He knew he could never earn such a love or fully repay God for it. It would always remain a free gift for the asking.

So how do you run and hide when you've been asked to go back to earth by the One who has given you all of the above?

You don't.

You can't.

Your conscience won't let you.

Ben thought about how God never laid a guilt trip on him. It isn't His way. He knew this. And it was in the realization of such a great love that the answer became clear.

He would go back gladly.

If for no other reason, it would, in a small way, give him an opportunity to say thanks to the Lord for what He had done for him.

Ben also thought long and hard about the difficult task he knew was ahead of him back on earth.

He knew he was changed, born again, not the same, but some of his old thoughts were creeping in already, and he didn't like what he was thinking.

How would his friends and colleagues relate to him? He knew his family would be glad, but what about everyone else?

Snap out of it, he thought. This type of thinking, he knew, was ridiculous.

What was he doing? Was his mind trying to trick him into slipping back to his super-analytical ways; ways that had kept him from God in the first place?

Ben closed his eyes and repented of his fears and doubts.

He repented for thinking too much like he used to. After all, he was still in heaven, and when he went back, a piece of heaven, the Lord Himself, would be right there with him, there in his thinking, there any time he asked for His presence.

And besides, the plan he was being asked to complete was beyond anything he could accomplish in the natural.

Because it was, he would have to rely on the supernatural.

This was something he vowed he would do. He would do so, not because it was the thing to do, but because it was the thing he would have to do, if he wanted to survive and complete such a daunting task.

He was up for the challenge.

And why shouldn't he be?

Chapter Forty-Seven

Elliott Hanrahan looked every bit the professor.

Smartly dressed in a blue suit and matching polka dot bowtie, he walked hastily across the stage, picked up a mic, and proceeded to welcome the crowds jammed into the Metro Centre.

The spontaneous applause was deafening.

Elliott had never seen anything like it; neither had any of the platform guests, singers, or musicians.

It was loud, thundering, and it went on for at least five minutes non-stop.

Elliot tried again to get through his opening remarks. This time he made it as far as the introduction of platform guests, and again, resounding applause and shouts broke out across the huge crowd.

Then there was silence.

An eerie, total stillness descended over the entire place.

Elliott was unsure what was happening.

He stopped talking and gazed across the vast audience, trying to pick up on what had caused the crowds to be so quiet, so still.

"Well, folks, I've never found myself to be that interesting as to leave anyone speechless," Elliott quipped, his voice cracking slightly.

No one laughed.

The silence continued.

Then, out of the corner of his eye, he noticed a slight movement at the end of the stage and to his right.

Glancing over, he saw the reason for the silence.

A huge, glowing angel, approximately twelve feet tall, was standing there, wings extended, with a large sword in his right hand.

Elliott didn't know what to do.

He tried as best he could to regain his composure.

Clearing his trembling voice, he spoke softly, almost in a whisper, into the microphone. "Well, now that I've got your attention, I'll finish introducing our guests, and then we'll proceed with a time of praise and worship."

Elliott didn't know if that was the right thing to say, or the right direction in which to go. There was no manual on the podium on how to proceed if a large angel showed up while he was talking. He'd just have to wing it.

He also didn't know whether or not to comment on the twelve-foot stranger that obviously everyone was staring at.

He chose not to say anything.

What could he say? What should he say?

One thing was for sure, it took the media no more than ten seconds to react.

Camera flashes suddenly started going off, lighting up the arena, like a fireworks display. Lights and TV equipment were turned and drawn like a magnet in the direction of the stalwart angel standing at the corner of the stage.

Whispers and chattering replaced the silence, as the crowd began to point at the majestic being standing there, right before their eyes.

Then, seemingly as quickly as the angel had appeared, he disappeared. The silence resumed.

People, all over the stadium sat in awe, seemingly frozen in time.

Elliott decided to say something.

"God is obviously in our midst. Let us stand together and begin to give Him the praise that is due His name."

Elliott's words were the right words to say and the right direction to take.

As people stood to their feet, in both the lower and upper bowls, he simultaneously asked the King's Quartet, one of seven musical groups taking part in the festival, to come to the stage and lead in a time of praise and worship.

Elliott decided to address the crowd in the few minutes it took the quartet and band members to set up.

"As we begin to praise and worship, let us remember who it is we have come here today to honor. As grateful as we are to witness one of God's mighty messengers, let us remember we do not worship angels; we worship only the Lord."

A boisterous chorus of "amens" and "hallelujahs" broke out everywhere.

A sea of hands were raised in adoration all across the stadium. Some people actually knelt down right at the base of their seat. Others could be seen at the end of rows, kneeling out in the aisles.

The minute the music started and the praise began, people here and there throughout the crowds could be seen crying; some softly, some not so softly. Though unseen, God was obviously working in the hearts and minds of the people.

A tear was even noticed on the faces of some of the seasoned journalists, though you'd never get any of them to admit it, and there would certainly be nothing about it reported on the evening news.

An electrifying charge of peace, warmth, and joy began to flow softly, gently across the people. It moved in waves, starting at the crowded floor level and moving all the way upwards, row after row, until it reached the rafters. When it did, the waves seemed to reverse and roll back down to the floor level again. The process kept repeating itself over and over.

The words of a song, started on the lips of the King's Quartet, and picked up by everyone in the building, flooded the air.

Repeatedly, for well over an hour, people kept singing the words: "Holy, holy, holy is the Lord." The more they sang, the more they wanted to sing, and did so for what seemed like forever.

It was nearly noon before anyone tired of that same song.

When there was finally a slight lull in the proceedings, Elliott arose from his seat and walked to the podium.

"We're going to bring the morning session to a close, break for lunch and begin our afternoon sessions as scheduled at two p.m."

The crowd immediately began to stir.

Some headed for the exits. Others remained in their seats, staring at the stage, watching the speakers and musicians leaving the platform.

Some instantly began to speak about what happened. Others couldn't bring themselves to say a word.

One thing was for sure, everyone was caught up in the excitement of having seen, firsthand, a twelve-foot angelic being on the stage of the Halifax Metro Centre.

There was no one more excited about the visit than the news media.

Journalists of all stripes were seen scampering as fast as they could in the direction of Elliott Hanrahan and any other festival organizer or clergy-type person they could corner for an interview.

The shocked press was indeed in a frenzy trying to get comments from anyone they could about the huge warrior angel seen on stage by thousands of people, including themselves.

Up to this point in the news world, all the stories about angelic visits were stories told to them by others.

Now it was personal.

And it was about to get a whole lot more personal.

People used the break to regroup, get a bite to eat, go to the bathroom, and talk on their cell phones.

Everywhere across the stadium, people could be seen talking on the phone, calling someone, calling anyone and everyone they could think of to relate what had happened on the platform.

And while the break continued inside the Metro Centre, it certainly didn't in the skies above the city.

Angelic warfare raged on intensely, furiously, and with no letup in sight.

The intensity had a lot to do with the enemy's desperate attempts to stop, at any cost, this festival from proceeding to who knows what end.

An oily, sweaty Zadar fretted the most of all the enemy commanders in the battle. He, of course, had the most to lose.

Zadar began to make serious strategic mistakes, often miscalculating where to send troops and how many to send.

Michael's forces remained calm. Though greatly outnumbered, they were focused, sure of victory. The result was a fiercer and more powerful force than the enemy was used to in this region.

Something else of strategic importance was going on.

A tsunami of prayer was building across the nation and was about to crash on the shores of Halifax. Its force would be enough to score a knockout punch to the forces of evil bombarding Nova Scotia's capital.

The genesis for the surge was most peculiar.

The media, no friend in times past to anything Christian, was indirectly responsible.

The newsprint journalists, who had scrambled out of the centre, were now reporting in to their news desks. The morning papers would be full of stories and photos of what had happened.

For the TV outlet crews, big and small, things were incredibly faster.

Many of them convinced editors to interrupt normal programming and go live, blending footage of the angel with their on-the-spot interviews. The frenzy was incredible.

Before you knew it, actual footage of the giant angel was being beamed across the country.

News of the angel took on a life of its own as Christians nationwide began to pray for what was going on in Halifax.

And of course, the more prayer that went up, the more troops and power came down from heaven, landing in Michael's lap, and giving him greater leverage against his opponents.

During the break, something else not quite as intense had unfolded.

Aaron, who was covering the festival for the *Herald*, managed to meet up with Anna.

They had both discussed, before the day began, to meet each other at noon in the mezzanine near the main doors on Brunswick Street.

Their rendezvous was a success despite the press of the crowd.

Aaron and Anna shared a sandwich as they stood pressed against the wall. They said their good-byes, and headed back to their respective posts—hers the seat Ann had promised to save for her, and his a seat in the first two rows from the stage, an area set aside for the media and all of its paraphernalia.

Chapter Forty-Eight

Just as the best wine in the miracle at Cana was saved for the last, the festival saved Esther as the final speaker, and waited for the third day of the explosive event to introduce her.

The afternoon and evening of the first day and all of the second saw incredible results; results beyond the organizers' wildest dreams.

Festival leaders estimated at least five thousand people came forward for salvation at the Metro Centre. According to conservative estimates, close to another three thousand re-committed their lives to Christ.

The other two venues also recorded a large number of converts and rededications. An estimated two thousand went forward at the Forum; approximately five hundred re-committed their lives. Similar numbers were recorded at the Dartmouth Sportsplex.

Nobody connected with the festival dreamed such numbers were possible.

In particular, a hardened, skeptical press, even though a few tears were noted earlier among their numbers, wasn't about to cut a whole lot of slack regarding the sincerity of the festival, that is until some of their own started going forward when the invitations were given.

This was the case when the *Herald's* well-respected, award-winning journalist, Aaron Cummings, made his way to the front of the platform, bowed his head, and joined a festival worker in saying the sinner's prayer.

They all knew Aaron.

Why would he do such a thing?

Not only did they see him up front praising God, but within minutes, a beautiful young girl walked over to him, slipped her hand into his, and appeared to be saying the same prayer.

One of his colleagues turned to another and commented that they had never even seen Aaron with a girl in the five years they knew him.

A tearful, smiling Aaron turned toward the crowd and began to maneuver his beloved Anna through the throngs of people and back to her seat.

There would be much to talk about when the night was over.

It was Esther's turn to speak.

Her diminutive stature initially fooled many people in the Metro Centre, but not those who knew her.

Meet Esther the evangelist.

To her relatives, friends, and church family, nothing was a surprise. The little dynamo, so dear to Sarah's heart, was quite comfortable with public speaking, despite her size and youth.

A teary-eyed Sarah—flanked on one side by fiancé Matt, and her son Joshua on the other—focused a steady glance at her pigtailed ray of sunshine bouncing around on the stage.

The young miss stood still only long enough for someone to attach a tiny mic to the lapel of her dress. When it was in place, she was off chattering again to yet another platform guest.

When the time was right, Elliott Hanrahan went to the podium, introduced Esther, and asked the crowd for a welcoming round of applause.

After approximately two minutes of thunderous clapping, the dimpled spitfire beckoned with her hand for the people to be seated.

"Thank you very much for the wonderful welcome. Isn't this festival great? Do you like my orange dress?"

For a split second, there was silence, followed immediately by outbursts of laughter, then applause, and lots of it.

The audience wasn't quite sure how to take her at first, but within a very few minutes, a love bond was struck between them and her, which lasted the remainder of the evening.

Esther continued.

"I wore this orange dress and matching shoes, in honor of my guardian angel, Angelo."

The crowd grew silent, not quite sure what she meant.

Beneath the silence, however, slowly but surely, pockets of belief began to rise up. People immediately began to believe the words she spoke. And why wouldn't they? Sweeter than sugar, she had such a way of wooing her audience with equal doses of sincerity and truthfulness.

Everyone loved her.

They especially seemed to like the fact that nothing about her, or what she would say, was predictable. There were no pieces of paper, no binder of notes in sight. The young evangelist had a real knack for speaking straight from her heart. And without question, her every word found its mark.

Something else about Esther: she never stood at the podium looking stiff, still, and boring.

For openers, if she had latched onto the podium, all the audience would have seen was a pair of small, twinkling eyes peering out over the top.

When Esther spoke, she liked to be on the move, back and forth across the platform, speaking directly and intimately, into the minds and hearts of the people.

Her smile, and girlish giggle, was infectious to the thousands who settled into their seats, preparing to hear her speak.

The audience grew still as she cleared her throat.

"I am going to share with you this evening, how much the LORD loves you and wants to see His best poured out on you, and those you love.

"For me, some of God's best seems to be letting me see and visit the other world that few people seem to believe in or think very much about.

"It is not because He loves me more. How silly that would be. God is so wonderful that He loves all people the same. It's just that, for some reason, He wants to show me things I didn't know existed.

"This morning while I said my prayers, God told me He wanted to show you what is happening all around us, even in this place.

"What I am going to tell you might seem strange, but I want you to believe me. Everyone is excited about the great big angel we saw two days ago. But I want to tell you, he is only one of several who was here and is still with us.

"I know this to be true because I've seen them."

Within seconds of the little miss making her shocking statement, the entire stadium came alive, as one world was peeled back to reveal quite another.

The giant angel, who had caused all the fuss two days earlier, was back, and he wasn't alone.

Gasps joined puzzled looks, as shock began to ripple across the audience.

Four gigantic, angelic warriors had taken up positions on the platform, one at each corner.

All four of the majestic, daunting beings, peered intensely out across the stage. Their huge, drawn swords glistened in their hands, as the lights of the stage and cameras bounced off their long blades and beamed out into the crowd.

Hundreds of other angels, not as big as the sentinels, could be seen hovering over the platform guests. Each guest kept looking up and squinting as they tried to shield their eyes from the intense brightness.

There were also other angels, too numerous to count, flitting back and forth above the stadium crowds.

Some seemed to fly right through the roof only to return seconds later to complete a task known only to them.

The audience, glued to their seats, not only witnessed their coming and going, but also watched their intense conversations, carried out before their eyes. Obviously, some were in charge of others, who seemed to be listening attentively to their orders before flying off.

None of the creatures appeared to pay much attention to the people below. All seemed to have been given tasks to do, and were determined to go about their business.

The news media, gathered below the stage and in the first two rows, swung into action after swallowing the initial shock of what they were witnessing.

Lights flashed, and cameras rolled in all directions. Journalists reached for cell phones faster than a gunslinger would reach for his gun.

The frenzy was on.

Television producers throughout TV land were stopping programs and going live to the Metro Centre.

What happened next defies reason.

Instead of images of winged creatures invading the Metro Centre, there was nothing showing up anywhere except the shocked looks on the faces of thousands of people and one cute, pigtailed kid, smiling on the platform.

There were no angels anywhere to be seen.

The people could see them, as could the camera crews, but nothing was showing up on their screens. There were simply zero images appearing on anyone's equipment, anywhere in the building.

No one but the journalists could hear the screaming of editors and producers on the other end of their phones. It was just as well. Fits, anxiety attacks, and unspeakable profanity flowed as a rushing river going nowhere.

The ten minutes that had gone by since the fiasco began seemed like an eternity.

Finally, a still, small voice—Esther's voice—spoke above the confusion.

"I hope you are enjoying watching my angel friends. Though they are beautiful, I want you to know that there is a serious side to their mission.

They are here to fight for me, to fight for you, to fight for our city, and to fight for our country.

They will go about their business until I am finished speaking, and the festival is brought to a close, in just a short while.

In my time of praying, God also told me many other things."

Maybe it was the soft voice of a little child, so sure of herself, so unafraid, that calmed the crowds. People kept looking around, but they also listened, and listened intently to Esther.

"Don't be afraid. Angels are God's messengers, and they won't hurt you. They are here to protect us. They in themselves are a message.

The news people will not be able to record the message in pictures, because God has said He doesn't want them to."

The truth be known, Michael's orders were to block the sightings, so as not to create chaos, such as had been the case in the debacle of the Orson Welles's 1938 radio broadcast. The broadcast of H.G. Wells's *The War of the Worlds* set off pandemonium in the cities and towns that heard it.

The crowds, seeking further consolation, continued to fix their gaze on Esther.

"God wants us to know that we must seek Him in prayer. We must stop thinking only about the things we can see. Instead we must focus on the things we cannot see. Though we cannot see Him, He is here, and He loves us. He loves us so much that He allowed His Son, Jesus, to die for us, so that we might have eternal life. All we have to do is accept His gift of salvation and follow Him."

Weeping broke out here and there, all across the stadium, at the very second the tiny-framed speaker finished her last sentence.

A strong feeling of peace and joy began enveloping the audience, and magnifying the truth of Esther's words.

People looked on in shock as the angels slowly began leaving their midst. One by one, they disappeared through the walls and roof. Within a minute, or so, a little girl and her four giant friends, one on each corner of the stage, were all that remained.

Her invitation for people to give their hearts to Jesus brought a phenomenal response.

She wisely asked the people not to come forward to the stage because of the jam it would create. Those who wanted to become a Christian were asked to raise their hand. Thousands, upon thousands did so. No one knew for sure how many; the numbers were simply too numerous to count.

Elliott Hanrahan came to the podium, thanked Esther, and led the people in a prayer of acceptance and thanksgiving for their salvation.

It seemed the number of dry eyes in the house could be counted on one hand, as Elliott thanked all those who came. He concluded with a prayer of benediction to bring an end to the three days of meetings.

With heads bowed and all eyes closed for the prayer, no one actually saw the four giant angels leave the stage.

When the people opened their eyes, they were gone.

Chapter Forty-Nine

Big news stories can quickly come and go with the wind. They can be hot one week, and cold the next.

The story of what happened at the Metro Centre was extremely hot and would show no signs of cooling for a long, long time.

As a matter of fact, it would be the catalyst for a Canada-wide revival, the likes of which had never been seen before, and probably would never be seen again. It wouldn't happen overnight, but for sure the birth pains had begun.

The rarity of the Metro Centre story, the lives it touched, and its scope were the glue that kept the tale stuck in the minds of the people.

Halifax became a city in 1749. Not since its founding, at least not ever recorded in the press, was there an account detailing such a sighting of angelic beings, and one witnessed by so many people.

Then again, perhaps another reason the media stuck with the story was the embarrassment issue.

You might say their "no story" became "the story."

In their defense, they did capture images of one of the angels. One out of hundreds was better than none, though most journalists for years to come would still be haunted by the failure of not capturing them all.

The frustration would lead some reporters, like Aaron Cummings, to keep digging deeper to find out more about the fascinating spiritual world the natural world so often ignores.

One story, in particular, had a profound effect on what physical eyes saw at the Metro Centre.

That was the story of Zadar's final defeat.

It began in earnest months before the festival meetings ended.

Since everything that takes place in the natural world has roots in the spiritual world, it must be understood that the Metro Centre events didn't just come together by chance.

Zadar had been working overtime for months trying to stop the seeds of revival from taking root.

The Metro Centre, if you will, was his Alamo, his last stand.

He well remembered when the message came through. It was a few days before Halloween, his favorite time of the year.

He had called a meeting of the approximately one hundred powerful demons assigned to corrupt the minds of key people at the universities.

The motley crew of dark forces were all there in the black of night, hidden among the fortress ruins near the beach at Point Pleasant Park. Yellow, cat-like eyes and snarls could be seen and heard for hours. Luckily no earthly beings, no lovers holding hands in the moonlight, came near the sight.

The message from his superior was clear. Hell's elite had gotten wind of a growing increase in prayer in the province's capital, and it had to stop. Its power would later fuel the success at the Metro Centre, something that would infuriate the blackened heart of Satan himself.

The consensus of the meeting was to go after the professors like never before. The presence of demons of depression, drinking, drugs, gambling, jealousy, and pornography was to be tripled on every campus in the city.

The extra pressure paid off. It wasn't long after that meeting that the plan was hatched to get Ben's best friend Elliott to try and kill him.

The scenario was only one of hundreds of similar attacks against universities, churches, and other institutions known to be threatening the cause.

Specially trained demonic hit teams went after every facet of society, in an attempt to deal deathblows to as many people as possible.

The press, incapable of understanding spiritual warfare, never could get the connection. All they knew was that they were increasingly being given assignments about the alarming increase in murders, drug-related crimes, gangs, arsons, and rapes.

Such was the genesis that led up to the end for Zadar and his power base.

One might say that it is true that for every action there is a reaction.

Both good and evil forces had to up the ante on a daily basis to keep up with the changing face and pace of a region that had quickly become a battleground.

The mix of stories on the decadence in the region was countered by an increase in articles about angel sightings and other supernatural phenomenon. These stories climaxed the incredible events that took place at the Metro Centre, events that proved fatal for the diabolical commander Zadar and those under his command.

Just as kettles whistle when water reaches the boiling point, so Zadar's plans and schemes were about to blow.

The ego-bloated, fat guy of demons decided to throw all his eggs into one basket and go for the jugular. He would smash the seedlings of revival in one final battle by bringing the bulk of his forces across the Atlantic region to one spot—Halifax, and in particular, the Metro Centre.

What he hadn't anticipated was the snowballing effect of the enemy, an enemy he knew would counter his efforts, but not to the extent that he did.

Confusion had broken out when the festival finally did get underway. It led to Zadar making fatal mistakes.

Zadar was sure his original plan was fail proof.

His approach would involve a two-pronged attack. He would send his secondary forces into the air to fight at the Amherst border. A diversionary main force would attack over land, pushing toward the outskirts of Halifax.

Those left undefeated in the air battle were to return under the cover of night to join up with the land forces hiding in the forests and small coves on the outskirts of the city.

The first kink in his plans was an utter defeat at Amherst that allowed only a fraction of his forces to rejoin the land contingent.

Try as hard as he may to stay secretive and hidden, Zadar's army of demonic forces traveling over the land were soon detected. All it took was one man praying incessantly in the small village of Purcell's Cove, directly across the Northwest Arm waterway from Point Pleasant Park.

The man had a horrible encounter with a small scouting party of demons. They had become enraged with the man's praying and praising God. In a move of total frustration, they visibly appeared before the man in hopes of scaring him into a heart attack or killing him outright with one swipe of their disgusting claws.

The man's screams to God sent angels to the rescue, and an uncovering of the plot.

Heaven and hell collided that day like never before in this part of the world. It was definitely not a coincidence that it was opening day of the festival when the major battles began.

Bill Jackson was livid.

The loud thumping of his fist on the desk said so.

"Aaron, come in here," screamed the *Herald's* irate managing editor.

The young reporter entered Bill's office and for a moment just stood there, wondering what his friend, and boss, was so upset about.

"Look," he blurted out, as if Aaron was to blame. "It's bad enough that I'm stretched to the max trying to cover too many stories with too few reporters, but now here comes yet another one."

"What's up boss?"

"'What's up?' you say. Open the window and take a smell, if you want to know what's up."

Aaron half giggled, not meaning to be disrespectful. It was just that being as close to Bill as he was, he knew the finer points of the man's personality, and sense of humor.

Bill looked straight at Aaron and burst out laughing.

"I'm sorry about all that, Aaron."

"No problem."

"Three of us are working on the stink story. The phones have been ringing off the hook since we came in, but we haven't yet got any leads. I got my contact at the Dartmouth oil refinery out of bed at 7:30 this morning, but he swears they're not doing anything over there that would cause the smell."

"Okay, Aaron, keep on it, but you have to drop the story in an hour and get over to the Metro Centre for the opening. Give us what you've got before you leave."

"Sure thing," said Aaron, as he closed the door behind him.

Bill knew a rotten egg smell across the city was one thing, but no matter what it was, it wasn't as big as the festival opening. Missing that would have caused an even bigger stink.

Aaron didn't know it, but by the time he had made his way to the Metro Centre, the smell had gotten worse, resulting in more calls than the newsroom could possibly handle.

The strong sulfuric smell drifting across the city wasn't the only thing unusual in the air.

It had been a beautiful, cold, but clear day when he stepped onto the street. In an instant, the sky became sullen, black, and overcast. Strange, short, intermittent vertical flashes of lightning began to appear across the sky.

When Aaron slipped into the backstage press entrance of the Metro Centre, he remembered looking up and wondering what on earth was going on.

The press would never get to the bottom of the story or see the correlation between what was going on inside the Metro Centre and what was happening outside the building and across the city.

But the supernatural world knew only too well what was going on, especially a trembling Zadar.

Sulfuric smells and blackened skies were all too familiar when the supernatural world exploded in battle.

For the same three days the festival went on inside the Metro Centre, the fight raged on fiercely outside, both in the skies and on the land.

Michael's warriors, by the second day, had all but driven back and eliminated the vast majority of Zadar's demon forces.

By the third day only minor skirmishes were breaking out.

Zadar was nowhere in sight, and Michael was on the hunt.

It didn't take long for a group of scouts to locate the retreating Zadar, seen shifting in the shadows of the Citadel's moat, encircled by at least ten members of Satan-trained master guards, an elite group of demonic killers.

Michael should have taken other members of his army with him, but he wanted Zadar for himself.

Swooping down from the skies above the stadium, he set foot on snowy Citadel Hill, on the side facing the Metro Centre. From there, he had a perfect view of the winding moat below and the harbor in the distance.

He spotted Zadar at the same time Zadar spotted him.

The master guards turned quickly to face their opponent.

All ten of them shook their swords and fists in defiance as they cursed and swore profusely, all the while encircling the pitiful Zadar.

The cowardly commander hadn't yet drawn his sword and was seen cowering in the midst of them like a frightened, whimpering pup.

The clash of swords rang out in the cold, crisp air.

Michael scored the first blow. A charging guard, so enraged with his adversary, had broken ranks with the others and came right at him, both hands securely grasped on his extended sword as he charged toward him.

Michael stepped quickly to the side and was able to slice the demon wide open as he passed by. The demon landed up against the stone inner wall of the moat and fell to the ground in a heap.

The agility of Michael took the other demons by surprise. It also somewhat weakened their resolve when they saw how skillful a warrior he was.

Despite their growling, hissing, and promises of what they were going to do to Michael, their skills fell short of their bragging.

In a flash, Michael ducked as two of them swung their swords at his head. One he pierced through; the other he slammed up against the wall with such force that he disintegrated right there on the spot, in a puff of yellow smoke.

Instantly, the remaining guards dropped their swords to the ground and shot straight up in the air, out of the moat, and out of sight.

The pitiful Zadar—the Zadar who had terrorized the entire Atlantic region for eons of time—now sat alone on the ground at Michael's feet, sweating profusely with both forearms raised to his head in a gesture of begging for mercy.

"Please! Please! Let me go! Don't hurt me!"

Michael looked at Zadar in disgust.

"You expect me to show you mercy? Are you not the one who has caused the death of untold thousands of earthlings and brought so much misery to this region?"

Zadar by now was frothing at the mouth and slithering on the ground before Michael.

There was no longer any need for conversation.

Michael lifted his sword skyward with both hands on the handle and, in one motion, thrust its blade into the fat, enormous body of his adversary.

The stench and sight of what poured forth was revolting.

In one motion of his powerful wings, Michael rose up from the moat floor and stood for a moment on the snowy embankment above. He turned and looked below, catching a glimpse of the disintegrating mass that once was Zadar. All that remained was the reddish-black outline of a defeated foe.

What was left of Zadar's forces would carry the disgusting beast back to hell. There his punishment for defeat would be far worse than the blade of Michael's sword.

Meanwhile, heaven's commander turned eastward and headed toward the main body of his forces. There he would tend to the wounded and regroup for the journey home.

Chapter Fifty

The interior of Crossroads Christian Assembly never looked so festive, and never quite so red.

Super-organizer Sarah, envisioned from the get-go how she wanted the decorating to unfold. She knew from the very night she and Matt had announced that Valentine's Day would be their wedding date.

Now here it was, the night before the big event, and the church and downstairs reception hall were decorated just as she had imagined.

An army of helpers saw to it.

Sarah, putting on her coat in the foyer, turned to thank all those who had worked so hard.

"Just a minute; I want to take one last look."

Matt laughed as his over-the-top fiancée ran across the foyer, opened the large double doors to the sanctuary, and peeked inside.

There before her was indeed the sea of red she had imagined.

A white wedding aisle runner, with a background pattern of red rose petals, extended from the door to the altar. Homemade, heart-shaped pew markers, trimmed in white lace, added to the décor. A white, silk banner draped the podium. On it was stitched two intertwined red hearts displaying, in large letters, the words: "Two hearts become one."

Matt stood there smiling at Sarah as she took one last look at all of her creations.

"Come on, Sarah, we've got to get you home."

On their way home, Sarah thought about how their goodnight kiss at the door would be their last as single people.

A short time later, both stood under the light of Sarah's porch.

"So, Mr. MacKeen, this is my last night as Sarah Jacobs. Tomorrow I'll be Mrs. Sarah MacKeen. What do you think of that?"

Matt smiled.

"It sounds great."

"Sleep well!"

As it turned out, Sarah didn't sleep well. As a matter of fact, she never slept a wink. Matt slept like a baby.

It was nine o'clock in the morning.

Matt, along with the other three male members of the wedding party, was in the final stages of getting his shiny, black tuxedo and red bowtie, just right. Well, almost right.

Joshua wore the biggest smile of the foursome. He was so proud to be with the "men" at Matt's apartment, getting ready for the biggest day of his life. Ever since he awoke at seven o'clock, he was thinking how glad he was to be officially getting Matt as a dad.

Across town at Sarah's Fairview home, things weren't exactly peaches and cream. The four female members of the wedding party were, more or less, in a panic mode.

Most of the last-minute upsets had to do with hair and the preparation thereof. Brushes and mirrors became the choice of weapons in the battle to get ready on time.

Pieces of clothing, opened shoeboxes, and tissue from said boxes were strewn everywhere throughout the house.

Esther was the only one who seemed remotely calm. Like Joshua, she was too excited to be nervous.

"Mom, you look beautiful."

"Oh, thank you darling, you look great as well."

And, indeed, Sarah did look quite stunning.

The soon-to-be Mrs. MacKeen wore a simple but elegant gown.

Sarah loved her dress from the moment she first saw it. Now the day had finally arrived when she could wear it for the man she loved so dearly.

In her hand, she fidgeted with a bouquet of red roses in the shape of a heart. Two white carnations stood out in the center.

It was nine twenty when the limousine arrived at the door. It was nine forty before the girls finally all piled into the limo and headed for the church. Fortunately, it wasn't that far away.

Matt and the men had left the apartment at nine fifteen and were already there and in their places at the front of the church when the women arrived.

Ben couldn't get over how strange and tired he felt.

His body seemed constrained, weighted down. He was sweaty, nervous, on edge. Maybe he was dreaming? After all, it was dark in the room, but why did he feel so different, so agitated?

The answer came in the form of a voice speaking to him in the dark.

"You're back, Ben, and we've got work to do."

With the voice came a light. Actually, the entire room lit up. He somewhat recognized the voice, but couldn't quite see who it was because of the brightness in the room.

Finally, he could see a figure standing at the side of his bed.

There before him was none other than his old friend Malak.

Startled, Ben sat straight up in bed, and strained his eyes for a second look.

Was he dreaming?

"Malak! Malak! Is that really you?"

"Well, of course it is. Who were you expecting—your fairy godmother?"

A broad smile came over Ben's face. It was Malak, all right. No one else he knew had that kind of a sense of humor.

"Malak, where am I? What's going on? How long have I been here?"

Looking around, Ben came to the quick realization he was in a hospital or nursing home of some sort—an obvious conclusion evidenced by the machines and wires he was hooked up to.

Something else hit him with full force. He realized he was no longer in heaven and must be back on earth, back in his earthly body.

He knew this day was near, but the knowledge didn't lessen the shock of actually being here, back in Halifax, back in a bed that held him hostage.

His emotions scattered in all directions.

He felt alone, scared, glad to be home, sad to be home. He stared straight ahead, for the time being not really seeing, or registering anything in the room.

Malak picked up on his emotional state.

"It's okay, Ben. It's okay."

It wasn't what Malak said that snapped him out of it. It was the kindness in his voice when he spoke.

"I'm sorry, Malak. I just seem to be so overwhelmed," he said, trying to fight back tears. "By the way what are you doing here? I thought you were off helping Michael as one of his high-ranking generals?"

"I was. But the campaign is over. I've been reassigned to the likes of you," he said, sporting his trademark boyish grin.

"So, what is going on with my family? How are they? When can I get out of here to see Sarah and my grandchildren?"

"A lot has happened in the past six months. I'll fill you in on the way," said Malak.

"On the way, where?" asked Ben.

"We're going to a wedding," said Malak.

"Whose wedding?" asked Ben.

Malak smiled. "Oh, didn't I tell you? Sarah is getting married at ten o'clock, and you're walking her down the aisle."

"She's what? I'm what?" Ben was obviously both shocked and confused. "Who is she marrying?"

"I'll tell you on the way."

"Malak, I don't know if I'm strong enough to go anywhere."

"You will be as soon as your feet hit the floor. I've been told so by the Lord Himself."

Suddenly faith began to arise in Ben.

Malak leaned over his charge, unhooked all of the monitors and tubes, and told him to get up and walk.

Ben did as he was told.

As his foot touched the floor, a burning heat shot through him. It continued to shoot up and down his body for at least thirty seconds as he stood there practically naked on the cold floor.

When it left, Ben was not the same man he had been just moments before.

"Malak, I feel great! I feel great!"

"Sure you do. Now let's get a move on. In the closet over there you'll find your clothes for the wedding. Go in the washroom and put them on. Also, look in both front pockets when you're dressed. In your left pocket, you'll find a red bow tie. In your right pocket there's a gift for your daughter."

While getting dressed, Ben had a good look at himself in the mirror.

For being almost seventy-three, and having just spent six months in a coma, he thought he looked pretty good.

What he didn't know was that the second he had put his foot on the floor, the Lord saw to it that the thirty pounds he had lost were now back on his frame. Color had also been restored to his cheeks, as well as the twinkle in his eyes.

Remembering what Malak had said, he put his hand in his left front pocket, pulled out the bow tie, and put it on. Then he reached in and took out the gift in his right pocket.

Inside the gold plated box was the most beautiful necklace he had ever seen. Its centre was a very large ruby in the shape of a heart, surrounded by a second heart-shaped arrangement of small diamonds.

Ben estimated it must be worth a small fortune. Turning it over, he realized it was engraved with the words, "Crafted by Karli."

Ben was touched. His heavenly friend had thought enough of him to craft a present for his daughter. How it ended up in his pocket, he wasn't sure, and wasn't about to ask questions.

"Are you ready in there?"

"I sure am."

Out walked Mr. Ben. T. Jacobs, looking quite dapper and sporting a broad smile from ear to ear.

"Okay, Mr. Debonair, we've got to get a move on. Here's the deal. When we walk out that door, alarm bells should go off but won't because I've created a diversion in a room down the other end of the hall. We have five minutes to get to the cab waiting outside. When they return to the central desk and realize your monitors are all off, they'll come running, but we'll be gone. Leave a note on the table telling them where you've gone."

Ben grabbed a pen and some paper and wrote these words: "*Gone to my daughter's wedding in fine health. Thanks for all the care. Love, Ben.*"

It was nine fifty-five when the cab pulled up to the back entrance of the church.

Ben paid the cabbie, walked briskly into the building, through the reception hall, and up the stairs leading to the foyer.

No one saw him standing in the doorway. He took the moment to drink in the beauty of his daughter. She looked absolutely stunning as she stood there in her wedding gown, being fussed over by her attendants.

Elliott Hanrahan was standing in the entranceway with one arm slightly crooked, waiting for Sarah to put her arm in his so they could begin the march down the aisle.

In short order, Ben walked over to Elliott and tapped him on the shoulder.

"Excuse me, sir, but I think that's my job."

A round of loud screams, yells, and cries of disbelief went off everywhere. One of the bridesmaids fainted. Sarah, with her arms extended, burst into tears as she ran to her father, yelling, "Dad! Dad! Dad!"

The pianist stopped playing.

The entire congregation strained their necks to the max trying to figure out what all the commotion was about.

With his long legs set to running, Matt was down the aisle and into the foyer in seconds. After quickly assessing the situation, all he could do was join the others in their expressions of shock, mixed with absolute joy over seeing Ben.

Pandemonium had broken out.

It took fifteen minutes to calm everyone down.

When the emotional dust settled, Matt calmly walked to the front of the church and briefly explained what was going on.

While Matt was telling the people what had taken place, Ben was proudly presenting his overjoyed daughter with her necklace and helping her secure it in place.

The pianist started again, and the march down the aisle began.

Needless to say, an unusual amount of pictures were taken during the long walk to the altar, especially of the bride and her dad, a dad who practically no one expected to ever again get out of bed, let alone walk his daughter down the aisle.

When Ben reached the front of the church, he was smiling so hard he thought his face would crack.

"Who gives this woman to be married to this man?" asked the minister.

"I do, and I'm so proud to be able to do so," replied Ben.

Turning in the direction of his soon-to-be son-in-law, Ben kissed his precious daughter on the cheek and placed her hand in Matt's.

"Take good care of her. She means the world to me."

"I certainly will, sir," replied Matt.

As Ben turned to take his seat in the second row, he noticed a faint glow in his peripheral vision. Stopping dead in his tracks, he glanced upwards to find the source.

There in the balcony stood his beloved Melanie, trying her best to hold back tears and being consoled by none other than her faithful servant, Mosoo. At first glance, it was hard to tell who was consoling whom.

Off to the other side stood Malak, peering intently over the congregation like a nervous secret service agent.

Ben knew only he could see them. It was just as well. There had been enough excitement for one day.

As he sat down, he thought about how gracious the LORD was to grant Melanie the chance to see her only child get married, especially to someone as nice as Matt.

With his knowledge of how heaven worked, Ben also knew Melanie and Mosoo would return there as soon as the ceremony was over.

In one sense, he would like to go with her, but in another, he knew it wouldn't work. He had been sent back to do a job, and he would do it with gladness, joy, and in the strength of the LORD.

Besides, he figured the day would come soon enough when he would walk forever on streets of gold.